THE WINTER WAR

The Prince Warriors Series

Book 1
The Prince Warriors

Book 2
The Prince Warriors and the Unseen Invasion

Book 3
The Prince Warriors and the Swords of Rhema

Unseen: The Prince Warriors 365 Devotional

NEW YORK TIMES BEST-SELLING AUTHOR

PRISCILLA SHIRER

with GINA DETWILER

THE WINTER WAR

A PRINCE WARRIORS SEQUEL

B&H
PUBLISHING GROUP
Nashville, Tennessee

978-1-4627-9675-5

Published by B&H Publishing Group
Nashville, Tennessee

Dewey Decimal Classification: JF
Subject Heading: SPIRITUAL WARFARE—FICTION

1 2 3 4 5 6 7 8 • 22 21 20 19 18

For Jerry

Contents

Contents

Prologue

Gavreel frowned at the creature that slithered before him, leaving a trail of inky goo on the crystal floor. It was making a terrible mess. He drew his sword; kaleidoscopes of color leapt from the blade and swirled around Gavreel's tall, shining form, making the cowering creature before him recoil as if in pain.

"What are you doing here, Ponéros, you miserable worm?"

Ponéros, prince of the dark world of Skot'os, did look a bit like a worm that had just been run over by a car. But he had taken an extremely bad beating from the Prince Warriors, so it was understandable.

With great effort, Ponéros pulled himself together, re-forming a head with eyes, a nose, and a squiggling hole that acted as a mouth. A single, tentacle-like arm popped up from the goo on the floor.

"I . . . demand . . . an audience with the Source!" Ponéros's voice sounded like the gurgles of a plugged-up sink. It made Gavreel's ears ache.

"Request denied." Gavreel raised his sword to strike. But then he stopped and turned toward the crystal staircase behind him. The staircase led to an enormous throne, upon which sat a ball of flame so white-hot it looked like a burning star, its light stretching endlessly in all directions. Smaller, twinkling lights spun in the flame's orbit, each one humming a note that joined the others in perfect harmony.

Gavreel was still for a long time, listening to the glorious music emanating from the throne. A huge golden lion lying at the bottom of the staircase swished its tail and stared intently at the unwelcome visitor mucking up the floor.

Finally, Gavreel turned back to Ponéros and lowered his sword. He sighed. "State your business. You will be heard."

"My business is this," said the gurgling voice. "I demand a rematch."

The lion sat up and licked its lips.

Gavreel almost laughed, his eyes blazing. "A rematch? You are no match for the Prince Warriors. Haven't you seen that already? There is nothing you can do to penetrate their armor."

Ponéros made a strange noise that might have been a snicker. "Perhaps not. But this war is not over. In fact, it has just begun."

"You're wrong, worm," Gavreel said. "You have no idea how wrong. You will see. When the time comes."

"I have nothing but time."

"Wrong again. Your time is just about up."

Just then a great darkness passed over both Gavreel and Ponéros, and the colors ceased to shine. The lion leapt to its feet with a low growl as another figure appeared. It was small, yet it cast a long, dark shadow that seemed to consume everything it touched. Ponéros shrank back as the shadow approached, gathering himself into a ball, so he looked like a slimy armadillo.

"Come no closer!" Gavreel's voice lost its light tone. He raised his sword. Lightning burst from the white flame on the high throne. The figure retreated just enough so that its shadow did not touch Gavreel or the lion. Yet it remained on Ponéros.

"Does it make you nervous to have that one so close?" Gavreel regarded Ponéros with disdain. "Then you'd best be gone."

"I'll go," Ponéros replied, more than eager to leave now. He uncurled himself and began to slink away from the figure with the great shadow.

"But do not doubt. I will return. In Winter."

Part 1

A Time for Everything

CHAPTER 1

Armor of Lies

Ponéros was delighted.

He gazed upon his new creation, a Forger far different from the other Forgers in his army, those slave-soldiers who guarded his stronghold and fought his wars. He decided to call him Thayne. The perfect name, he thought, for the one who would destroy the Prince Warriors once and for all. Thayne was bigger, stronger, and smarter than any Forger before him. He had something else the other Forgers did not.

A suit of armor.

Ponéros's Weavers had spent eons crafting this armor to make it stronger and more resilient than the armor of even the most powerful and experienced Prince Warrior. Thayne's helmet was fused to his body armor, so thick it could never be separated or infected by the call of the Source. The helmet had a long, gleaming scythe, sharper than any sword, set right at the top. Around his waist, Thayne wore a Belt of Lies made of a magnetic metal that would repel any Prince Warrior's sword. His heavy breastplate was riveted to the belt, protecting the orb in the center of his chest from ever being pierced. His boots were so massive they could crush ten Prince Warriors with one small step.

Ponéros could almost taste the victory to come.

But that was not even the best of it. Ponéros had another surprise in store for his enemies. A weapon more devastating than any he had made before. The armor of the Prince Warriors would be useless against it.

He called it *Askalon*.

"We are ready," Ponéros said, savoring the moment. "Just in time."

"Yes, master."

Ponéros slid off his throne and moved to the portal of his new lair, which lay at the bottom of the boiling sea in the deepest crevasse of Skot'os. A better hiding place than the skypod he had previously occupied, which had been too easily discovered by that turncoat dragon Tannyn. No one from Ahoratos, not even Tannyn, would ever find him here. It was only temporary, anyway, until Thayne invaded Ahoratos and secured the Mountain of Rhema. Such a defeat would be so debilitating to the Prince Warriors that they would certainly never rise again.

Ponéros opened the portal, but the boiling sea did not flow in, held in check at his command. Huge, reptilian creatures with snakelike tails and spiked heads glided by, swift and silent, yellow eyes piercing the murky depths. Ponéros reached out to touch the edge of the acid-green water, causing a stirring among them. Another creature swam into view, one with the same snakelike tail as the rest but with a more streamlined body and green-gold gills that fanned out like wings on either side.

The creature slid into the bunker and raised itself upright, balanced on its coiled tail. Two small flippers on its body suddenly grew into long, tapered arms, ending in sharp talons. It bowed its spiked head and peered at Ponéros with slitted yellow eyes.

"Master," whispered the creature in a soft slithery voice. "What do you require?"

"Sybylla, you are looking lovely today."

The creature tilted her head slightly in silent acknowledgment.

"Gather your children," Ponéros said. "Take them to the boiling pool, under the mountain. Make sure no Prince Warrior passes through."

Sybylla closed her eyes and nodded her head. "Your will be done."

CHAPTER 2

A Gathering of Princes

Day 1

The Cave was filled with Warriors.

It seemed to have grown, stretched to accommodate this massive gathering—Prince Warriors from all over the world who had been called for a single purpose. None of them had ever seen such a large assembly of Warriors in Ahoratos before. There was an electric energy in the atmosphere. Something big must be happening.

They stood shoulder to shoulder, back-to-back, Warriors of all ages and sizes and colors and languages. Their armor, too, was quite varied. Some armor was very plain and simple, others more elaborate and detailed with fancy engravings or intricately scrolled edges. Above their helmeted heads, tiny white puffs called Sparks darted about, filling the darkened Cave with spectral light. Long, jagged stalactites, glowing blue as if lit from the inside, dripped from the ceiling. The walls were rimmed with more glowing stalagmites and rock formations on which some Warriors sat in small groups, fingering their seed-shields and their Krÿsen nervously. Others shifted about, murmuring to each other, filling the air with anticipation.

All were wondering the same thing: *Where is Ruwach?*

Evan never knew there were so many other Prince Warriors besides him and his friends. He looked around, admiring some of the fancier armor. His own armor had grown with him in the past two years; his breastplate was bigger and thicker, now embellished with the Crest of Ahoratos, the funny symbol that looked like an *N* but really was an *A*. Every mission he went on seemed to make his armor a little stronger. He hoped someday he would have really cool armor like Mr. J. Ar's.

"Whoa," he said, even though it was something he was trying not to say so much. His brother, Xavier, kept pointing out that he said that way too often. Xavier liked to point out all the things Evan did that he didn't like. Not that Evan got to see his big brother much anymore since Xavier was just too busy these days, between high school and basketball and his new crowd of friends. Evan relished those times Xavier would challenge him to cannonball contests in their pond, or practice sword fighting with him in the backyard. He even looked forward to Xavier's criticisms, because at least that meant he was paying attention.

"They must come from all over the world," Evan said. He jumped up to get a better look and came down on the boots of a tall Warrior standing near him.

"Oh, sorry," he said, embarrassed.

"Ei hätää," said the Warrior with a quick smile.

Evan stopped and stared, his jaw dropping open. Because not only had the Warrior spoken in another language, but Evan had actually *understood* what he said: "No problem."

"Whoa." Evan turned away and nudged Xavier. "Did you hear that?"

"What?"

"Watch this!"

He tapped the Warrior on the back. The Warrior turned around to look at him again.

"Pardon me. Do you have the time?" Evan asked.

"Ei ole aikaa Ahoratos," said the Warrior.

There's no time in Ahoratos.

"Okay, thanks," said Evan. He looked at Xavier. "This. Is. Awesome."

Xavier nodded, his eyes widening in amazement.

They pushed through the crowd, calling out for their friends. They heard the chatter of the other Warriors as they went, and every different language they heard they found they could understand perfectly. Evan had to stop himself from tapping people on the shoulder and asking them questions, just to hear their answers.

Finally, Evan spotted Ivy's red hair spilling out from her helmet. Brianna was with her, wearing her signature lip gloss, though it wasn't as glittery as it used to be. She'd switched to less sparkly shades now that she was older.

Next they found Finn and Manuel, who were together, because they'd been practicing sword fighting in Manuel's backyard when they were called to Ahoratos.

"Where's Levi?" said Brianna, looking around.

"Haven't seen him," said Finn. He was the oldest and felt it his duty to look out for the others. "Maybe he didn't come."

"The Rec-ing Crew isn't complete without Levi," said Evan.

"The what?" said Manuel.

"It's the name I came up with. For us. Because we all pretty much met at the rec center. Get it?" Evan looked at his friends, waiting for some reaction.

"I get it," said Ivy. "Pretty cool, Ev."

"Yeah, not bad," said Finn, giving Evan a fist bump. Xavier rolled his eyes.

"Stellar," said Brianna, looking around. "Levi must be here somewhere." She pushed through the crowd, calling Levi's name until she found him, sitting all alone on a rock, staring at the wall. He had a strange look on his face, and it seemed as though he didn't even know where he was.

"Levi!" said Brianna, giving him a little hug. "There you are!"

"Oh, hi," Levi said, barely even looking at her.

"You okay?"

"Sure."

"Are you sure you're sure? 'Cause you look like somebody just died." Brianna laughed, but Levi didn't. His face scrunched up as he turned away quickly. He looked as though he might start to cry. Brianna frowned, concerned. She started to ask him something when her attention was caught by a sound—a melody, beautiful and sweet—and the darkened Cave filled with spellbinding light. All the Warriors stopped talking and stood at attention, listening. It was as if the light and the music were connected, one giving shape to the other. The Sparks were instantly drawn to it, gathering and forming an image the Warriors all knew well.

Ruwach.

The Warriors watched in awe as the Sparks created a hovering vision of the small, purple-robed creature who was their guide in the Kingdom of Ahoratos, the Unseen world. Unseen by *most* people, anyway. But Ruwach himself did not appear in person. Instead, his voice came through the music, the notes translating into words that each Warrior understood in his or her own language.

"Welcome, Warriors," said the Spark-created version of Ruwach. "I have gathered you here for an important mission. Perhaps the most important mission of your lives." Trembling murmurs swept through the crowd. "The enemy is preparing to cross the Bridge of Tears and invade Ahoratos."

"But he can't!" Evan yelled out. Everyone looked at him. Evan's face reddened. "I mean, he's not allowed to cross the bridge, right?"

The question hung in the air for a long moment.

"That is not quite true, Prince Evan," the image of Ruwach finally responded. "Ahoratos must be defended, as must any kingdom. That is why you are all here. To defend Ahoratos. Beware, for the enemy is always looking for a weakness. This is the danger. For your weakness is often the thing you refuse to see.

"Stand firm, Warriors. Stand *together*. And you will have victory." He added: "Remember, you have everything you need."

"Man, I wish that guy Ponéros would just stay dead," Evan mumbled. "How many times do we have to beat him?"

"Only the Source can really do that," said Finn. "And he will, one day. In the meantime, we need to make sure Ponéros stays out of our territory."

"Right," said Xavier, impatient to start. "Let's get this show on the road."

The image of Ruwach disappeared as the Sparks dispersed. They flew to one wall of the Cave and re-formed into a sparkling archway. The wall of the Cave dissolved, revealing the landscape of Ahoratos through the arch.

The Warriors gasped at the sight, for Ahoratos looked quite different than it had before. The sky, usually golden, was slate gray. The trees looked as though they had lost all their leaves, and the grass was brown and dead. A harsh wind fell upon their faces as they began to march out, their boots crunching on the dried grass. But they kept moving forward, following the steady beam of their breastplates, which pointed them in the direction they were to go.

Evan couldn't see much at all because of the taller Warriors marching in front of him. But he didn't like the way the air felt, or the way the few trees he could see were completely bare. Or the way the sky was gray and ominous.

"This doesn't look like Ahoratos," he whispered.

"It's looked different every time we've come here," Xavier said, although Evan could tell he was concerned as well.

"I didn't think there was weather in Ahoratos," said Brianna.

"Where do you think we're going?" Evan asked.

"We'll know when we get there," said Xavier.

Evan had a sudden thought that wherever they were going, he wasn't going to like it.

CHAPTER 3

Battle Lines

After nearly half a day of marching, the army of Prince Warriors arrived at the battlefield, which lay on the plain at the edge of the chasm. Before them lay the Bridge of Tears, the only bridge that spanned the endlessly deep chasm between Ahoratos and Ponéros's kingdom of Skot'os. The Warriors stopped marching and formed into three sections. Evan and the rest of the "Rec-ing Crew" ended up in the middle section, directly in front of the bridge.

Evan glanced at his brother, who looked pleased. Xavier wanted to be on the front line, leading the rest into battle. But Evan didn't like being so close to Skot'os. The memory of his last visit there was still very raw, as if it only happened yesterday.

That had been only their second time in Ahoratos. They hadn't even gotten all their armor yet, and Ruwach had sent them on a mission to rescue a prisoner who was held in Ponéros's fortress. That prisoner was Rook, a Prince Warrior who had gotten trapped by Ponéros's schemes. Evan still remembered the look on Rook's face when they had first seen him in the prison cell, chained up and half turned to metal. That was what Ponéros did to his prisoners. It was a terrible sight.

"Maybe if Ruwach just got rid of that bridge, Ponéros wouldn't have a way to cross," he said aloud. "Why doesn't he just get some dynamite or something and blow it up? That's what they do in movies."

"Blowing up the bridge *would* make the most sense, strategically," said Manuel. "I don't believe Ruwach would even need dynamite."

"He must have a reason for leaving the bridge there," said Ivy. "Maybe it's so the prisoners in Skot'os can still come back."

Evan looked from Xavier, standing to his right, to the tall Warrior standing on his left, the one whose foot he had stepped on. He reminded him a little of Rook, although this guy was much younger.

Whenever Evan thought about Rook, a hard little lump formed in the middle of his throat and wouldn't go away. Like a cherry pit he'd accidentally swallowed that got stuck. He had to fight to swallow that cherry pit all over again.

"I wish Rook were here," he murmured.

"Who is Rook?" The tall Warrior next to him looked down at him. Once again, Evan realized he could understand what the Warrior had said.

"Oh, a friend. A Prince Warrior, like us, but all grown up. He's . . . dead."

"Oh, I'm sorry. I'm Kalle, by the way."

"Kalle? That's a cool name. I'm Evan. Where are you from?"

"Finland."

"Really? Awesome. I have a friend named Finn. That's him down there. But I'm pretty sure he's not from Finland." Evan shivered. "It's so cold. I don't remember it being this cold before."

"It is often this cold where I come from," said Kalle.

"Man, I'm glad I don't live there," murmured Evan, too softly for Kalle to hear. He fell silent, as did the entire line of Prince Warriors. There was no sound but the mournful breeze blowing a few brown leaves across the plain.

"This is kind of . . . eerie." Brianna shivered.

"I agree. Something doesn't feel right," Manuel said.

"All we have to do is stand firm," Ivy said, although she sounded as if she were trying to convince herself. "And stand together."

Evan looked up and down the line of Warriors. He felt reassured by how many there were. Certainly such a great army could stand up to anything, couldn't it?

Suddenly they saw movement, shapes emerging from the dense fog on the other side of the chasm: a long, unbroken line of Forgers. They were Ponéros's slaves—massive metal soldiers with round, red orbs for eyes and similar glowing orbs on their chests. Whispers and gasps swept down the line of Warriors. The sight was truly terrifying.

"Forgers," Evan said. "I hate those guys."

"There's got to be a thousand of them," said Manuel.

"We've taken down Forgers before. It's not that hard," said Xavier. "Remember, aim for that orb on their chests. It knocks them out of commission."

"Or cut off their heads," said Brianna. She nudged Levi, who stood beside her, as if waiting for him to make a snarky comment. But he didn't say anything. "C'mon Levi, don't you want to cut off some Forger heads?"

He looked at her and blinked. "Oh, yeah. Sure."

"So who starts this battle?" Evan asked in a hushed tone. He looked around. "Does someone have to say *go* or blow a whistle?"

"Of course not," Xavier said, clicking his tongue in disgust. "It's a battle, not a kickball game."

"Okay, so . . . what are we waiting for?"

As if in answer to his question, a thunderous roar rose up from the other side of the chasm. In the next instant, the cold air was filled with blazing heat—the Olethron, the giant flaming arrows, burst forth from the dense fog.

The Warriors pulled their seeds from their pockets and raised them in their fists. The seed-shields deployed, launching streams of tiny red lights that created force fields around them. The fiery arrows soon began smashing into the shields, instantly extinguished.

"Stand firm!" The voice of Ruwach echoed in their ears as the Olethron attack continued. Through the onslaught, the Warriors could see that the Forgers were now advancing to the bridge, preparing to cross.

"Here they come," Brianna whispered, her voice threaded with fear. They had not been in a full-scale battle since Rook died. That had been almost two years ago, the last time Ponéros tried to take over their town of Cedar Creek and steal their armor. They always knew Ponéros would eventually come up with some new way to try to destroy them. But since the Battle of Cedar Hill, things had been pretty quiet, and their visits to Ahoratos had been few and far between. Although they had tried to keep up their skills, they were all feeling a little rusty.

"Move forward, as one!" Ruwach commanded. Sparks suddenly swooped down in front of the army to lead the charge. The Prince Warriors stayed in close formation with shields deployed, marching toward the chasm under a storm of flaming arrows. The Forger army was moving as well, heading toward the bridge, using the Olethron attack as a cover for their advance.

Ice crystals whipped against the shields of the Warriors as they marched.

"Is it raining?" Evan asked, looking up at the sky.

"More like sleet," said Manuel.

The sleet worsened quickly, creating patches of ice under their feet. Several Warriors almost lost their footing before their boots sprouted cleats to give them traction. The marching slowed.

"Hey," said Xavier, staring ahead at the Forger army. "I think I see a way to stop them from crossing the bridge."

"We should stay in formation," Finn said. "Ruwach said to stand firm."

"Yeah, we do *not* want to go over here," said Ivy. "Especially in this weather. I'm staying here."

"Look—the bridge is narrow enough that we can push them back before they cross all the way over. Let's go!" Xavier pulled his Krÿs from his belt; the small, harmless-looking utensil suddenly lengthened into a long, shining sword.

"I don't know about this," said Manuel looking at his breastplate, which had not illuminated. None of them were crazy about getting on that bridge. It could disappear, for one thing; it had done that before. And halfway across, its ivy-covered stone changed to treacherous metal girders. "I think we should stay with the rest of the army. . . ."

But Xavier was already running, brandishing his sword.

CHAPTER 4

The Iron Chariot

Xavier ran all the way to the bridge, ignoring the worsening weather and the sleet that now deluged his shield, making it difficult to see. Yet the closer he got, the more he realized how perfect his idea was—they would stop this invasion dead in its tracks. He imagined another trip to the Hall of Honor, another medal around his neck, words of praise from Ruwach. His friends would admire him for having so much courage and taking the initiative. The Prince Warrior army might even pick him up on their shoulders, like a crowd might do after a big basketball victory.

When he looked back, he was glad to see most of his friends following him, all but Ivy, who stayed with the main army and kept shouting at him to come back. He ignored her. She obviously couldn't see the opportunity he saw. Of course she wouldn't. She was much too young and inexperienced.

He stopped running when he got to the bridgehead and turned to gather his friends. Ice coated their shields so that the sparkling seeds could barely shine. The other Warriors panted for breath and extended their Krÿsen into swords.

"Okay, listen up," Xavier said. "If we stay together, we can block the bridge and keep them from crossing."

"There aren't enough of us," Manuel said, his voice slightly strained. He glanced back at Ivy and the others.

"Yeah," said Evan. "We'll get polarized!"

"He means pulverized," said Manuel.

"No, we won't," said Xavier.

"I can hardly see," said Brianna.

"My shield is getting too heavy," said Manuel, struggling to keep his arm out straight. "The ice seems to be building up on it."

The Forgers were thundering over the bridge, bearing down on them. Xavier thought he could hear the heartbeats of everyone else, as well as his own, pounding in his ears. They were about to face far more Forgers than ever before. But he had no doubt they could do it. Forgers were pretty easy to defeat, once you got the hang of it.

The enemy soldiers reached the center of the bridge, their pounding boots making the entire structure shiver and quake, their thick metal arms beating the air. Forgers didn't fight with swords, but their grip created an iron shell around their human victims that would penetrate their skin, slowly turning their blood to liquid ore, casting their hearts in iron.

"Now!" Xavier cried out. He surged forward and thrust his sword into an advancing Forger's orb. It stumbled backward, knocking over another Forger behind it. Xavier was encouraged. He shouted for his friends to fight, and soon the hectic clanging of steel on iron filled the air as the others joined in.

They had developed a pretty good system for fighting Forgers. Evan and Manuel worked together, Evan ducking and slashing at their legs and forcing them to topple forward so Manuel could thrust upward into the orb. Brianna and Levi did the same thing, taking turns slashing legs and orbs while their shields protected them. Xavier and Finn were tall enough that they could each take on their own Forger, shouting encouragement to each other as they did. The Forgers began to fall backward into the others behind them, many of them tumbling over the side of the bridge into the chasm below.

As the Warriors fought, the ice storm worsened, forcing them to lower their shields. Ice crystals clung to their arms and helmets.

"We need to pull back," said Finn. "They're getting tired. They can't even hold their shields up—"

"We can't pull back now. Keep going!" Xavier shouted. The Forgers were flagging; in another moment they would be in full retreat. This was going to be even easier than he thought. "Forward!" He started advancing across the bridge as the Forgers fell back, his friends struggling to keep up.

"I don't know about this," Manuel said. He was breathing hard. "This ice is making my armor feel heavy. I don't think I can go much farther—"

"No one's following us," Finn said.

Xavier glanced back, but he couldn't even see the army now through the storm.

"The Forgers are retreating! We have to go after them!" Xavier cried. He was already moving, chasing after the enemy soldiers. His breastplate began to blink rapidly, telling him that he should not proceed in that direction. But he ignored it.

"I can't go on," said Brianna, slowing to a walk. The bridge was now like a sheet of ice, made all the more slippery by the smooth metal girders on the Skot'os side. Even their cleated boots had a hard time keeping a firm grip. And the icy coating on their armor made it harder for them to move with ease. "The breastplates . . . blinking . . . we need to go back. . . ." Brianna stumbled and almost slipped off the edge of a girder. Levi grabbed her in time to pull her to safety.

"Xavier," Levi shouted. "We need to go back!"

Xavier ignored him and pressed on over the bridge, despite the increasing numbness in his own limbs. Even his sword felt ten times heavier. His breastplate was telling him to turn back. But he saw that the Forgers were thrown into chaos, and he just couldn't resist the chance to finish them off once and for all.

Finally, Xavier made it over the bridge. His friends followed more slowly, struggling against the added weight of the ice on their armor. Yet it seemed Xavier had been right, for the Forgers were actually running away, deserting the bridge altogether. The Warriors charged after them but soon lost them in the heavy mist. They stopped and looked around in wonder. The Forgers were gone.

Xavier raised his sword in a victory cheer. "We did it!" he shouted so that the army on the other side of the bridge could hear him. "We did it!"

"Did we?" said Manual, finally grinning a little, though still trying to catch his breath.

"Woohoo!" Evan shouted, thrusting his sword into the air.

"Why did they run off like that?" Brianna asked.

"Must be scared of us," said Finn. "Wait . . . what's that noise?"

The Warriors stopped celebrating to listen. A low rumble resounded from somewhere in the fog. It grew louder, as if the thing making the noise was coming very fast.

"Sounds like an engine of some sort," said Manuel.

"A truck," said Finn. "A big truck. With a bad muffler."

Suddenly a monstrous object smashed through the fog, a machine unlike any they had seen before.

"A tank!" Evan cried, shocked at the sight. But not a normal tank. This machine was covered in blades and horns and spikes, with a great metal horn sticking straight out front. Long, spiked scythes projected from each of the four wheels, designed to slice through anything in their path.

"More like . . . a chariot," murmured Manuel. "An iron chariot. Except without the horses."

The massive iron helmet of a Forger protruded from the top of the chariot. But the helmet looked different from a normal Forger helmet. It had a long, sharp spike sticking out of the top and two curved horns on either side. And the eyeholes were pitch black, as if the helmet was completely empty.

"Who is that?" asked Evan. "*What* is that?"

The machine paused before them, belching out steam and revving its engines. Then it made another noise, like a fog horn or an air raid siren. More machines burst from the mist, smaller but no less terrifying. They surrounded the Warriors, the sound of their engines like several jet planes about to take off.

And then they charged.

CHAPTER 5

Nowhere to Run

"Run!" Xavier shouted. But there was nowhere to run. Xavier spun around to lead his friends to the bridge, but a chariot was already there, rolling onto the bridge, cutting off their escape.

"We're trapped!" said Brianna.

"Get your shields back up!" Levi shouted. The Warriors banded together in a tight circle and struggled to raise their shields, though the shimmering lights were still dimmed by the coating of ice. The main chariot with the big Forger came barreling toward them. But instead of plowing into them, the chariot merely veered around them and continued on its way to the bridge. The other chariots did the same, until all of them were rolling over the bridge and into the midst of the army on the other side.

The Warriors there scattered in all directions as the chariots fanned out over the field.

Then a curious thing happened. The steaming and belching suddenly ceased. The terrible machines fell silent. For a long time, nothing and no one moved.

"Maybe they can't work over there," whispered Manuel.

"Let's hope they can't," said Brianna.

"Quick, let's get across the bridge," said Xavier. But before he could take a step, Evan let out a yelp. Xavier turned and gasped.

The Forgers had returned.

On the other side of the bridge, the Prince Warriors started to circle the strange, iron chariots in their midst, trying to figure out if they were really broken or just pretending. They inched closer as time went on, their curiosity overcoming their fear.

"Stay away!" shouted Ivy. "Get away from them!" Some Warriors hung back, but many continued to move in closer, lowering their shields, thinking they were out of danger.

"Ruwach must have disabled them!" someone shouted. "They are powerless here!"

"Of course! Ponéros's schemes cannot work here!"

Others joined in, until there was general commotion among them about what was really going on. More and more Warriors were moving toward the chariots, eager to get a closer look.

Suddenly trapdoors on the chariots sprang open, releasing a torrent of . . . snakes.

At least they *looked* like snakes—enormous creatures with long silvery bodies like writhing icicles. They sprang from the chariots and slithered toward the Prince Warriors, wrapping around their legs and coiling up their bodies, freezing them in place. The Warriors screamed in terror, some slashing at the snakes with their swords, even as they were being trapped.

Commotion turned to chaos as everyone ran to escape the ice-snakes. Before they could regroup, the chariots began to move, spewing blasts of ice that formed giant webs. Those trying to run away were caught in the webs like flies. They cried out for help, but all who came to help were caught as well.

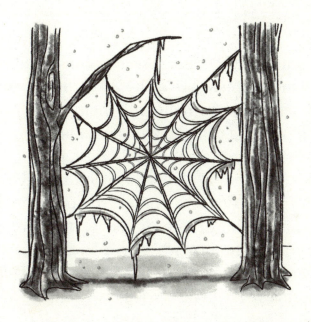

Ivy had stayed far away from the chariots and kept her shield raised, so she managed to escape the snakes. She ran toward a trapped Warrior and hacked at the snake with her sword. She recognized Kalle, the Finnish boy who had spoken to Evan before the battle began.

"Hold still!" she shouted, as she broke a few pieces from the snake, enough to allow Kalle to free one of his arms. Another Warrior soon joined her to help. The two of them kept hacking until Kalle was able to wriggle out of the ice-snake's grip. He shook off the last of the ice.

"Thank you," Kalle said. He was shivering so badly even his voice shook.

Ivy paused to stare at the two Warriors before her. They looked exactly alike.

"I'm Kristian," said the one who had helped to free Kalle. "We're twins."

"Right." Ivy stopped to take a breath, gazing around at the chaotic battle, Prince Warriors on all sides struggling to fight off the snakes. The Warriors caught in the ice-webs screamed for help until their voices froze and they could no longer make any sound at all.

"We should try to free them," said Kalle.

"Look! The bridge!" Ivy said. Even through the ice storm she could see the Forgers reappearing on the Skot'os side of the bridge. If Xavier and her friends couldn't hold them off, they would be dealing with not only the chariots but Forger foot soldiers as well. "Let's gather as many free Warriors as we can. We've got to keep those Forgers from crossing the bridge."

Ivy and the twins began to call to the others who were still free to help them protect the bridge.

But then Ivy saw something that made her sick with horror.

The ice-belching machines were plowing through the army of Prince Warriors, mowing down anyone who didn't get out of the way in time. They left a trail of frozen and wounded Warriors in their wake as they headed to the Mountain of Rhema.

––––––

Xavier realized the metal soldiers had never really retreated in the first place. They had only pretended to in order to lure the Prince Warriors over the bridge. And Xavier had fallen for it.

"This is not good," murmured Manuel.

"We can do this," Xavier said. But he wasn't sure he believed it himself.

Ruwach. Help us. Help me.

Xavier glanced back to see that Ivy had managed to rally a remnant of Prince Warriors to stop the Forger advance at the bridgehead, which was where Xavier should have stayed. Now he was cut off, with no chance of escape and unable to help Ivy and the others stop the invasion.

We can at least try and stop them from here, he thought. He raised his sword and shield, preparing for the Forger attack. His friends banded around him, struggling to keep their shields raised.

"Here they come," Xavier said.

"I can't . . ." Manuel said. "Too tired." He fell to one knee.

"Get up, Manuel!" Finn said, hauling Manuel back to his feet.

"It's too heavy . . ." Brianna said. She slumped forward, dropping her shield. Levi caught her and pulled her upright.

The Forgers closed in. A strange darkness had fallen, causing their red, glowing eyes to magnify a hundred times, like monsters in a nightmare. The whole world seemed filled with terrible noise—the bellows of the Forgers and the screams of the Prince Warriors being trapped in ice on the other side of the bridge.

Then a new sound pierced the air, a warbling shriek like many trumpets all playing different notes. Everyone, both Forgers and Prince Warriors, stopped to see what it was.

"Tannyn," Evan gasped. "It's Tannyn!"

A moment later, the big green dragon dove out of the clouds. He swooped over the embattled armies and breathed jets of fire onto the Forgers that surrounded the kids. The metal soldiers fell back with hideous screams, for the fire from Tannyn's breath was hotter than a blowtorch, able to melt their metal bodies into shapeless gobs.

"Yay, Tannyn!" Evan yelled. The others joined in, calling to their old friend, who had rescued them many times before. Tannyn swerved and sped toward them.

"He can't land here—there's no room," shouted Finn. "Belts!"

Everyone knew what he meant. Quickly, they took off their plain white belts and touched them to each other. The end of each belt fused with the next one, forming one large, unbroken belt. They strapped themselves all together in the large belt as tightly as they could.

Finn waited until he could see one of the dragon's huge rear legs about to skim over his head. "Hold on!" he yelled. He reached up and grabbed the leg with both hands, and Tannyn lifted all of the Warriors up into the air like a bundle of sticks. Finn's muscles bulged as he fought to hold on, while the others clasped their arms around each other. Xavier managed to grasp Tannyn's other leg, giving Finn a little relief.

As Tannyn flew over the battlefield, the kids could see the devastation below them—hundreds of Prince Warriors standing in their battle poses, frozen in place, their swords now reduced to tiny Krÿsen. A small group of Prince Warriors was still on the bridge, beating back the last of the Forgers. The air was suddenly filled with small white specks flying every which way, coating the bridge, the ground, and the frozen Warriors themselves.

"Look! Sparks!" said Evan.

"No," said Finn. "Not Sparks. Snow."

It was true. The snow went from flurry to squall to storm, covering everything below them in a blanket of white.

Winter had come to Ahoratos.

CHAPTER 6

The Garden

The dragon flew for miles through the darkening sky, carrying the small group of Warriors. They did not speak to each other; they were too shocked and too sad. And too cold. Only the heat of the dragon's body kept them from freezing solid, although their tears formed little ice crystals on their faces.

They passed over the Mountain of Rhema, which was now surrounded by the iron chariots. Despite the storm, smoke rose from the top of the peak. It was not the gentle wisps of the Breath that the Warriors had seen on their first trip to the mountain. This smoke was dark and violent, born of a bright orange-yellow substance that now churned at the crater.

"Lava," Manuel said. "The mountain has become a volcano."

The Warriors gazed at the newly formed volcano in shock.

After what seemed like forever, Tannyn let out a loud "Gorp!" The sound was half warning, half burp. The Warriors braced themselves as Tannyn dove straight down, letting go of the children, who gasped as they dropped to the ground, landing on a soft pile of snow. Tannyn shot back up into the air, twirled around to waggle his wing in farewell, and flew away.

The belts had separated before they landed, allowing the Warriors to roll away from each other, rubbing their sore elbows and knees and backsides. Everywhere they looked was snow, glowing faintly under the night sky. Before them stood a large stone arch, the kind that might lead to a garden. The kids pulled themselves to their feet and trudged wearily toward the archway, buckling on their belts as they went.

"I think that's the Garden of Red," said Evan as they neared the entrance. There was no snow here, only large patches of dirt and bare trees along the path. Dried-up vines hung from the tree branches, looking like creepy spider legs. "Look! There's the stone."

The Warriors paused before the large stone near the entrance with the words "Garden of Red" engraved on its surface. This Garden was where they had first received their seed-shields. Back then it had been lush and green and fragrant, filled with plants of every variety. But now there didn't seem to be a single thing alive.

"At least it's warmer here as they entered the garden," said Manuel. The heavy crusts of ice on their armor began to melt, allowing them to breathe more deeply and stand up straight without feeling as though they were weighed down by some unbearable burden.

"It must be the Garden," said Brianna. "But everything is . . . dead."

"Not quite," said a whispery voice. The kids jumped, spinning around to see who had spoken.

"It was Ru," Evan said, his voice quavering a little. "It must have been Ru."

"It didn't sound like him," said Levi.

"What's that smell?" Brianna wrinkled her nose in disgust. "It's awful. Like a garbage dump."

"No, more organic," Manuel said. "Like compost or . . . rotting leaves."

"It's weird to see this place so . . . empty," Evan said with a shiver.

"Empty," said Brianna. "That's exactly how it feels."

"A *giant* empty," said Evan.

"Warriors." This time it was definitely Ruwach's voice, coming from somewhere in the Garden. They whirled around, searching for him, but not seeing him. "Come to me."

"Where is he?" whispered Brianna.

"I can't tell," said Manuel, looking all around.

They started down the narrow garden path, searching for the familiar form of Ruwach, their friend and guide. They could still hear his voice calling to them, but for some reason they couldn't see him. The path broke into several different paths, and soon they were confused and filled with panic. The smell of rottenness had become nearly overwhelming.

"He's not here," said Brianna, fear rising in her voice. "This is a trick. We're in Skot'os; we're in Ponéros's prison. . . ."

"No," said Levi. "He's here." Levi headed down a small, winding path alone. The others followed him. The path was very dark, but the smell receded as they walked.

"Are you sure?" Brianna asked, but Levi didn't answer.

Then they saw him: Ruwach. The small figure stood in the center of the path under a large, barren tree, his purple cloak glowing in the darkness, accentuating the emptiness of his hood. Levi got to him first. Ruwach extended his long arm, a brilliantly glowing hand emerging from his cloak. He placed his hand on Levi's shoulder. Levi's head dropped, but he didn't speak. The others caught up, and Ruwach withdrew his hand, hiding it in his voluminous sleeve.

"Boy, are we glad to see you," said Evan. "There's something weird going on in this place. What's that smell? Have you been fertilizing or something?"

"Evan," Xavier huffed.

"I was just asking. This place could use some fertilizer."

"What's happened, Ruwach?" Brianna asked. "Is it really winter in Ahoratos?"

Ruwach nodded his hood silently. The kids looked at each other.

"For how long?" Brianna whispered.

"Forty," said Ruwach.

"Forty?" said Manuel, hope and fear mingled in his voice. "Forty what? Days? Weeks? Years?"

Ruwach didn't answer.

"Hey, guys."

They turned to see Ivy coming toward them down the path. She had taken off her helmet, but her red hair remained plastered to her head. She was out of breath.

"Ivy!" Brianna rushed over to hug her friend. "I'm so thankful you're all right."

"Yeah, I'm fine." Ivy brushed past Brianna and joined the others.

"How did you get here?" said Evan.

"I'm not really sure. We were fighting the Forgers, and then the Sparks came, and all of a sudden I was here."

"Did you see the Finnian guy?" Evan asked. "Is he okay?"

"Finnish," corrected Manuel.

"Yeah," said Ivy. "There's actually two of them. Twins. Kalle and Kristian. We stopped the Forgers at the bridge, thanks to Tannyn, but we couldn't stop those chariots. They took the Mountain of Rhema. The Breath . . . is gone."

Everyone was silent a moment, the truth almost too awful to bear. It was the Breath of the Mountain of Rhema that had given them their swords. The Breath was the core of Ahoratos. It didn't seem possible that something so mighty and enduring could be cut off by the evil schemes of Ponéros.

"We really blew it." Evan said aloud what everyone was already thinking. "We shouldn't have gone over the bridge. If we'd stayed where we were supposed to be, maybe we could have stopped those tank things."

"It was his fault," Levi said, rounding on Xavier in sudden fury. "You did exactly what Ponéros wanted you to do! You could have gotten us all killed!"

"Hey, take it easy," said Brianna, stepping in front of Levi. "He made a mistake, okay? He did his best. . . ."

"I'm never following him again." Levi spun on his heels and stalked away.

"Levi, come back!" Brianna said, starting to follow him.

"Let him go," commanded Ruwach. "I will speak to him."

"I'm sorry about that, Xavier," Brianna said, glancing at Xavier's stricken face. "He didn't mean it. He's not himself today. I don't know what's going on with him, but I'm sure he'll apologize when he realizes what he said."

"He's right," said Xavier, hanging his head. "If I hadn't gone over the bridge . . . I put everyone in danger. . . ."

"You couldn't have stopped those chariots anyway," said Ivy.

"We can still beat Ponéros, can't we?" Evan looked hopefully to Ruwach. "We can get him off that mountain."

"Yeah," said Finn. "Ponéros knows he can't win against us."

Ruwach finally spoke. "It was not Ponéros who drove the Askalons to the mountain."

"Aska-who?" said Evan.

"The Askalons—the iron chariots."

"That's what you call them? So weird."

"If it wasn't Ponéros, then who was it?" asked Brianna.

"It was Ponéros's new Forger-general, Thayne."

"You mean the big-monster guy in the tank?" said Evan. He threw his hands in the air. "So there's a new guy in charge now? Great. That's all we need!"

"But how could he get to the mountain?" said Xavier, ignoring his little brother. "I mean, how could Ponéros or this Thayne character cut off the Breath?"

Ruwach's hood bowed slightly. "Because it is Winter. Winter is the time of rest. Sleep. But also testing. It can be a difficult time. When life seems . . . absent."

The Warriors looked around at the barren garden, understanding what that meant. No one said anything for a long time.

Finally, Ruwach spoke again. "You must return to your world now. But before you do, I have a gift. For you, Xavier."

Xavier straightened, nervous and a little fearful. Ruwach didn't move at all, but next to him something started to wriggle out of the ground. A tiny green shoot. It grew up right before their eyes, until it was twice as tall as Ruwach. Small branches with tiny leaves popped up as it grew but then instantly withered and fell off. Its main trunk suddenly stopped growing and turned brown until it looked more like a stick.

Ruwach plucked the stick from the snow. He handed it to Xavier.

"This is for you."

Xavier took the stick and stared at it, befuddled. "Um . . . thanks, I think. What's it for?" It didn't look like much of a gift.

"You will soon find out," replied Ruwach. "Go now, all of you. You will know when it is time to return."

Then he disappeared, and so did the Garden.

CHAPTER 7

Bad Things Happening

Levi found himself back in the hospital waiting room, where he had been when the Crest had appeared and taken him to Ahoratos. His mother was standing before him, trying to get his attention.

"Levi, Levi," she said again. He looked up into her eyes, which softened instantly. "I've been looking all over for you. Where'd you go?"

"Oh . . . just took a walk," Levi said vaguely. He wondered how much time had passed. Time was weird in Ahoratos. Things happened in the blink of an eye. "Is he—?"

"Yes. He's back in his room. He's been asking for you."

Levi went with his mom down the hallway, passing attendants and nurses who smiled and said, "Hello, Dr. Arthur," to Levi's mom as they passed. Some had sympathetic looks on their faces, as if they knew where he and his mom were going, and who they were going to see.

Levi didn't like the smell of hospitals. That mixture of sickness and disinfectant made him think of bad things happening. He'd been in a hospital once before, when he'd had his tonsils out. He was only five then, but he remembered eating ice cream and playing Go Fish with the nurses. People came to visit and brought presents. It was almost fun.

Now everything was different.

Levi's mom stopped before a room and glanced down at him.

"Ready?"

He nodded and went in.

His father, James Arthur, Mr. J. Ar, lay on the bed.

There were machines and tubes all around him. Some of the machines were beeping steadily, little red lines jumping on the screens. His eyes were closed, and his cheeks were sunken. His arm, lying outside the cover and connected to all the tubes, looked terribly thin.

"Hey, Dad?" Levi said, approaching the bed. Mr. J. Ar's eyes opened, and he smiled weakly.

"Hi, son," he said, his voice raspy. "How you doing?"

"Okay. What about you?"

"Oh, getting there." Mr. J. Ar's eyes flicked to his wife, who lifted the blanket to examine the bandage. "What do you think, doc?"

"So far so good," she said. "We'll know for sure in a few days."

Levi knew what they were talking about. His father had had surgery to remove a tumor, but they weren't sure they'd gotten all of it.

He hadn't known until that morning that his dad was so sick. Mr. J. Ar had always been so healthy and active. He'd played football and basketball in high school and college, and he was the basketball coach at the Cedar Creek Rec Center. He was so broad and muscular that most kids were afraid of him at first, and no one *ever* messed with him. But in the last couple of months, things had changed. He'd been coughing a lot and losing weight. He kept saying he was fine—that it was just a bad cold or the flu. Finally his mom, who was a doctor herself, made him go for a checkup. The next thing Levi knew, his dad was scheduled for surgery. His mom had told him his dad had a tumor that had to be removed immediately.

Tumor. That was a word Levi didn't like at all.

"Hey, I'll be right back; just need to check on a patient down the hall," said Levi's mom. "Don't go away, either of you." She went out the door.

Levi sat on the chair beside his dad's bed. He wasn't sure what to say. He caught his father eyeing him in that way he had of looking into a person's brain and knowing exactly what was going on there.

"Been to Ahoratos while I was—busy?" Mr. J. Ar asked in a hoarse voice, a soft grin on his face.

Levi nodded.

"Something happen? I take it from your expression that it wasn't too good."

"Yeah. You could say that again. The enemy got past us and took the Mountain of Rhema."

Mr. J. Ar didn't say anything, but his forehead creased a little and his eyes half closed.

Levi continued. "It was cold, and everything was covered in ice. And there was this huge machine . . . it was real bad. Ru said it was . . . Winter."

Mr. J. Ar's eyes shifted back to his son's face. "Ah. Winter."

"Have you been to Ahoratos in the Winter?"

"No. But I've heard about it."

Levi let out a sigh. "I guess I wasn't a lot of help. And when Xavier led us over the bridge, I just followed. I shouldn't have listened to him. I wasn't thinking. I could have changed his mind, maybe. Then I got mad and said things . . . I shouldn't have said."

Mr. J. Ar gave Levi a gentle look. "I imagine that Winter can be pretty tough in Ahoratos. On all of us." He coughed slightly, his eyes closing. Levi leaned over him, worry etched in his face.

"Dad?"

"I'm okay, son. Just tired."

Dr. Arthur came back into the room.

"Hey, Levi, why don't we go down to the cafeteria and get something to eat?" she asked. "Give Dad a little break. He's had a tough day."

Mr. J. Ar's eyes were already closed. Levi whispered goodbye and followed his mom out of the room. They took the elevator to the third-floor cafeteria. Levi glanced around at all the people getting in line for food, chatting and laughing as if everything were going fine. Yet he felt a dark emptiness hanging over him, much like how he'd felt in the Garden of Red. He shivered suddenly, aware of a new scent in the air, replacing the hospital disinfectant. It reminded him of a time when he was little and had gone out to play after a rainstorm. The driveway had been full of earthworms, which made his nose wrinkle in disgust.

Levi glanced around, wondering where the smell could have come from. There certainly weren't any earthworms around.

"You okay?"

Levi looked at his mom and nodded silently. He took a bowl of soup from the shelf in the food line and put it on his tray.

"I know this is hard, Levi," his mom said as she reached for a salad. "It will get easier. Once your father gets home, he'll start feeling better. You can help him get back on his feet."

They sat down at a table. Levi stared at his soup. He thought he might be sick.

"Is he . . . going to die?"

His mom's fork stopped halfway to her salad plate. She set it back down and swallowed hard, preparing her words carefully. "I have to be honest with you, Levi. It's a possibility. We hope the surgery was successful, that the cancer hasn't spread. But we won't know for a few days or weeks."

Levi felt a huge weight press against his chest, and he fought back the tears that suddenly filled his eyes. *Cancer.* Another word he didn't like. He looked away, toward the windows that lined one side of the room. White flakes were flying in the air. Snow. It was snowing.

Levi's mom noticed as well. "Yes, the weatherman says it's going to be a big storm," she said. They were both silent a moment. Then she reached across the table and grabbed Levi's hand.

"Levi, we will get through this. Together. It's going to be okay. Eat something. You'll need your strength. You haven't eaten all day."

Levi picked up his spoon and took a small sip of the soup, which sat like a stagnant pool in his mouth. He struggled to swallow.

His mom was right. He had to be brave now. For the sake of both his mom and his dad. He just didn't know if he could do it.

Something Ruwach had taught him from The Book came to his mind, out of the blue.

Don't be afraid. I am with you.

Thanks, Ruwach, he said silently.

And then something else, as familiar to him as his own name.

You have everything you need.

PART 2

A Time to Build

CHAPTER 8

Snow Day

Day 4

It snowed so much that school was canceled three days in a row. And it showed no signs of stopping. Winters were usually pretty mild in Cedar Creek, which made this snowstorm, according to the weatherman, "epic."

Evan sat around the house, watching the snow pile up, bored out of his mind. The radio was saying there weren't enough plow trucks to clear the roads, so people needed to stay home and not go anywhere. Everything was closed anyway, so there really wasn't anywhere to go. Evan and Xavier had spent the morning helping their father shovel the driveway and the sidewalk, which were just covered up again as soon as they were done. Evan had some fun playing in the snow, throwing snowballs at Xavier, but Xavier never fired back. He didn't seem interested in snowball fights. Evan figured he was still sulking after his failure at the battle.

Their mom made tomato soup and grilled cheese sandwiches for lunch, which was Evan's favorite. But Xavier hardly ate anything. He went to his room right after and closed the door.

"What's up with your brother?" asked Mom as Evan helped her clean up the dishes.

Evan bit his lip. "Oh, he's probably just mad because he can't play basketball. You know how he is when he misses a game." He didn't want to tell his mom what he really thought. As soon as they had returned from Ahoratos, Xavier had taken that stick Ruwach had given him and gone right to his room. He clearly didn't want to talk about it.

Evan looked out the window. "It's still snowing. Will it ever stop?"

"It will be over by tomorrow morning," said his mom. "This is the most snow we've gotten all at once in a long time. Forty years, the weatherman said."

"Forty years." Something about this stuck in Evan's throat. *Forty.*

He wondered if there would be *forty inches* of snow too. There were at least two feet already.

Xavier had left his phone on the kitchen table. Evan stared at it, amazed that Xavier would have let it out of his sight. He was never separated from his phone.

Evan still had the phone they used to share, but it was pretty old and not nearly as cool.

Evan picked up Xavier's phone and hit some of the buttons, trying it out. Then he decided to send a text to Manuel, who lived right across the street, hoping he might want to get together.

> Hey, it's Evan. (I'm using Xavier's phone.) Want to hang out?

No answer. Manuel was probably deep into some sort of science project, like creating some electrical contraption to melt snow off the driveway.

Evan dropped the phone back on the table, disappointed. He went to his room and picked up the book his grandfather had given him, a large picture book that had lots of stories about a Prince Warrior. He had read it so many times the pages were starting to curl. He sat on his bed and opened the book; the pages fell open to a chapter called "Winter." He had never seen this chapter before.

The scene depicted a snowy landscape, much like the one he had witnessed during the battle. But on the side of the illustration was a big dark spot, like a shadow. He almost didn't notice it at first, but the more he stared at the page, the bigger that dark spot seemed to get. He blinked, wondering if his eyesight was somehow to blame.

There were words under the picture.

And then it was Winter for forty days, to test the heart of the Prince Warrior.

A strange chill ran up his spine. Forty days. Ruwach had just said "forty." So the Winter came to test them? And they had already failed the test. On the very first day. But what would happen at the end of forty days?

A weird smell suddenly came out of the book, just like the smell of something rotting that had been in the Garden. What had Manuel called it? Compress? Something like that. The smell was so bad that Evan shut the book.

Then he noticed the Crest on the front of the book was glowing slightly. And it was *turning*, like a 3-D image, rotating slowly, rising up from the cover.

"Xavier!" he yelled, jumping up from the bed. "Come on! I think we're being called back!" But Xavier didn't answer. Evan took a deep breath and put his hand over the top of the Crest.

Brianna texted Levi, but he didn't answer. Again.

She knew something was wrong. Levi just wasn't himself. Even in Ahoratos, where he was usually the fiercest of the Rec-ing Crew, he had barely wanted to fight at all.

Finally she went to Grandpa Tony, who was busy fixing the kitchen sink, as usual. That sink always seemed to be leaking. Besides, there wasn't much else to do in the house. Brianna's dog, Star, woke from a nap under the kitchen table and ran to her, demanding to be picked up. Brianna obliged, sitting down on the floor so the dog could jump into her lap. Brianna nuzzled her furry nose and scratched her behind the ears.

"Grandpa, something's bothering Levi, and I don't know what to do about it. I think he's mad at me. He was acting really weird in . . . you know where."

"You mean Ahoratos?" Grandpa Tony grinned. "You can say it out loud, you know. It's okay. No one's around."

"Well, you never know when one of my sisters might come barging in. They do that a lot."

"Oh, I see." Grandpa Tony pulled himself up from under the sink so he could see his granddaughter. His face was tight and grim, as if he had some bad news.

"I think I know what's bothering Levi," he said. "Mr. J. Ar's in the hospital. He had surgery."

"*Surgery?* What for? Is he sick?"

"I don't know the details. But I'm sure Levi will tell you about it when he's ready."

Brianna pushed the dog off her lap and stood up. "I should go over to the hospital. Can you drive me?"

Grandpa Tony chuckled. "In this weather? Sorry. You'll have to wait until Mr. J. Ar comes home. And for this storm to blow over. Can't go anywhere right now."

"I feel so bad. I was joking around with Levi . . . I didn't know . . . I should really apologize."

"Why don't you call him? He'd be glad to hear from you."

"I've been texting him for three days. He hasn't answered."

"I'm sure he will soon. Hey, how about finding me a bucket? I think there's one in the upstairs bathroom."

Brianna went upstairs, but her sister Crystal was in the bathroom. Brianna knocked on the door.

"I need a bucket," she yelled.

"Just wait!" said the annoyed voice on the other side.

Brianna huffed a little then went to her room to wait. Her sister Nikki was there, studying for a test.

"Don't make a sound!" she ordered.

Brianna tiptoed over to her bed and sat down. She could see the door of the bathroom across the hall, still closed. She sighed. With three sisters, chances were always good that one of them would be in the bathroom. It was the only room in the house where any of them could go to be alone. Brianna wished that just once she could have the bedroom to herself. Or any space other than the bathroom, for that matter. All four girls shared one bedroom, so they were almost literally on top of each other, though the oldest was away at college most of the time, which helped a little.

She picked up her phone, which was charging by her bed, and punched in Levi's number. No answer. She sent him another text.

Hey! Just heard about Mr. J. Ar. I'm so sorry!

Call me if you need someone to talk to.

After a few minutes, she sent Ivy a text too.

Hey, what's up?

She waited a few minutes, but there was no response. That was weird. Ivy must be home, probably bored like she was. Ivy would be all alone too, because she didn't have any brothers or sisters to bother her. She lived with her mom; her dad didn't live with them anymore. Ivy didn't like to talk about her dad much, but Brianna knew she really wanted him to come back home to live.

Brianna never knew her own father. And she hadn't seen her mother in a long time. She wondered where her mom was now, what she was doing. If she ever thought of the daughters she left behind. Nana Lily said that her mom just couldn't take care of her right now, but that someday she would be better. And she would come to get her daughters. But the more time passed, the more Brianna thought that probably wouldn't happen. Still, it was okay. She loved Nana Lily and Grandpa Tony so much. They were the best parents any girl could ask for.

Brianna watched the snow fall out the window for a few minutes. While waiting for a text to come in from either of her friends (and for the bathroom door to open), she reached under the mattress and pulled out her Prince Warrior book. Grandpa Tony had given her this book, which was filled with stories and secrets. It even had a special page where she kept her Krÿs to charge when she wasn't using it.

Before she could even open the book, she saw the golden Crest on the cover glow and rotate, calling to her.

Suddenly the bathroom door opened.

"Okay, I'm done!" shouted Crystal.

Holding the book close to her chest, Brianna quickly ran into the bathroom, brushing past her sister. She grabbed the bucket from under the sink and raced down to the kitchen to deliver it to her grandfather.

"Gotta go!" she said, running out of the kitchen before Grandpa Tony could ask her where she was going.

But he probably already knew.

———

Evan found himself in the dark, scary forest he had been in the very first time he and Xavier were summoned to Ahoratos. Except this time, his older brother wasn't with him. The sky above was red and stormy looking. Blackened, decaying trees loomed over him. The wind whipped through the branches, making them move like arms about to grab him.

Evan ran. The trees were even more frightening now than they had been the first time. And Ruwach wasn't here this time to show him the way.

He had to get to the Water. That was the important thing. Whenever the Prince Warriors "landed" in Ahoratos, they were in a place Evan called the In-Between. It was usually dangerous, because they didn't yet have their armor. But they had to get to the Water, which would take them to the Cave. The Water was always marked with the Crest of Ahoratos, and a red-colored hue rippled across the surface right after anyone went through. Finding the water seemed like an easy task, but it usually wasn't.

Evan kept running in a roughly straight line, dodging tree roots and branches that seemed to be shooting out all around him, as if trying to stop his momentum. They scratched his face and arms as he struggled to push them away. The wind howled mournfully; it sounded like someone crying.

Evan stopped for a moment to catch his breath. He didn't know which way to go. He thought he might be running in circles, despite the fact that he had tried to go in a straight line. The trees were closing in, blocking out the sky.

He sensed something move behind him and spun around. But there was nothing there. Or was there? All around him, rustling noises made him spin in circles.

And that smell again. Something rotten. It filled his nostrils, making him gag. He realized too that he was very cold, colder than he had ever felt before. The cold felt as if it had fingers trying to clutch at him, hold him in place.

He started to run again, but the smell and the cold stayed with him. Something whizzed by his head and he almost fell, filled with fear. He looked up and saw a large bird landing on a tree branch in front of him. The bird was pure white—even its beak was white. Bigger than a crow, it was the most majestic bird Evan had ever seen. It had a noble head with black, intelligent eyes. Evan felt strangely drawn to the bird; it was looking right at him, as if it knew who he was and why he was there. But just as Evan moved in for a closer look, the bird took off again. Evan jumped backward, startled. The bird flew a short distance through the tangle of trees and landed on another branch. It turned to look at Evan, who got the impression it was waiting for him to catch up.

Follow me.

Evan wondered where the voice came from. Was it the bird? Or was it something bad and evil, leading him to a dead end?

Follow me.

Evan ran toward the bird. He suddenly found his path quite easy; the branches were no longer scraping his face, the roots no longer tripping him up. As soon as he reached the bird, it took off again, swerving and dipping around the branches. Evan sprinted to keep up.

Finally, he came to a small clearing. The bird was nowhere in sight. A stream ran through the clearing, and the Crest flickered faintly on the surface of the water. He'd found it! The Water! He tried to jump into the stream, but found his feet were stuck, as if his sneakers were frozen to the ground. Instantly the cold descended upon him, its icy fingers crawling up his shoulders and encircling his neck. His sneakers wouldn't move.

Desperately, he bent down and undid his laces. And then he jumped straight out of his sneakers, landing with a splash in the Water.

CHAPTER 9

Difficult Gifts

That was a close one."

The words were out of Evan's mouth before he even realized where he was. Usually, after coming through the Water, the Prince Warriors arrived in the Cave, where Ruwach would meet them and give them instructions from The Book, which had been written by the Source of all life, all truth, and all wisdom.

But Evan wasn't in the Cave this time. He was in the Garden of Red. That was pretty strange all by itself.

Then he saw that Brianna and Manuel were also in the Garden. They were wearing their armor as he was, but without their helmets and swords. From the looks on their faces, he assumed they'd been through the same terrifying experience he had.

"That was the worst," said Brianna, still breathless from the experience. "I've never been so scared in my life."

"Me neither," Manuel added, his voice raspy.

"The forest?" said Evan.

Brianna and Manuel both nodded.

"I didn't think I'd ever get out of there," Evan confessed. "If it weren't for that bird—"

"You saw the bird too?" asked Manuel.

Evan nodded.

"I did too," said Brianna. "But then it disappeared. I thought I'd gone the wrong way. And my feet froze to the ground—"

"Mine too!" said Evan. "I had to jump out of my shoes!"

"So did I," said Manuel.

"But I didn't see either of you guys there," said Evan. "How could we have been in the same place and not seen each other?"

"Beats me," said Brianna. "But anything can happen in Ahoratos."

Evan spun around. "Did you hear that?" He peered up into the branches of a tree behind him.

"Maybe it was just the wind," Brianna said, her voice quivering a little.

"What wind? There's no wind here," said Manuel.

"I'm sure it's nothing," Brianna said.

"Warriors." The three kids jumped at the voice. They turned to see Ruwach striding toward them down the garden path. His face, as usual, was invisible inside the hood, but his voice was lighter than it had been the last time. Not nearly as ominous. "You are wondering why I called you here. Only you three."

"Sort of," said Evan.

"I have something for each of you. Follow me."

The three children followed Ruwach down a new path, to a part of the Garden none of them had seen before. It looked just as dead and barren as the rest.

Ruwach stopped suddenly, reached down, and picked up a smooth gray rock. He handed it to Evan.

"This is for you."

"A . . . rock?" Evan stared at the gift, mystified. It looked like a plain old rock, but it fit perfectly in his palm and felt comfortingly warm. "For me? Wow, you shouldn't have."

The other two kids chuckled a little, but Ruwach did not make a sound. Evan cleared his throat and tried again.

"Uh . . . thanks. I guess. What's it for?"

"It is a Stone of Remembrance."

"Okay . . . so . . . what am I supposed to remember?"

"Me."

"You?"

The hood nodded slightly.

"That's it? I mean, I don't think I actually need a rock to help me remember you. You're pretty . . . memorable."

"Keep it, all the same," said Ruwach. "You may take your gift back to your world with you, just as Xavier did with his gift. Don't lose it." Evan saw Ruwach's hood focused on him. Evan swallowed. He had once thrown away a gift that Ruwach had given him. He would never do that again.

"I won't," he said.

Ruwach turned away and continued quickly down yet another path. The kids were beginning to realize that the Garden was a lot bigger than they'd thought. They came upon a small pool of water. The water was so clear and still that it reflected everything above it perfectly, like a mirror.

"At least it's not frozen," said Evan.

Ruwach put one of his shining hands into the water, which trembled at his touch. He pulled something out and turned to Manuel.

"Hold out your hands."

Manuel did, and Ruwach placed a wet, brownish lump into them. It looked like a small, misshapen potato. Manuel looked from the lump to Ruwach, his eyes narrowing.

"A flower bulb?" he said.

Ruwach nodded.

"It looks a bit like a water-lily bulb."

"Exactly," said Ruwach.

He swiftly turned and started moving again, gliding over the dirt path as if his feet never touched the ground. As if he had no feet at all. The three kids scrambled to keep up. They were getting tired when Ruwach finally stopped again, under a large tree. He bent down and picked up one of the stringy, tangled roots that stuck up from the ground. He snapped it off and gave it to

Brianna, who looked at it with disappointment etched on her face.

"A . . . root?"

"That's almost as nice as a rock," Evan said under his breath.

"These gifts mean something unique to each of you," Ruwach said. "You will soon discover that meaning, if you are patient, and you listen carefully."

"But what about the others?" said Brianna. "Levi and Xavier and Ivy and Finn?"

"Do not concern yourself with the gifts of others."

A light fell upon them as if from a distant star. The children turned to see a soft glow at the very end of the Garden, which grew larger and larger until it took on a shape they recognized.

The Book.

The Book of the Source, speeding toward them on its golden pedestal. It stopped just before it was about to crash into them, hovering for a moment before gently setting itself down on the ground. The golden cover projected the image of the Crest of Ahoratos, which rotated slowly in midair. The Book opened, and the pages began to turn, making a soft, tinkling music that appeared as tiny spangles of light in the air. Then the pages stopped turning, and words floated up from the page, forming themselves into a sentence.

You have not been given fear but power.

"So these things have power?" Manuel asked, gazing down at his innocent-looking water-lily bulb.

Evan looked down at the dirty rock in his hand, wondering how it could be powerful. The worst it could do was break a window if he threw it hard enough. And the flower bulb and root seemed equally un-powerful. Yet he knew that the tiny seeds they'd been given before from this very Garden had grown into mighty shields when they had raised them up in their fists. Evan gripped the rock and raised his arm in the air to see if the rock would do something.

It didn't.

"Are we going on a mission now?" he asked.

"The time is not yet," Ruwach said.

"But we only have forty days right?" said Manuel. "Or, technically, thirty-six days."

"The time is not yet," Ruwach said again.

"Ru," said Brianna, "I just found out that Mr. J. Ar . . . is in the hospital. Is he sick? Can you make him better?"

"What's wrong with Mr. J. Ar?" said Evan, alarmed.

"I don't know. He had surgery."

"Surgery? Maybe it was just something easy to fix, like an . . . apple-deckamy," said Evan.

"Appendectomy," Manuel corrected. He frowned. "If it was something like that, Levi would have told us." He turned toward Ruwach and said in a soft, trembling voice, "Is Mr. J. Ar really sick? Like . . . my mom was?"

Ruwach was silent for a moment. "James will fulfill his mission," he said finally, in a voice so faint the Warriors almost missed it. "As will all who serve the Source with whole hearts."

Evan's brow furrowed, and he scrunched up his nose, displeased with how vague Ruwach seemed to be at the moment. "When can we see him?" Evan asked, impatiently. "The Source, I mean. Why can't we see him in person?"

Ruwach's hooded head nodded slightly. "You already have."

CHAPTER 10

The Big Stick

Xavier stared at the stick.

It was leaning up against his dresser in the corner, where it had been since he'd gotten back from Ahoratos. He'd been staring at it for three days now, as snow continued to pile up outside. School would probably be cancelled for a week. He didn't know how much longer he could stand it, sitting in his room, doing nothing but trying to figure out what he was supposed to do with the "gift" Ruwach had given him.

He wondered if this was his punishment for messing things up in the battle. Like he should be using the stick to beat himself up. But that didn't make a whole lot of sense. For one thing, he couldn't easily hit himself with a stick this long. And he doubted that Ruwach would want him to.

So what do you do with a big stick?

He remembered a quote from Teddy Roosevelt he'd learned in history class: "Speak softly and carry a big stick." Roosevelt meant that the big stick was used to threaten people. You didn't have to yell when you had a big stick in your hand. But that didn't seem right either. Ruwach never taught the Prince Warriors to threaten others. Yet it could be some kind of weapon. He'd seen martial arts experts who fought with sticks, and that had seemed pretty cool. But the Krÿsen had completed their armor. They didn't need any more weapons.

He wished Rook were here to talk to. Rook had always had a word of wisdom or encouragement to offer, even if he didn't have all the answers. Rook had saved Xavier's life and given his own in the process. Xavier still felt a pang of regret when he thought of that. If only he had been paying attention when that dragon was coming for him, then Rook might still be alive.

And then . . . this last battle. If Rook had been with him, he would have told Xavier to stay where he was, to not try to advance over the bridge, and Xavier would have listened. Or if Mr. J. Ar had been there . . . but neither of them were. Rook was gone, and Mr. J. Ar— where *was* Mr. J. Ar anyway? Xavier hadn't seen him in quite a while.

He reached into his pocket for his phone but realized he didn't have it. He must have left it on the kitchen table. He got up and opened his door, hoping

Evan wasn't there to ambush him. Evan had wanted to go outside and build a snow castle or have a snowball war, and Xavier was trying to avoid him.

Evan wasn't there. He wasn't in his room either. Xavier relaxed, thinking maybe his little brother had gone to hang out at Manuel's house. He went downstairs.

His dad was sitting at the kitchen table, reading the newspaper, a cup of coffee in front of him. The phone was still there too. Xavier went over to pick it up. He was going to leave when his dad spoke.

"Don't even want to say hello?"

Xavier turned back. "Sorry. Just needed my phone."

"Sit down, Xavier." Mr. Blake folded up his newspaper. Xavier groaned inwardly. He knew he was in for some sort of talk. He sat down opposite his father, fingering the phone, trying not to look at it.

"Tough day?" said his dad.

"Nah. Just bored."

"That's not like you. Sure you're all right?"

"Sure." Xavier tried to smile. "Everything's cool."

Mr. Blake peered at him a moment longer. "Okay then. But if you ever need to talk, you know I'm here, right?"

"Sure. Thanks, Dad." Xavier got up to leave and then turned back. "Hey, Dad?"

"Yes?"

"What do you do when . . . when you make a big mistake, and you don't know how to fix it?"

"Hmmm. Tough question." Mr. Blake sat back in his chair, thinking. "You have two choices. You can learn from it, move forward, and make sure you don't do it again. Or you can let it eat at you until you are unable to move forward at all." He paused. "Which one are you doing?"

"The second one, I think."

Mr. Blake nodded slightly. "I've been there. My dad used to tell me: 'Don't look back, unless you plan on going there.'"

"Right," said Xavier. "But . . . it's hard."

"Yes, it is. But you can do it, Xavier. I'm sure of that."

Xavier thanked his dad and went back to his room. He put the stick in the closet and shut the door so he wouldn't have to look at it again. Then he lay down on the bed and turned on his phone.

There was a message from Brianna.

Mr. J. Ar in hospital!!!

Xavier felt his heart sink farther into his chest, so he could barely breathe. Next to his dad, Mr. J. Ar was his most important role model. He hoped it wasn't anything too serious.

There was a knock on the door. Evan's voice: "Can I come in?"

For once, Xavier welcomed the idea of talking to his little brother. He needed some distraction. "Yeah," he said.

Evan opened the door slowly, looking around as if he expected to be hit by a pillow or have a pile of dirty laundry fall on his head.

"What's up?" said Xavier, trying to sound annoyed.

"Nothing." Evan came into the room and shut the door. He sniffed the air. "What's that smell?"

"What smell?"

"It smells like dad's aftershave. Are you using aftershave?"

Xavier sighed and rolled over on the bed. "What do you want, Evan?"

"I was in Ahoratos."

Xavier rolled back and sat up. "You were?" He wondered why Evan had been called and he hadn't. Was he no longer welcome? After what he'd done, maybe he deserved that.

"Yeah. And . . . I got this." Evan showed him the rock. "This was my 'gift.' Ruwach said it was like your stick." He handed the rock to Xavier, who examined it carefully.

"It's a rock," said Xavier.

"I know that. Duh."

"Does it do anything?"

"Not that I can see."

"So it *is* just like my stick." Xavier gave him back the rock. "Useless gifts for useless Prince Warriors."

"You think we're really useless?"

"I don't know anymore." Xavier paused. "Brianna texted and said that Mr. J. Ar is in the hospital."

"I know. He might be really sick too. I wonder why Levi didn't tell us."

"I don't know. Maybe he doesn't want it to be true. Sometimes, when you say something out loud, it becomes more real, and you have to . . . face it."

"I don't want it to be true either," said Evan. Then he told Xavier about his trip through the scary woods and the rotting smell, the thing he called the giant Empty.

"Something bad is going on. It's like the Empty is . . . taking over. Eating up Ahoratos."

"Yeah." Xavier let out a deep sigh. He had thought a lot about that strange feeling in the Garden. The Empty. It was more than a feeling. It was like an—entity—a being or a thing that had a definite presence. He didn't want to tell Evan, but he had an idea what it might be.

CHAPTER 11

Ginger Girl

Day 8

Ivy slumped in the plastic chair outside the principal's office, her arms folded over her chest, her knees pressed tightly together. She could hear Mrs. Loomis, the principal, talking in a loud, stern voice through the closed door. The shadowy outline of the principal loomed over the smaller one of her mother through the frosted glass of the door, making it look as though Mrs. Loomis were about to devour her. In the middle of the glass was an engraved sign: Sybil Loomis, Principal.

Though her mother's replies were too soft to understand, Ivy knew what she was probably saying all the same: "Don't worry, Mrs. Loomis. I'll talk to her. It won't happen again."

Finally the door opened, and her mom came out, followed by the principal, who was possibly, at least according to the majority of the kids at the Cedar Creek Middle School, the meanest woman on the planet. She might also be the tallest. Her hair was whipped into a perfect French twist and piled high on her head with not one strand out of place. She wore a tailored green suit with a snakeskin belt. She gazed down at Ivy, her lips pursed into a disapproving line. Her black, horn-rimmed glasses reflected the light so Ivy couldn't see her eyes at all, only wide, blank discs that silently

72

pronounced judgment. She did not speak. She didn't have to. Next to her, Ivy's mom looked small and sad and beaten.

"Come on, Ivy," said her mom in a tired voice. "Let's go home."

Ivy followed her mom out of the office without looking back at Mrs. Loomis, but she could feel the principal's gaze boring a hole in the back of her head. They got into the car, and Ivy's mom started driving home.

"First day back at school after a week of snow days, and I'm called into the principal's office," said Ivy's mom after a long period of silence. "What is going on with you, Ivy? You never used to do things like this." Ivy didn't respond. She just stared out the window at the huge piles of snow on either side of the road. Her mom heaved a sigh. "You want to tell me what happened?"

"This kid at my lunch table keeps calling me 'ginger girl' and 'carrot top' and 'freckle face,' and he gets all the other boys to laugh at me. I was just sick of it. So I dumped a carton of milk on his head." She paused. "He deserved it."

Ivy glanced at her mom in time to see her stifle a small smile. "And you think that was an appropriate response?"

Ivy shrugged. "It was all I could think of at the time. Honestly, Mom, you have no idea how mean and stupid those kids are."

"Oh, I probably do. I was your age once too. You know there is nothing wrong whatsoever with having red hair. Some bullies like to tease, that's all. You shouldn't pay any attention to them."

"Everyone always says that. But it's just hard."

"I know. But this is not like you. You never used to do things like this."

That was true. Ivy didn't even know why she had reacted the way she did. She liked her red hair. It was different. It made her stand out. Yet when those kids made fun of her, it just seemed so mean and rotten. She'd lashed out in anger.

Ivy looked out the window. The sky was gray and lifeless. Everything was frozen and still.

Her phone beeped. She took it out and saw a text from Brianna.

I looked for you at lunch. They said you got sent home. What happened?

She deleted the text without answering. What she did was probably all over the school by now. She wished she didn't have to go back ever again.

"Mrs. Loomis said she would deal with the kid in question and she wants you to tell her if the teasing continues," said Ivy's mom. "But if there's another milk-carton incident, you'll be back in her office. I need you to promise me that you will not do that again, no matter what anyone says to you."

"I promise," said Ivy, choking back tears. She hated to cry, especially in front of people. It frustrated her that in Ahoratos she could be a fearless Warrior, but in this world she was such a useless, ugly mess.

When they got home, Ivy helped her mom put away the groceries. Then she went up to her room and pulled a guitar out from under her bed. She'd gotten the guitar for Christmas the year before and had started taking lessons. She loved to sing and play, especially when she was upset.

Halfway through her song, her phone started to ring. She stopped playing, annoyed. It was probably Brianna again, bugging her to find out what happened. She pulled out her phone to decline the call, but then she saw the large image of the Crest floating on the screen.

She had never been so happy to see that Crest.

CHAPTER 12

An Unexpected Encounter

Finn paused in his shoveling and wiped his brow. He was sweating, even though it was freezing. He'd had no idea there were so many sidewalks at the Cedar Creek Rec Center. He had to clear them all before it opened for after-school programming that afternoon.

The whole day before he'd spent clearing the driveway and parking lots, using the pickup truck fitted with a snowplow blade. Driving that truck had reminded him, eerily, of the Askalons, the giant tank-chariot things that had plowed their way through Ahoratos to the Mountain of Rhema.

That was probably why it was taking him so long to finish the snow clearing. He couldn't get his mind off those chariots, or the ice-snakes, or the ice-webs, or anything to do with the battle. Or with Ahoratos. He was aching to go back. In fact, he often wished he could just stay there. To never return to this world and his boring life as caretaker for the rec center. He'd wanted so much more for his life. It was only a few years ago that he was the star of his high-school football team, dreaming of going pro. He'd blown up that dream with the mistakes he'd made. Curiously, though, he didn't have that dream anymore. Being in Ahoratos, learning to be a Prince Warrior, and making new friends had changed him more than he even realized.

Finn had been rescued from Skot'os by Rook, with a little help from Ivy. Rook had been like a big brother to him, had understood him like none of the others could because he'd been a prisoner in Skot'os once too. Finn had even taken over Rook's old job at the rec center.

But now Rook was gone. Finn knew that Rook wasn't *really* gone. Ruwach had promised that Finn would see Rook again one day. But still, not being able to see him or talk to him right now was hard.

Now Finn just wanted to do what Rook did: rescue prisoners like him. If he could, Finn would just stay in Ahoratos and go on rescue missions. He'd beaten a whole squadron of Forgers once, even before he had gotten his sword. He knew he could do it. Whenever he had a chance, he asked Ruwach when he could go back. But Ruwach always said the same thing: "There is a time for everything."

Finn bent over to start shoveling again. He supposed he'd just have to wait on Ruwach's time.

He got to the end of the sidewalk and turned the corner. There he saw a figure in a dark green coat spraying the back wall of the rec center with graffiti.

"Hey!" he shouted. The kid saw him and dropped the paint can. He started to run. Finn ran after him, his strong legs leaping through the snow, the shovel held over his head. "Stop!" he yelled. He could see that the boy was struggling against the deep snow, unable to move as fast. Finn caught up to him, dropped the shovel, and tackled him. The two fell into the snow, the boy struggling to get free before finally giving up. Finn raised himself up so he could see who he had tackled.

"Landon?"

He knew this kid. He was often at the rec center, but he usually didn't participate in any of the activities except for basketball. Mary Stanton had told Finn that Landon had once bullied Manuel relentlessly.

"What are you doing?" Finn barked at the kid, holding him by the collar in the snow.

"Nothing," Landon said, trying to pull himself away.

"You call that nothing?" Finn pointed to the large blotches of green spray paint on the wall.

"I was just . . . messing around."

"Why aren't you in school?"

"Didn't feel like going."

Finn pulled a phone from his pocket. He showed it to Landon.

"I'm about to call the police. Do you want me to call the police? Report you for defacing a public building?"

Landon hesitated, then shook his head.

"Okay then, here's the deal. You are going to clean that paint off today, before the rec center opens. And, you'll come here every Saturday for a month and help me with the maintenance."

"What? I'm not doing that!"

"Then I'll start dialing." Finn hit the numbers 9-1-1 on his phone. His finger hovered over the Send button.

"Stop." Landon sighed and grumbled. "Okay, fine."

"If there's a day you don't show up, I will be coming to look for you. And believe me, you don't want that."

"I get it." Landon pushed Finn away and struggled to his feet.

"You'd better go get some soap and a scrub brush," Finn said.

"I don't have that stuff."

Finn sighed. "Fine. You can use our supplies. Come inside, and I'll get them for you." Finn turned to head toward the door.

"Hey," said Landon. Finn turned back to look at him. "Why didn't you just report me? Why are you . . . giving me a chance?"

"Because I was just as dumb as you once," Finn said. "And someone gave me a second chance."

Finn took Landon into the building and got him a bucket of cleaning solution and a scrub brush. Then he sent Landon out to clean the wall, with the warning that if it wasn't absolutely spotless, he would call Landon's parents. Landon grunted but did as he was told. Finn left him to his work and went back to retrieve his shovel. But when he got there, there was something hovering over the top of the shovel handle. The Crest. Solid and bright, rotating slowly in midair. Finn smiled to himself.

Guess I won't finish the shoveling after all.

CHAPTER 13

Scouting

"There it is."

Finn and Ivy paused at the edge of the wood. They had been walking for quite a long time, their boots forming snowshoes so they could move quickly in the deep snow. The trunks of tall trees rose up all around them, bare branches crackling in the stiff wind.

The Mountain before them was covered in snow and ice. They couldn't see the very top because a dark cloud ringed the entire summit. But smoke continued to pour into the sky, creating a black cloud overhead. Thin rivers of red lava trickled down the mountain, like blood, slowing and steaming when it hit the snow.

"He's taken over the whole mountain," Ivy said.

"Probably building some new fortress at the top," Finn said.

"Do you think those Askalons are still around?"

"Probably. And see those skypods?" Finn said, pointing to the large lumpy, rock-like objects floating in the air near the top of the mountain. "He's probably got spies on them, keeping a lookout. Maybe even dragons."

"Great." Ivy sighed. "And we know what's in those skypods, so we definitely don't want to mess with them."

"Ruwach told us just to scout out the situation," said Finn. "To gather information and report back. Without being captured."

"Sure. Piece of cake," Ivy said sarcastically. It still seemed odd to her that only she and Finn had been tasked with this job. She had a feeling it was because she and Finn were the only ones who had been prisoners in Ahoratos. Maybe Ruwach thought that gave them a special sort of ability to sense Forger traps.

Seeing Ahoratos so frozen and desolate filled Ivy with an unnamed dread. And then there was that smell. Ahoratos used to smell sweet and fresh most of the time. Now this pervasive stink just seemed to hang over the whole land. There was no escaping it.

"Let's see if we can find a way up the mountain," Finn said. "A secret way."

"If we go out into the open, we'll be seen," she said. She glanced at her breastplate. "Breastplate says to keep going this way. Let's stay in the trees; it's easier to hide if we see any of those chariots around."

She and Finn turned and started walking again, staying in the cover of the trees, which hugged the base of the mountain. To her surprise, her boots glided over the snow soundlessly, almost like skis. Finn's did too.

"That's cool," she remarked.

They glided in silence, gazing around them, searching for something promising. But the landscape didn't change much. Snow and ice and bare trees. The mountain rose so steeply that she couldn't see any way they could actually climb up without being seen, let alone try to lead an attack.

"It looks pretty hopeless," she said.

Suddenly two figures with swords raised jumped into their path. Ivy shrieked. Finn reached for his sword, but then Ivy started to laugh.

"Kalle! Kristian! Where did you come from? You scared us half to death."

"Sorry," said Kalle. Or was it Kristian? Ivy wasn't sure which one was which. "We heard movement and thought it was a Forger patrol."

"Forger patrols? Have you seen any?"

"Nope," said the other twin. "But the Askalons are roving around. You can see their tracks in the snow. And there are Bone Breakers on all the skypods."

"Bone Breakers?"

"Big birds. They look like giant vultures with blood-tipped feathers. Very keen eyesight. They will see anyone who attempts to climb the mountain."

"Great," said Ivy. "What are you doing here anyway?"

"We're searching for a path up the mountain," said Kristian. Or Kalle.

"So are we. Did you find one?" asked Finn.

The twins shook their heads. "There must be something we're missing."

"I agree," said Ivy. "Nothing we can do but keep going."

"Kristian and I will join you, if that's all right with you," said Kalle.

"Sure. You guys are good at sneaking around in snow."

"We are used to it," said Kristian with a grin.

The four of them moved single file through the deep woods, keeping an eye out for Forger patrols or ice-belching machines lying in wait. Ivy led the way, following the steady beam of her breastplate, with the twins behind her. Finn stayed in the rear, as he usually liked to do, so he could look out for anyone who might try to attack from behind.

They had walked about a mile when Finn spoke up in a harsh whisper.

"Look!" The others turned back to see Finn pointing to the ground at their feet, where something appeared to be moving under the hardened snow. "Does that look like water to you?"

"Yes! Running water," said Kalle, his voice now buoyed with hope. "That could indicate an underground spring. Spring water wouldn't be frozen yet."

"How does that help us?" asked Ivy.

"If there is a spring, it's probably coming from under the mountain. We should follow it. We might find the source of the spring through a tunnel or a cave. It's not much, but it's worth a look."

They followed the trickle of water until it formed a crack in the snow and flowed more freely. The stream led them out of the cover of the trees. Ivy paused, unsure if they should proceed in the open. The wind was picking up, and icy snow stung their faces like a swarm of flying ants.

"Something doesn't want us going this way," said Ivy, raising an arm to shield her eyes.

"There!" said Finn. The narrow stream led directly to the base of the mountain, where the Warriors could make out a small opening in the ice. "That's where the water leads."

"Looks small," said Kristian.

"Maybe we can dig it out," said Finn.

"What's that smell?" Ivy asked, wrinkling her nose. "It's different from the Empty smell. But still bad. Like rotten eggs."

"Sulfur," said Kalle. "Don't worry; it's not dangerous. Just stinky."

"Great." A gust of wind nearly knocked Ivy over. The snow seemed to be falling sideways, blasting them with more stinging ice. "Maybe we should go back to the Cave!" she cried over the roar of the rising wind. "I don't think we can make it in this storm."

"We have to go now," said Finn. "The storm will be our cover!"

"I agree!" said Kalle. "We came this far. We have to try!"

Finn was the first to move, dashing across the icy expanse toward the small opening in the mountain. Kalle, Kristian, and Ivy soon followed, struggling against the wind that seemed to want to blow them back as far away as possible. Ivy thought it might succeed.

"Come on!" said Kalle. He reached back to grab her hand. "I'll help you!"

When they got to the opening, Ivy could make out Finn on his knees, trying to punch a hole in the ice with his Krÿs. His whole body was coated in ice and snow, but he kept working. Kalle and Kristian soon joined him, hacking away at the ice until the hole was big enough to crawl through. Water streamed from the enlarged hole, smelly and steamy.

"The water's really hot," Finn yelled to the others. "Don't touch it with your bare hands!"

"Let me go in first." Ivy ducked and crab-walked through the ice hole, holding on to the sides to keep from touching the water. She straddled the small stream and stood up unsteadily, directing her glowing breastplate deeper into the tunnel that lay before her. Inside, the noxious smell was so pungent she had to plug her nose. Her breastplate glowed steadily, indicating that she was supposed to keep going in this direction, but she wasn't sure she wanted to.

"See anything?" yelled Finn from the entrance.

"A tunnel!" Ivy called out. "I think we're supposed to follow it!"

She moved forward a few steps to make room for the boys, who tumbled in behind her. Kalle, followed closely by Kristian. Or vice versa.

"Hot in here," said Kalle, finding his footing on either side of the spring.

"A sauna," said Kristian. "We have lots of saunas in Finland, but this one smells very bad."

A few more hacks at the ice, and Finn wormed his way through the opening. Outside the storm raged, but the sound of the wind seemed to be dampened by the warm, humid tunnel. The four Warriors took a moment to catch their breath and adjust to the sudden change.

"This must lead deeper into the mountain," Ivy said. Following the light of her breastplate, she started to move, the boys close behind her. The tunnel curled around boulders and sometimes became so narrow they had to squeeze sideways.

"It's getting hotter," said Kalle, pausing to wipe his brow.

"As if we didn't know that," said Kristian with a slight scoff.

The smell grew stronger the deeper they went. Just when Ivy was certain there was no end to this tunnel at all, it widened into a large cavern filled with bubbling water that glowed green, steam rising from its surface. The ceiling hung with massive stalactites, and the walls dripped with slime. The four Warriors stepped out of the tunnel and onto a narrow ledge that ran the circumference of the pool, trying to keep from touching the slimy walls.

Ivy coughed. "Wow, that really stinks. I thought the Empty was bad, but this is worse."

"The Empty?" asked Kristian.

"It's what Evan calls . . . the feeling up there on the surface. You know. Whatever is causing that rotting smell that seems to be everywhere."

"I see. Empty." Kristian nodded.

"Should we try to cross?" said Kalle. "The tunnel continues on the other side. And it looks dry over there. Perhaps there is some sort of path up to the top."

"The water is too hot to swim," said Finn. "And it might be toxic."

Ivy glanced down at her breastplate, which had gone dark. "No. I think we should go back."

"Why would Ruwach send us here just to go back?" Kristian stuck his foot into the water. Ivy gasped, shocked. But instead of sinking, Kristian's boot just stayed right on the top. He took another step onto the pool and stood there, on the water. "Look. We can walk on it," he said with a big grin. "The boots are like flotation devices. This is cool!"

Kalle went next, taking a couple of steps on the water. "Yes, it's true," he said. "Awesome."

"Guys, I really think we should turn around," Ivy said. "The breastplates—"

"Come on. Don't be a chicken!" said Kalle.

Ivy threw back her shoulders. "I'm not a chicken," she said, her face turning red.

Finn put a hand on her shoulder. "You go on ahead," he called out to the twins. "We'll wait here—"

He never finished the sentence. For something exploded from the water, something massive and green, covered in scales, and with sharp, snapping teeth.

CHAPTER 14

Leviathan

Ivy yelled, grabbing her Krÿs. "Look out!"
Kalle and Kristian had no time to react before the monster was upon them. It curled its long, spiked neck and lunged at Kristian. Kalle managed to raise his sword and smash the thing's massive snout, knocking it sideways. It flailed and splashed, creating a near tidal wave.

"Come back!" Ivy stood in frozen terror as the twins tried to make a run for it back to the ledge. But the water was no longer still; it rocked with waves churned up by the monster, making it hard for the twins to keep their footing. If they fell, they might be burned by the boiling water or locked in the creature's jaws before they were able to recover.

The creature rounded for another attack, its serpentine body just visible under the turbulent water. Ivy saw that it had a head like some prehistoric alligator. It breached again and snatched one of Kalle's boots in its jaws. Kalle let out a scream as his foot was pulled down into the water.

"It's trying to take my boot!" Kalle cried.

Kristian spun around and grabbed his brother's arm, smashing his sword against the creature's head. It let go once more, but Kalle's boot was so mangled he could no longer keep his balance.

"Help!" Kristian yelled. "I can't hold him!"

"We need to help them!" Ivy said. She turned to Finn. "I'll try to distract that thing so you can rescue the boys. Okay?"

Finn nodded.

Ivy stepped onto the rolling water, struggling to keep her balance. She took several steps away from the twins, then pulled out her seed and deployed her shield. She waved her other arm in the air, making loud, whistling noises.

The creature swerved to look at her. She called to it. "Hey! Toothy! Come and get me!"

The creature dove under the water and rocketed toward her. It broke the surface but collided with the shield and fell backward with a high-pitched scream. Ivy took a few steps backward, drawing it farther away from Finn, who had gone out to help Kristian bring Kalle back to the ledge.

Ivy braced herself for another attack, but it never came. She stared down into the depths of the pool as the water calmed. There was no movement. The creature had suddenly disappeared. She wondered where it could have gone.

Ivy lowered her shield and looked up to see Finn helping the brothers to safety. She walked over the water to join them, though her legs were shaking so badly that she was afraid they might go out from under her.

"You okay?" Finn asked her as he let go of Kalle. Kristian helped his brother to sit down on the ledge to rest.

"I . . . think . . . so," she said between gasps for breath. "Just give me a minute." She crouched down next to Kalle, who was holding on to his crushed boot. "How are you?"

"The leviathan almost got my boot. It's pretty mangled," Kalle answered in a pained voice. "Not sure about my foot. It really hurts."

"A leviathan? You mean, you've seen one before?" Ivy asked.

"Not really. Just read about them. Giant sea creatures. Part snake, part alligator. But how did it get in here? In an underground pool? The leviathans are supposed to be in the open sea."

"This pool must go pretty deep," said Finn. "If that creature came from Skot'os, then this water must come from Skot'os too. Maybe there's an underground river or something."

"So the leviathans are guarding the mountain too," said Ivy with a sigh. "From underneath. Awesome."

"We should get out of here, I think. The leviathan will probably be back with more like it." Kristian turned to his brother. "Can you walk?"

"I think so," said Kalle. "I might be a little slow."

"Looks like this tunnel isn't going to help us much, after all," said Ivy, disappointed. Their scouting mission seemed like a total failure.

The four of them made their way slowly to the opening of the spring, Kalle leaning on his brother's shoulder. But instead of the outside world with a storm raging, there was only a plain wooden door. Ivy went forward, puzzled, and pushed it open. Something flashed before her eyes. She shut them against the blinding light. When she opened them again, she realized she was back in the Cave with Finn, Kalle, and Kristian by her side. Sparks danced all around them. Kalle collapsed to the floor, grunting a little. The Sparks instantly went into action, gathering on his mangled boot. Soon there were so many Sparks on the boot that the boot itself appeared to be made of tiny lights. The Warriors watched in fascination as the boot began to unravel, the crushed parts filling out, the punctures disappearing. Kalle's breathing came easier, as if the pain had been instantly relieved.

When the Sparks departed, the boot looked as if it had never been damaged.

"How's it feel?" Kristian asked.

"Good." Kalle got to his feet and gingerly tested out his foot. He then put his full weight down and smiled, glancing up at the Sparks buzzing around his head. "Thanks, guys."

"You're welcome." The Warriors whirled to see Ruwach standing before them, as if he had been there the whole time. Ivy laughed.

"Ru! Thanks for the shortcut." She threw her arms around him in a hug. "We're really glad to see you."

"As I am you. So. Tell me what you have discovered."

"We found a spring that led us inside the mountain," said Ivy. "We were hoping it might be a way to the fortress, but it only led to a green pool with this weird, alligator-snake creature that almost killed us."

"A leviathan," said Kalle.

"Ah. Leviathans." Ruwach mused on this. "Creatures without fear. The coiling serpents of the sea. The most powerful ever created by the Source."

"The Source made the leviathans?" said Finn, tilting his head to one side. "Why?"

"For the same reason he created you. The Source gave the leviathans a wide sea in which to play. They will not hurt you if you leave them alone."

"We weren't bothering it at all—it bothered us!" said Kalle. "We were minding our own business."

"In the mind of the leviathan, you were trespassing," said Ruwach. "The water is its domain."

"Great," said Ivy. She heaved a big sigh. "Well, it doesn't look as though we are going to get to the fortress through the underground tunnel. Not with those creatures patrolling it."

"Perhaps not," said Ruwach. "But there may be a way after all."

"Oh? How?"

"You will know when the time comes."

Ivy let out a sigh. "I should have known you would say that."

"Hold out your hands, all of you," said Ruwach.

The four Warriors obeyed, holding their hands out flat. Instantly they felt them tingle with warmth. And then a soft glow appeared from the center of their palms, radiating outward in a star pattern.

"This is my gift to you," said Ruwach.

"I don't see anything," said Kalle, staring at his hand. The glow was already gone.

"You will in time."

CHAPTER 15

The Comeback

Day 15

Xavier was having a hard time concentrating on schoolwork. All he could think about was the basketball game that night. The Cedar Creek Lions were playing the Riverview Sharks, and Xavier was suiting up as one of only two sophomores on the varsity team. He couldn't wait to get back on the court, especially after the disaster in Ahoratos. He needed a win. Coach Cavanaugh had been impressed with his playing and promised he would put Xavier in this game.

He just wished Mr. J. Ar would be there to give him some pointers and cheer him on. His strong, steady presence encouraged Xavier. Made him want to play harder and better than he had before. But Mr. J. Ar wasn't even home from the hospital. The news was not very good. He didn't just have his appendix out. He was still pretty sick. It would be weeks until he would be able to come to a game.

Xavier opened his locker and quickly took out the books he needed for his geometry class. He glanced at his phone. Ten text notifications, and more kept coming in. Most of them about the game. He swiped the screen and started to read them as he slammed his locker door shut and headed to class. But he wasn't looking where he was going and rammed into someone walking past him. His phone went flying, along with the other person's books.

"I'm sorry," he said, glancing at the student he'd run into. She was bending down to pick up her books.

"No problem," she said. She grabbed his phone and handed it back to him. "My fault." She smiled. She had long brown hair and pretty brown eyes.

"No, I wasn't looking. . . ." Xavier just stared at her.

"It's okay," she said. "I hope your phone's not broken."

"Uh, it's fine." Xavier stuck it in his pocket without looking at it.

"You're Xavier, right? You play basketball?"

"Yeah."

"Cool. I'm Cassie."

"Oh."

Cassie waited for him to say something more, and when he didn't, she shrugged. "Good luck at the game."

"Thanks."

She smiled again and turned to walk down the hall. Xavier watched her go.

The gymnasium was filled to capacity. Fans for both the Sharks and the Lions were already cheering as their teams filed in from the locker rooms and sat on their respective benches on either side of the scoring table. The Sharks' mascot ran across the court, waving his fins and pretending to scare the onlookers. The Lions' mascot roared crazily and chased the Shark around.

On the bench, Xavier had to keep his hand on his leg to stop it from shaking. He looked up at the bleachers, searching for his family and friends. He saw his parents sitting three rows up from the floor along with Evan, who waved at him. Xavier smiled but didn't wave. He hoped he'd get a little playing time so his family wouldn't have come to the game for nothing. Brianna was there with her grandfather, holding up a sign that said "Go Xavier!" They both waved.

Xavier didn't see Levi anywhere, though he wasn't surprised. They hadn't spoken since Levi's blowup in the Garden of Red. He wasn't mad at Levi, but he did think Levi was still mad at him.

At the very top of the bleachers, Xavier saw Cassie, the girl he'd run into in the hall, sitting with a bunch of other girls. She caught his eye and waved; he smiled and turned around quickly.

"Ooh, Cassie Cavanaugh . . . I think she likes you." Daryn, the other sophomore, gave him a shoulder shove. "Nice work, Romeo."

"Nah," said Xavier, shaking his head. He looked away so Daryn couldn't see his face redden. "Wait, did you say Cavanaugh?"

"Yep. Coach's daughter."

Xavier felt the heat creep up the back of his neck. *Coach's daughter. Why didn't I know that?*

Just then Coach Cav walked into the gym and gathered his team around him for a huddle.

"Listen up, boys," he said. "Remember what we talked about in the locker room. I know you're nervous. We missed a week of practice with the snowstorm. Turn those nerves into energy. Have fun out there. This team likes to drive to the basket, so be on guard. Keep it steady and work together. Be respectful—be a good sport. Got it?"

The boys nodded and agreed. The coach put up his hands for high fives all around.

"Hey, Coach," Xavier said once the huddle broke up. "Are you going to put me in?"

"Yeah, in a bit. Just be patient, Blake."

Xavier sat down on the bench with the other guys as the starters took the court and got into position. The ref tossed the ball into the air; it was tipped off by the Lions' point guard, Eric, and the game was on.

Xavier spent the whole first half of the game on the bench, cheering on his team. Every time coach signaled for substitutes, Xavier sat up, hoping it would be his turn. It never was. But the Lions led 24–16 at the half.

The team went into the locker room for halftime, while the cheerleaders and the mascots entertained the crowd.

"Doing great out there," Coach Cav said. "But we need to keep up the pressure. Some of you boys are getting tired, so I'm going to mix up the subs in the second half." He turned and looked right at Xavier. "Blake, you're on point."

Xavier nodded, but his insides started to churn. He was going to play point guard in his first varsity game.

As the team headed back out to the court, Coach grabbed Xavier's shoulder.

"You think you can handle this, Blake?"

"Yes, sir. I can."

"That's what I like to hear."

Xavier's heart hammered, the blood pulsing in the center of his throat. He dared not look up at the stands.

When the second half was about to begin, Xavier took to the court with the other players and readied for the tip off. The lights seemed very bright, the sound of the crowd magnified in his ears. Xavier kept his eyes on his teammates. He knew their strengths. Bryce was their best long shooter. Jonathan, the tallest, could get under the basket and layup without even leaving the floor. Daryn and Scott were quick, precise dribblers. Xavier had confidence in them, and in himself. He was so excited he could barely wait for the tip-off.

The ref tossed the ball into the air. Jonathan jumped for it, tipping it to Xavier, who spun around and passed it to Daryn. Xavier called to Daryn and Scott, telling them where he wanted them to go. He focused on his strategy rather than the cheering crowd and the piercing stare of the coach.

Daryn took the ball down court and, under pressure, passed it to Scott who dribbled around two defenders and passed to Jonathan. Jonathan did a layup and sank the ball in the basket for two points. The crowd cheered.

They made two more baskets, and Xavier started to relax. He took the ball on a rebound and dribbled down court, faked a pass and then ran around to the outside. He spun and passed to Bryce, who hit the rim. Jonathan recovered for the basket, and cheers exploded again.

The Sharks got control and sank a basket. The score was 30–18. Still a comfortable lead, but Xavier didn't want to take any chances. Sweat poured down his face in rivers; his hair was plastered to his head, but he was in the zone. This is what he needed to get beyond the disastrous battle in Ahoratos.

He got the ball and dribbled down court, focused on which teammate he would pass to. He saw Daryn was open and bounce-passed the ball, then spun around and ran smack into one of the Sharks. He fell, his knee slamming into the floor. Pain shot through his leg. The ref blew the whistle to stop the play.

The coach ran out to the court, but Xavier was already on his feet, testing his knee.

"It's cool," he said to the coach. "I can play."

Coach shook his head. "Why don't you sit out for a bit. Make sure. Great job, Blake."

The coach walked him to the bleachers. Xavier tried not to limp. *It's fine. Doesn't even hurt.* He stole a glance at the crowd in the bleachers cheering for him. Evan was screaming his name and fist pumping the air. Mom had a worried look on her face. Cassie, up near the top, was standing, watching intently. She smiled at him.

"Nice footwork," said Eric, giving Xavier a high five on his way out to play.

"Thanks," said Xavier. He sat down on the bench, fighting the urge to rub his knee.

The game resumed. The Lions continued to gain ground, widening the lead to fifteen points. Xavier jumped up and went over to the coach.

"Hey, Coach, can I play some more?" he asked. He did a few jumps to prove his knee was fine. "I'm good."

Coach looked him over and sighed. "If we get to twenty points up, I'll put you in." Xavier sat back down but continued to cheer as the Lions gained an eighteen-point lead. He felt his heart skip when the scoreboard read 54–34.

"Okay, Blake, check in," Coach said.

Xavier jumped to his feet and went to the scorer's table to check in. He bent and unbent his knee a few times. It still hurt a little, but it worked fine. The buzzer sounded, and Xavier ran onto the court. Wild cheers erupted. His heart soared.

Xavier played harder than he ever had—running, dribbling, passing, shooting. His knee hurt, but he'd played through pain before; it was no big deal. His team made two more baskets in a row. Xavier knew they were going to win, but he continued to pour it on. He got the ball on a rebound and dribbled down the court. He saw Jonathan open but ignored him, preferring to do a snake run around two of the Sharks and go in for a layup himself. This last basket would be all his. He jumped for the basket and felt something pop, a jarring shock radiating through his entire leg. By the time he landed his leg wouldn't hold him, and he collapsed on the floor.

The buzzer sounded just as the ball swished through the net.

A new, more intense pain exploded in Xavier's leg. He grabbed hold of his knee, aware that something terrible had happened, for this was unlike anything he had experienced before.

"Blake, you all right?" He looked up to see Coach Cav and a ref gazing down at him. His teammates crowded around, concern on their faces.

"Yeah, I'm fine . . . just felt something go pop in my knee." He winced with the pain and tried to get up, but every movement of that knee brought instant agony.

The coach and Daryn helped him up. Xavier hopped on one leg, leaning on them until he got to the bench. Jonathan's dad, who happened to be a doctor, knelt in front of Xavier and felt around his knee.

"I don't think it's broken," he said. "But you'll need an MRI. I suspect it's a torn ACL."

Xavier groaned. A torn ACL was a season-ending injury.

The doctor put an ice pack on Xavier's knee and wrapped it in a gauze bandage. Xavier's mom and dad came down from the bleachers, their faces painted with worry. Someone ran in with a wheelchair. Xavier wanted to refuse. "I can walk. Just give me a minute!" But in the end he got into the wheelchair. His mom wheeled him out of the gym while his dad went to the locker room for his clothes.

Xavier sat in the back of the car, the throbbing in his knee made worse by the realization that he was out for the season. No more basketball.

Evan got into the seat beside him. Xavier turned away from him, looking out the window to avoid his gaze. Evan was wise enough not to try and talk to him.

Once home, his parents helped him get to his room and into bed. His mom gave him a fresh ice pack and some Tylenol for the pain.

"I've already made an appointment," she said. "Thankfully, the office is open late tonight. We'll get in for the MRI first thing in the morning."

"Mom, what will they have to do if it's my ACL?"

"Well, you might have to have surgery, and rehab," she said with a sigh. "Could be a few months."

Xavier said nothing. His mom left the room, turning out the light.

Xavier lay on his bed a long time, unable to sleep, thinking about what had happened. He glanced over at his closet door, which was open, and saw the stick Ruwach had given him.

"So that's what it's for," he said to himself, the bitterness rising in his throat. "It's a crutch."

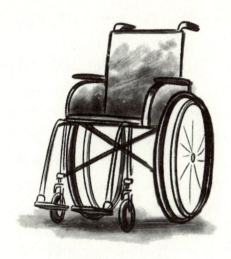

CHAPTER 16

Home at Last

Day 16

Levi sat in the back of the car, waiting for his mom to emerge from the hospital entrance with his dad. He played a game on his phone to pass the time and squash his nervousness. He tried to picture Mr. J. Ar walking out of the hospital, hand in hand with his mom, straight and tall as always. He longed for that.

When the sliding doors finally opened, Levi saw his dad in a wheelchair, pushed by his mom. His heart sank. But then Mr. J. Ar stood up—a little slowly, but he stood. On his own two feet. He grabbed his wife's hand, and she walked with him toward the car. They were moving really slowly, but that was probably because there were still patches of ice and snow on the sidewalk.

Levi jumped out of the car. "Hey, Dad!" he said, running over to him.

"Levi!" said Mr. J. Ar. He grabbed Levi's head and pulled him close. Levi used to feel nearly smothered by his dad's hugs, but not this time. He wrapped his arms around his dad, careful not to hurt him.

The three of them walked the last few steps to the car. "Still a lot of snow around," Mr. J. Ar said as Levi's mom helped him into the passenger seat.

"Yeah," said Levi. Usually snow in their area melted pretty quickly, but it had remained cold, and the snow had stayed. "They said on the news that we got forty inches."

"Forty, huh?" Mr. J. Ar took a deep breath. "Not surprised."

"They had to bring snowplows in from other states to clear it all. School was out for a week."

"Man, I missed a lot," said Mr. J. Ar.

"Everyone got their seat belts on?" asked his mom. Mr. J. Ar reached for his belt but had trouble buckling it. Levi's mom had to help him.

"Still a little sore," was all he said.

As they drove home, Levi's mom told her husband that so many people were waiting to come and see him that she had to start an appointment list.

"Let them all come at once," said Mr. J. Ar. "The more the merrier." He coughed slightly. The sound made Levi's hair stand on end. "What's this I hear about Xavier?"

"Oh yeah. Guess he took a bad fall at the game last night," said Levi's mom. "Torn ACL. He's out for the season."

"Oh, that's a shame," said Mr. J. Ar. "That's gotta be tough for Xavier."

Especially after he messed up the battle, Levi thought to himself, though he didn't say that out loud. He was trying not to blame Xavier too much. After all, Levi hadn't really been much help in the battle, being so distracted by the news he'd just gotten about his dad's illness. He wished he could get a do-over, replay the battle, stay with Ivy and those Finnish twins instead of following Xavier. If he'd been thinking more clearly, he might have even been able to talk Xavier out of doing what he did.

He also wished he'd had a vision of what was really there, as he had at the battle on Cedar Hill against the Glommers. Then he had seen the unseen warriors aligned with them in battle. That was the gift Ruwach had given him. But at the Bridge of Tears, he'd seen nothing.

Maybe it was because he hadn't even been looking.

Levi's mom started talking about all the flowers and baked goods that had come for Mr. J. Ar, especially from the parents of rec center kids who were so grateful to him for all he'd done for them. He'd provided their kids a safe place to hang out; he'd encouraged them to work hard and keep fighting for what was right. He was like a dad to many kids who didn't have a dad of their own.

Levi began to wonder, for the first time, why his dad did those things. Why he had decided to give up his career as a salesman for a big company to work a part-time job at the rec center, coaching basketball and helping kids with their problems.

Levi suddenly remembered the metal scar on his dad's elbow that Ruwach had healed the last time Mr. J. Ar had been in Ahoratos with them. That scar had been a reminder of something in his past he had never told Levi about. Maybe he was still ashamed or embarrassed. Maybe it was something so terrible he couldn't even tell his own son about it.

When they arrived home, Levi helped his dad get out of the car and walk into the house. Mr. J. Ar's hand rested upon his shoulder, giving him an assurance that everything was going to be okay now.

"I don't know about you, but I'm hungry," said Mr. J. Ar.

The house was full of flowers and gifts. Handmade get-well cards graced every surface. The kitchen table was set for three, with a big soup tureen in the middle and a basket of warm bread. The smell was heavenly.

"Looks like some angels have been here already," Mr. J. Ar said with a deep chuckle. "Although if those angels really loved me, they would have brought me a double-stacked cheeseburger and a bucket of french fries."

"Well, the angels know you are only allowed to have soup right now," said Levi's mom with a grin.

The three of them sat down at the table. Mr. J. Ar said grace, as he usually did, and Levi's mom started dishing out the soup.

"Gumbo! My favorite," said Mr. J. Ar.

Levi's stomach had been all in knots, but the aroma of the food awakened his appetite. He dug into the soup and grabbed a roll from the basket. He glanced up once to see his mom smiling at him. Then she reached over and grabbed her husband's hand.

"Do you think you'll be able to come back to the Rec soon?" Levi asked. "I mean, everyone wants to see you."

"Oh, I'm going to try," said his dad. "How are the kids doing?"

"I don't really know. I haven't been around them much."

"I see." Mr. J. Ar considered his son for a long moment.

"Well, I need to get back to the hospital for rounds," said Levi's mom, glancing at her watch. "You two be okay for a while?"

"Sure," said Levi. "I'll take care of . . . everything."

"I'm trusting you to make sure your dad doesn't go out and start shooting baskets," she said with a stern smile. "He's got to behave himself until the sutures are removed."

"Okay."

Dr. Arthur said her goodbyes and left the house. Levi started to clear the table. There was a long silence before Mr. J. Ar spoke.

"Why don't you tell me about the battle?"

Levi started telling him all the details, including the way Xavier had made a bad decision and led them all into a trap. He couldn't hide his own bitterness at this turn of events.

"I understand your feelings, Levi. But wouldn't it be better to think about what you can do to change things rather than focus on what other people did or didn't do?"

Levi sighed. "Maybe." He sat back down in his chair, slumping a little. "It just made me mad. Xavier is always the leader. He thinks he knows how to do everything better than the rest of us. Ruwach seems to think so too. He even gave him a gift."

"Oh? What was it?"

"Some big old stick."

"I see." Mr. J. Ar sat back in his chair, smiling a little. "A big old stick," he murmured to himself. He seemed to be thinking of something else, as if the mention of the stick had triggered some long-forgotten memory. Then he heaved a big sigh. "Well, I'm sure that will come in handy, one way or another. Hey, son, help me up the stairs, will you? Think I'll take a little nap."

Levi swallowed a lump in his throat. His big, strong father needed help climbing the stairs. But he got up and once again put his arm around his father's waist and helped him get to his room.

"We'll talk more later," Mr. J. Ar said. "I love you, son."

"I love you too, Dad."

The bedroom door closed. Levi turned around to head back down the stairs.

But something was in his way.

The Crest.

CHAPTER 17

The Way Up

L evi found himself in the middle of nowhere.
Literally.

At least, that's what he thought. He knew he had to get to the Water, but there was nothing around that looked remotely like water. All he saw was red dirt stretched out on either side of him, kicked up by a hot wind so that it stuck to his skin and coated his eyelashes.

At least it's not winter here, he thought.

Not sure what to do, he pulled his shirt up over his nose to avoid inhaling the dust and started to walk. In a few minutes, he saw a group of square yellow buildings that looked like abandoned warehouses.

He picked up his pace and headed toward the buildings. Maybe one of them held the Water. He'd learned to expect the unexpected when traveling to Ahoratos, especially in the In-Between.

He noticed that the buildings were laid out in straight rows. He counted. Four rows with ten buildings in each row.

Forty.

He started walking down the first row, trying the doors. There was only one door to each building, and no windows. The first door was locked. So was the second. In fact, all the doors were locked. The first row and the second. Levi started to get nervous, moving from a walk to a trot.

But the first door of the third row was unlocked. He turned the knob, then hesitated. He suddenly wasn't sure he should go in. And yet, an unlocked door seemed like an invitation. Maybe the Water was inside. Besides, the more time he spent outside, the more dangerous things might get. He took a deep breath, turned the knob, and opened the door very slowly.

It was completely dark inside. Even with the door open, no light spilled into the room.

"Hello?" Levi said. He stood in the doorway a moment until he was sure nothing was going to jump out at him or fall on his head. Then he took a few steps inside. He couldn't see any water. He couldn't see anything.

"Why are you here?" said a voice from the dark.

Levi was startled but not afraid. For some reason, the voice didn't sound scary. It sounded old and a little tired. It wasn't a friendly voice, but it wasn't unfriendly either.

"The door was unlocked." Levi tried to guess where the voice was coming from. But it seemed to be coming from everywhere. And nowhere. There was a weird smell too. Kind of rancid and sweet at the same time. Like the smell in the Garden the last time he was there.

"What are you looking for?"

"I was looking for the Water. But I guess it's not in here." Levi turned to leave but then stopped. "Who are you?"

"You don't know me?"

"You sound familiar. Are you . . . a friend?"

There was a silence.

"No," said the voice. "But I am not an enemy either."

Levi considered that. "Why can't I see you?"

"That is not allowed. Just yet."

"Are you . . . the Source?" Levi held his breath, waiting for the answer.

The voice let out a low chuckle. "No. We are— acquainted, however."

"What is your name?"

"Go quickly. Find the Water. The way up is down."

Suddenly a violent burst of wind coming from inside the building blew Levi off his feet and backward through the doorway. He landed on his backside, and the door slammed shut on him. Stunned, he picked himself up, brushing the red dust off his pants. The red . . . it reminded him of the Garden.

Levi tried the door again. This time it was locked.

He stood for a moment, wondering what to do. He realized it was starting to get dark. Although he could see no actual sun, it was as if something were pulling a shade down over the world.

He had to hurry.

Forty buildings. Forty doors. He ran down the rest of the row, trying the doors. All locked. Then it occurred to him that if the unlocked door had locked, perhaps another one had opened. He raced up and down the first two rows again, trying door after door. The dark was coming on quickly. The hot wind turned colder. Levi felt his heart racing like mad in his chest. He sensed the dark actually pursuing him, searching him out, just around each corner.

And then, a knob turned. Levi threw himself against the door as the dark fell hard and the cold wind blasted his back. He rushed into the building and slammed the door shut behind him.

He leaned against the door, struggling to catch his breath. He could no longer hear the wind. All was silent. He looked around, shocked.

He was not in a building at all. In fact, he was back outside, staring at rows of buildings in an endless red landscape. But it was still light. He wondered if he had just passed through some sort of time portal. He needed to find the Water. Quickly.

When his knees stopped shaking, he started to run again, trying all the doors to see if another one would open. Once again, the dark began to fall, starting at one end of the rows and working its way toward him. Levi frantically searched for the right door. None of them opened.

He got to the last locked door and dropped to his knees in despair, certain the dark would get him this time. There was no escape. Then he noticed that at this end of the rows, the ground was not red but white. A large white, rounded bowl, like a dry lake bed.

He got up and went over to the white area, kneeling to touch it. Maybe it was snow.

No. Salt.

The dark was so close. It had already covered all the buildings and was headed right for him.

Then he remembered the voice.

The way up is down.

Levi bent forward and started digging through the salt. Almost immediately, he found water. It was thick and briny with salt. Levi kept digging. That's when he saw it: The Crest. Bubbling to the surface, crystallizing. Like salt. Levi gasped in relief.

He shut his eyes, held his nose closed, and dove in headfirst.

CHAPTER 18

The Glimmer Glass

"Welcome back, Levi."

Ruwach was there in the Cave, waiting for him. Levi was glad to see Ru, but also curious, because he was the only one there. That was unusual.

He wondered if he was in trouble. Maybe for not helping more in the battle. Maybe for yelling at Xavier and blaming him for getting them trapped in Skot'os. But he was sure Ruwach knew what he was going through, and he would understand.

Levi took a slow breath. "Ru," he said, "I met someone, in the In-Between. Well, I didn't actually see him; I just heard his voice. Who is he?"

"Didn't you ask him?" said Ruwach.

"Yes. Well, no. It was weird. He actually helped me get here."

"Did he? How interesting."

"Does he work for you?"

"In a way. But he doesn't know it."

"Ru, what's going on? I mean, this guy—he's here because of the Winter isn't he?"

"Yes."

Levi waited, but Ruwach didn't explain any more.

"I brought you here to give you something." Ruwach glided toward Levi and raised up one long, glowing hand. In it lay a thick round piece of glass marked with

114

a series of concentric ridges. Levi picked it up. It was about the size of his palm.

"Thanks," Levi said. "What's it for?"

"It is a Glimmer Glass. It will help you see . . . the things you cannot normally see."

"Oh. Cool." Levi held the Glass up to his eye and peered through it. He gasped. The Sparks, those tiny specks of light bouncing around the Cave like dust motes, appeared now as huge shining warriors in full armor.

"It's like on the hill, before the battle with the Glommers," Levi said. "I could see them then."

"Yes, this gift is an extension of the one I gave you then. But with this Glass, you will now see more than you have ever imagined. It comes with a warning, however. This gift is the most difficult and perhaps the least desired. But it is essential."

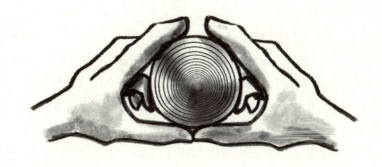

Levi took the Glass from his eye. "You mean I'm going to see things . . . I don't really want to see."

Ruwach's hooded head dipped once. "It is your choice. To accept it, or not."

Levi stared at the Glass. A huge part of him wanted to give it back. He sensed in Ruwach's words a terrible responsibility attached to this gift. But he knew as well that Ruwach wouldn't have given him the Glass if he didn't think he, of all the Warriors, could handle it. He closed his fingers around it tightly.

Ruwach understood. "Now, I will show you something. Your father has asked this of me. Do you want to see it?"

Levi nodded.

"Look into the Glass."

Levi held the Glimmer Glass up to his eye once again. This time, instead of seeing the Sparks, he saw the image of a young man who looked remarkably like him, except his hair was longer and his clothes were really out-of-date. He realized it was his father, Mr. J. Ar.

"Dad?" he asked.

Mr. J. Ar looked really young, like he was in high school. The images changed quickly—first he was playing football, then hanging out with his friends, then arguing with a woman Levi assumed was his grandmother. Then Mr. J. Ar was wearing his football uniform and holding up the state championship trophy. Levi was impressed. His dad had never told him he won a state trophy.

The setting changed again. To a group of kids on a dark night, setting off bottle rockets on a baseball field. They all had on football jackets with big letters on them. Everyone was laughing, having a good time. Levi's dad was among them. He held up a large firework, the kind used in big displays. Everyone wanted him to set it off. He said he had to wait for his uncle to do that. But the others kept pressuring him until finally he put the firework in the tube, ran the fuse, and lit it. But something went wrong. The tube fell over, and the rocket went sideways, exploding close to one of the kids. Everyone screamed. The kid just lay on the ground, badly injured. The grass caught fire. Sirens started to blare. Levi's dad ran to his friend, threw his jacket over him. He screamed his friend's name. A large burning piece of ash fell on his arm . . .

The Glass went dark. Levi put it down. He couldn't even speak.

"The boy did not die," Ruwach said, seeing the unasked question on Levi's face. "But the injuries were severe. He could no longer play football."

"He never told me."

"He would have, in time."

"I . . . don't want to lose him."

Ruwach didn't respond. Instead, he did something he had never done before. He moved to Levi and wrapped his long, robed arms all the way around him. The warmth of that embrace overpowered Levi's pain. He had never felt so engulfed in love, except when his own father would give him one of his big bear hugs. He felt tears well in his eyes, knowing that whatever happened, he would still be loved well.

He closed his eyes, thankful.

When he opened them, he was in the doorway of his father's bedroom, staring at his sleeping form. Mr. J. Ar seemed to sense his presence, for he awoke suddenly. Levi went to stand at his bedside.

"Levi," he said, his voice groggy. "Where'd you come from?"

"Ahoratos," Levi said.

Mr. J. Ar heaved a sigh. "Did you have a mission?"

"No. Ruwach just gave me a gift." Levi pulled the Glimmer Glass from his pocket. "It helps me . . . see things."

"That's a wonderful gift."

"Yeah. Maybe. Dad, I'm . . . I'm scared. . . ."

"Don't you worry about a thing, son," said Mr. J. Ar, grabbing hold of Levi's hand. "Everything is going to be all right. The battle is already won."

Levi hoped that was true. But at the moment, he couldn't see how.

PART 3

A Time to Live

CHAPTER 19

The Fortress

Day 25

Ponéros clung to the back of the leviathan named Sybylla as she swam through the tunnels of boiling green water that led from Skot'os to the mountain. He was anxious to see the new fortress Thayne had built on the top of Rhema. Thayne had succeeded in cutting off the Breath and turning the mountain into a roiling volcano, spewing lava and gasses that hung in a poisoned cloud over the land. He was now building his army of Lava Forgers. Once the army was at full strength, they would be ready for a full-scale invasion of Ahoratos. They would take over every inch of Ruwach's territory, even the Cave itself. This would be Ponéros's crowning achievement—to defeat Ruwach and his band of Prince Warriors once and for all.

Sybylla surfaced in the large green boiling pool. She shook the water from her gills and pulled herself up to the ledge, her two short flippers growing into long, tapered arms. With Ponéros still clinging to her back, she began to crawl steadily through the tunnel, which wound upward in a spiral, deep into the heart of the mountain and eventually emptied into a steam vent close to the crater.

From there, Sybylla carried her master up to the rim of the crater. The fortress, a mammoth pyramid of sleek black obsidian, rose up from the crater into the clouds. It sat on a foundation of steep ramparts and ledges, surrounded by a moat of churning, fiery lava. Hundreds of Lava Forgers—huge lumpy creatures with hard rock shells and molten cores—were on the ledges, busily building giant catapults that could hurl fireballs of lava down the mountain.

Sybylla crawled along the rim of the crater until she came to a bridge that led over the moat to the bottom of the ramparts. The bridge was made of obsidian, black and smooth as a newly paved highway. She slithered across the bridge and up the rocky slope as the Lava Forgers stopped their work to bow to their master.

Thayne was there in the entrance to greet Ponéros when he arrived. The Prince of Skot'os slid from the leviathan's back, observing the activity around him. He looked more human than the last time Thayne had seen him, although he had three sets of long, pulpy arms and a thick tail. His head was elongated, with large eyes that bulged out from both sides. Thayne bent to one knee and slammed an iron fist against his chest.

"My prince."

Two Lava Forgers stood on either side of Thayne. They also bent low and grunted, for they could not speak.

"Welcome to your new stronghold," said Thayne. "I hope you are pleased with what I have done in your service." He stood aside so Ponéros could enter the fortress.

Ponéros moved slowly into the pyramid, his long limbs gliding over the obsidian floor. It was clear he wasn't used to moving on solid ground, having recently spent so much time underwater. He stopped at a huge pit of lava in the center of the vast room. The crusty black surface rumbled softly, revealing orange veins of molten lava underneath. The floor all around the pit was littered with bones. Three tall skeletal figures in red robes tended the pit, stirring the lava with long white bones. They turned to Ponéros as he approached, and they bowed deeply.

"Ah, Weaver," Ponéros said to one of them. "What are you brewing?"

The Weaver didn't speak but picked up a few bones from the floor and tossed them into the pit. The lava roiled and rumbled as the three Weavers continued to stir. It clung to the bones, building up a thick coating. The bones began to move on their own, drawing together as the lava formed legs, arms, a head, and a torso all around the bones. A huge lumpy figure rose up from the pit and stepped out onto the floor, its outer shell instantly hardening into rock. But the fire still glowed from its eyes. A Lava Forger. Thayne made a gesture with one arm, and the Lava Forger began to move, lumbering out to the ramparts to join the others.

"The Bone Breakers gather the bones," Thayne said. "They are scattered all over Skot'os."

"Prince Warrior bones?" Ponéros asked.

"No," said Thayne. "These are mostly the bones of escaped prisoners who never made it over the bridge. And dragon bones. We haven't yet been able to get any Prince Warrior bones. But in time, we will have more than we could wish for."

"Yes. In time." Ponéros let out a long, satisfied hiss. He continued his tour until he reached a black stone staircase that led to a massive throne made of sharpened spikes of obsidian. On either side of the throne, two enormous Bone Breakers sat on perches. Ponéros paused to admire the fierce-looking birds with their thick strong beaks, sharp talons, and ruffles of white feathers rimmed in red, as if they had been dipped in blood. Their eyes were perfectly round, concentric circles of red, white, and black that watched his every move.

Ponéros glided up the steps and sat on the throne. His arms slid over the sides and dribbled down the steps.

"You are certain the Prince Warriors cannot destroy this fortress?"

"I am certain. They will not get to the top of the mountain, even if they tried. They will not get past the Forgers, or the catapults. Their armor is strong, but their flesh is still . . . vulnerable."

Ponéros looked up to the round hole at the very top of the pyramid. "Can you take me up there? I wish to see all of my new kingdom."

"Nesher," said Thayne to one of the birds, "take the Master to the sky."

Nesher hopped down in front of the throne. Ponéros slid onto his back, wrapping two sets of arms around the bird's neck. Nesher spread his wings, each one more than six feet long. He soared all the way through the hole at the top of the pyramid and perched on the edge, folding his wings again.

Ponéros gazed down at the frozen landscape with immense satisfaction. It was the most beautiful sight he had ever beheld. He could see the Prince Warriors still in the field before the bridge, frozen in snake coils and ice-webs, new layers of ice forming over their trapped bodies. Soon the layers would be so thick there would be no possibility of rescue. Once the forty days were up, if they had not escaped or were not rescued, they would be nothing but dry bones and useless bits of armor.

Fifteen days to go.

Ponéros commanded Nesher to take him back down into the fortress where he settled himself once more on the throne, sighing with satisfaction.

"Well done, Thayne. You trapped many Prince Warriors, I see. But—did you get them all?"

Thayne hesitated a moment. "No, my prince. Not all."

Ponéros's body reddened in anger. "What do you mean?"

"There is always a . . . remnant."

"How many are left?"

"I do not know. There cannot be many."

"Have they made any move to counterattack?"

"No, my prince. We have seen no movement. There was one group of spies that found passage into the mountain, but they were repelled easily by one of the leviathans. They will surely be too afraid to enter there again."

"Repelled?" Ponéros turned to Sybylla. "Why were they not killed?" he demanded.

Sybylla bowed her head. "They were clever," she said. "They slipped away. It will not happen again."

"See that it doesn't." Ponéros seemed satisfied, but he was still quite uneasy. He did not want to be outmaneuvered by the Warriors again. "I must know what their plans are. Thayne, you must go into the Cave and see what that pest Ruwach is up to."

"I cannot go into the Cave. It is sealed. You know that, my prince. But I have sent Nesher to search for the Prince Warriors and to spy on Ruwach. He saw something quite interesting. In the Garden of Red."

"Well?" said Ponéros, sitting up straighter. "What did he see?"

"He spotted three Prince Warriors. With Ruwach."

"Ah, excellent! What were they doing? Discussing battle plans?"

"No," said Thayne. "They said nothing of a battle. Ruwach simply gave them gifts."

"Gifts? You mean weapons?"

"No. Just plain things. A rock. A root. A flower bulb."

"That is utter nonsense. Did they speak of destroying the fortress?"

"No."

Ponéros rose up from the throne and nearly flew down the steps, greatly agitated. "What is going on here? What is that hooded flea up to?" He paced about, flinging his arms in all directions. He was disturbed by the gifts, which seemed so useless as to be truly frightening. But this was how Ruwach worked. He used not the mighty, not the most powerful and impressive, but the smallest—the most insignificant. Children. Rocks. Roots. Flower bulbs. That was Ruwach's way. It was maddening.

"If only we could get into the Cave," Ponéros said as he paced about the pyramid. "There must be a way!"

"There is nothing to fear, my prince," said Thayne in a soothing voice. "Ruwach and the Prince Warriors can scheme all they like. We hold the power. We have the mountain and the skypods. We can see their every move."

"They got into the tunnel under the mountain, didn't they?" Ponéros spat out.

"That will not happen again. The tunnel has already been blocked. Frozen. As is everything else. Once they make an advance, we will utterly destroy them. Soon the forty days will be up. And then . . ."

"Then," said Ponéros, burying his worry in savage joy, "we will have true victory. We *must* have victory." He did not want to think about what might happen if he were to fail again.

CHAPTER 20

Visiting

Day 28

The kids filed into the living room, tiptoeing as if they were afraid to make any noise. Ivy held a bouquet of wilted flowers. Brianna had a basket of her grandmother's homemade cinnamon rolls and a large card she'd made herself. Evan held a mac-and-cheese casserole his mom had made. Xavier couldn't carry anything because he was on crutches. Manuel had a book he had wrapped in the comics page of the newspaper.

They gathered around Mr. J. Ar, smiling brightly and loading his lap and the coffee table with their gifts.

"What's all this?" said Mr. J. Ar, putting the recliner in its upright position. "You shouldn't have."

"Sorry about the flowers," said Ivy. "They didn't do so well in the cold."

"Still cold out there, huh?"

"Freezing."

"Why don't I put them in water, see if I can resuscitate them," said Levi's mom with a grin. "And I'll take that too, Evan."

"It's mac and cheese," Evan said, handing her the casserole. "I made it myself. Well, Mom helped a little."

"That's so sweet of you, Evan." Dr. Arthur took the flowers and the casserole into the kitchen.

"Nana Lily made these just for you," Brianna said to Mr. J. Ar, pointing to the basket of cinnamon rolls. "She knows they're your favorite."

"Oh, yes, they are," said Mr. J. Ar, smiling a little weakly. "I could smell them before you even stepped into the house." He opened Brianna's card. Inside was a picture she had drawn of Mr. J. Ar in his Prince Warrior armor, standing on top of the mountain with his sword lifted high.

"Not bad at all," said Mr. J. Ar with a little chuckle. He unwrapped the book Manuel had given him. *Venus Flytraps and Other Meat-Eating Plants.*

"I couldn't get to the store, so I just had this one in my room," Manuel confessed. "But you'll like it. It's really fascinating."

"I'm already fascinated," said Mr. J. Ar, flipping through the pages. "Who wouldn't love to know more about meat-eating plants?" He glanced at Xavier, who had sat down to rest his bandaged leg. "How's the knee?"

"Only hurts when I move," said Xavier with a doleful grin.

"Good one," said Mr. J. Ar. He coughed slightly, making Levi wince. "Surgery went okay?"

"Yeah. They said in three months I should be fine."

"That's good news."

"The season will be over in three months."

"There's always next season, right?" Mr. J. Ar smiled, but Xavier didn't return the smile. Mr. J. Ar turned to the others. "So what's been happening? Anything going on in Ahoratos?"

"Finn and I found a way into the mountain," Ivy said. "Through a hot spring underground. Unfortunately, it led to a pool with a leviathan. Kalle and Kristian almost got caught, but we helped them get out."

"You went on a mission?" said Brianna, frowning. "Without us?"

"A leviathan—like a whale?" said Evan. "That's so cool."

"It didn't look like a whale, but it was pretty big." Ivy described the leviathan while the others listened in amazement.

"How did a thing like that get into the mountain?" asked Levi.

"We think that underground spring must go all the way into Skot'os, or maybe Ponéros dug a tunnel or something. The tunnel might actually be a way to get to the fortress. But with the leviathans, it's going to be pretty hard to get there. And we didn't find any way to attack up the mountain without being seen. There are these giant birds called Bone Breakers staking out the skypods."

"Did you see any dragons?" asked Evan.

"No," said Ivy, "but that doesn't mean there aren't any. I'm telling you, attacking that fortress is going to be virtually impossible."

"Ah. A virtual impossibility. Just the sort of challenge Ruwach loves," said Mr. J. Ar with a tired smile. He turned to Xavier. "What do you think, Xavier?"

Xavier looked from Mr. J. Ar to the other kids. "Me?"

"You don't have any thoughts on how this battle could be won?"

"It's not my job to win battles." There was bitterness in Xavier's tone. He glanced at Levi, who looked away. "I mean, I haven't been called back, like everyone else. I'm . . . done."

"You so sure of that?" Mr. J. Ar arched an eyebrow. "You can't think of any way to attack that fortress?"

Xavier shifted uncomfortably. He put a hand on his knee, wincing, as if it hurt. "Not really."

"What if we sneak into Skot'os and capture the Olethron?" said Evan. "Then we could use them to take out some of those skypods at least."

"You're going to capture the Olethron?" said Xavier. "How? Do you even know where they are?"

"They've got to be *somewhere*," said Evan, folding his arms.

"That would never work," said Levi. "And even if it did, you might destroy the whole mountain, and then no one would ever get their swords ever again."

"I agree. Anyway, we've got to free the frozen Warriors first," said Brianna. "How are we going to do that? There are so many of them. And so few of us."

"There may be more of you than you think," said Mr. J. Ar.

"Maybe there's a way to get up the mountain before Thayne is able to counterattack," said Manuel. "Like if we had powered skis that could go uphill."

"That sounds fun!" said Evan.

"You can't bring anything into Ahoratos, remember?" said Xavier, shaking his head. "Or take anything out that Ruwach doesn't give you. And I doubt there are any ski shops in Ahoratos."

"Well, of course, we would have to build them there," said Manuel.

"Out of what?" Xavier grumbled. "Let's face it. There's no way we can take back that mountain."

Everyone was quiet, shocked by Xavier's discouraging tone.

"Let's table this discussion until after we have some cinnamon rolls," said Mr. J. Ar. He coughed again. "Brianna, take these into the kitchen. You kids go with her; I'll be along in a minute."

The kids got up and followed Brianna into the kitchen. It took Xavier longer to get up, so he was lagging behind.

"Hang with me here a moment, Xavier." Xavier sat back down again, staring at his leg so he didn't have to look Mr. J. Ar in the face.

"I know what you're feeling," said Mr. J. Ar after a moment. "But you've got a job to do, Xavier. You can't be sitting around feeling sorry for yourself."

"That's all I *can* do," Xavier blurted. "I failed. And now I can't play basketball. I can't even walk."

"I will say it again. You have a job to do. You are a Prince Warrior whether you are walking or hobbling or sitting or not even able to get up out of the bed. You are always a Warrior. Ponéros never stops, so neither do we. Why did Coach Cavanaugh put you in as point guard?"

"I don't know."

"Yes you do. Because you are a natural leader. You know how to get the most of others' abilities, right?"

"I thought so. Once."

"Well, that doesn't change just because you can't play."

Xavier thought about this. "I can't play point guard from the bench."

"Why not?"

"Because. I just can't."

"Listen to me, son. Right now you have to focus on what you *can* do, not what you can't do. Do you get me?" Xavier nodded, mute. "I know you think you messed up, and maybe you did. But that doesn't mean the Source can't use you anymore. If that were true, there would be no Prince Warriors in the world. Trust me. I know what I'm talking about."

"Okay," said Xavier. "But I still don't know how to win this battle."

"The battle is already won," said Mr. J. Ar in a soft voice.

"That's what Ru says."

"You need to believe it."

Xavier looked dubious. "I'll work on that."

"Good. Now help me up. I need to get me one of those cinnamon rolls before they're all gone."

CHAPTER 21

The Root

Ivy's mom gave Brianna a ride home from Levi's house since she only lived around the corner. Brianna wanted to ask Ivy more about the mission and the two Finnish boys; she wanted to know what had actually happened and why she and Finn had been sent alone in the first place. But Ivy seemed too absorbed with her phone.

She couldn't help but feel that Ivy had changed since they'd started eighth grade. Brianna couldn't remember the last time the two of them had hung out together like they used to. She had heard rumors about what Ivy had done to that kid in the lunchroom, but whenever she tried to talk to Ivy about it, she would change the subject.

"Hey," Brianna said once they'd turned onto her street. "Want to hang out? Watch TV or something?" Brianna had hoped that Ivy would invite her over to her house. It was hard having friends at Brianna's house, because it was small and overcrowded. Ivy's house was much bigger.

"Oh, sorry . . . I can't. I'm meeting some girls at the movies."

"Oh." Brianna felt her stomach drop a little. "What girls?"

"You know Emily and Jill? They're in my Spanish class. They asked if I wanted to come, so I said sure."

"Oh."

"Do you want to come too? I'm sure they wouldn't mind."

Despite her friendly invitation, Brianna didn't think she would want to be an add-on to that group. They weren't *her* friends, after all. "No thanks. I've got . . . chores to do anyway. And Grandpa Tony said he would give me a sword lesson later on. Do you want to come over for that—after the movies?"

"Maybe. That would be great. We'll see how it goes."

Ivy's mom pulled up to Brianna's curb.

"Thanks, Mrs. Foster," said Brianna, getting out.

"Anytime, Brianna." Ivy's mom gave her a warm smile. Brianna sensed she actually knew what she was feeling.

"Bye, Ivy."

"See ya." Ivy never looked up from her phone.

Brianna walked up the icy sidewalk into the house. She could hear her grandmother busy in the kitchen. She was making more cinnamon rolls; Brianna could tell by the heavenly smell. Nana Lily made the best cinnamon rolls in the world. And now that she had recovered from her stroke, she made them practically every weekend.

Brianna avoided the kitchen and went straight to her room, which was empty for once. Nikki and Crystal were apparently out. Brianna sat on her bed, took the root out from under her mattress, and stared at it.

Roots were buried underground, where no one could see them. Maybe that was her gift. To be invisible. She felt like she was becoming invisible to her best friends. Ivy had new friends now. And Levi hardly spoke to her; he was so preoccupied with his dad's illness. She wanted to be a friend to him, but whenever she tried to talk to him about how he was feeling, he just put her off.

Brianna couldn't bear the thought of spending the whole of this dark, cold Saturday alone in her room. Even her sisters weren't there to fight with.

Maybe I will go to that movie after all.

She jumped up from the bed, tossing the root on the mattress. She changed into her best outfit and spent half an hour in the bathroom doing her hair. Then she went down to the kitchen, where Nana Lily was pulling a pan of cinnamon rolls out of the oven with one hand while holding her cane with the other.

"You're just in time, girl," she said, setting the pan on the stove. "Can you help me frost?" She pointed to another tray of rolls that were cooling.

"What? Oh, sure," Brianna said. She grabbed the bowl of frosting and quickly slathered each of the rolls.

"Hey there, take it easy on those rolls. You're drowning them!" said Nana with a laugh.

"Oh, sorry. Hey, Nana, would it be okay if I went to the movies this afternoon?"

"Movies?" Nana Lily arched an eyebrow at her. "Who with?"

"Oh, just some friends from school. And Ivy too."

"Well, I don't know. I suppose it would be all right, if your grandfather takes you. But he's having some trouble with the car, so you better go out to the garage and ask him."

"Oh, thanks, Nana! And . . . could I have some money too?"

"Well, there may be a ten-dollar bill in my purse. You can check and see."

"You're the best, Nana!" Brianna gave her grandmother a quick kiss and ran to the closet where her grandmother kept her purse. She grabbed the money and dashed out to the garage.

"Grandpa?"

"Hey there, Breeny." Grandpa Tony had the hood of the car propped open and was bent over, staring at the engine compartment.

"Can you give me a ride to the movies?" Brianna rubbed her arms, shivering in the cold.

"Not today I'm afraid. I think I might need a new battery. This cold is really doing a number on this old bucket of bolts."

Brianna bit her lower lip, disappointed. "Do you know where Crystal is?" Maybe her sister could give her a ride.

"I think she's working today. She gave Nikki a ride to the library this morning."

"Oh." Brianna plopped down on the garage step, deflated. She took out her phone and flipped through some more contacts, searching for someone to hang out with. Finally, she texted Levi again.

> Hey, want to come over? No sisters here right now!

Levi responded:

> Sorry. Can't. Dad needs me.

She typed:

> Anything I can do to help?

The reply:

> No thanks.

She put the phone back in her pocket, got up from the step, and opened the door.

"Hey, Breeny," said her grandfather. She turned to look at him. "How about that sword-fighting lesson?"

"Oh yeah, sure."

"Okay, let me just finish this up here. In the mean-time, why don't you go check your chore list? I'm sure there's a thing or two you haven't done yet. I'll come find you when I'm done."

Brianna went back into the house and up to her room. She lay on her bed, staring at the ceiling, imagining Ivy with all her new friends, laughing and joking and having a good time without her.

She forgot all about her chore list.

When Grandpa was ready for the sword-fighting lesson later, Brianna texted Ivy to see if she was coming. But she didn't answer.

Ivy finally texted her back an hour later, when the lesson was almost over.

Sorry I can't. Say hi to Grandpa Tony for me!

Brianna didn't bother to respond.

CHAPTER 22

The Bulb

Manuel's dad dropped him off at the Cedar Creek Rec Center. He hadn't been there in a while, but Mary Stanton, who had taken over as director in Mr. J. Ar's absence, had asked Manuel if he could come in and do a science project with the younger kids. It was Saturday afternoon, and he didn't really have anything better to do anyway.

Manuel had decided to teach the kids about meat-eating plants. He had his own plant specimens in a special insulated container so they wouldn't freeze on the way. His Venus flytrap, his pitcher plant, and a new one he'd gotten for Christmas that was called a butterwort. He thought the kids would think that name was pretty funny.

He almost tripped over a broom that came charging at him. He stumbled and recovered, saving his container of plants just in time.

"Sorry, dude, didn't see you."

Manuel looked up to see Landon—the boy who once wrapped him in toilet paper in front of the entire rec center—at the end of the broom. Landon kept his head down and continued his sweeping. Manuel stared after him, shocked to see the big bully, of all people, doing chores at the Rec.

"Manuel! Thanks for coming!"

Still a little confused, Manuel turned to see Mary Stanton rushing over to greet him.

"Oh, hi, Miss Stanton." Manuel took another glance at Landon. "Why is he sweeping?"

"Oh, I'm not sure. Finn just said he was going to be coming in and helping out. I was surprised too."

"Oh. Well, anyway, where would you like me to set up my presentation?"

Mary brought him over to a smaller room off the main area, where she had already set up a table for Manuel to use.

"Will this work okay?"

"Sure." Manuel smiled at her. Mary Stanton still kept her long blonde hair in a ponytail, but otherwise she wasn't much like the old Mary from two years ago, who had spent most of her time drinking lattes, texting her friends, and studying for her college exams. Back then she hadn't had much use or interest in the kids. Now she seemed interested in everything. She read a lot, and whenever Manuel or the other kids were there, she would pepper them with questions about Ahoratos.

It had taken her a while to get over what had happened the day Ponéros, posing as a kid named Viktor, had come to the Cedar Creek Rec Center to steal the Prince Warriors' books and armor. Her life had changed that day. She'd seen ordinary people turn into Glommers. She'd seen the kids she used to supervise at the Rec become Prince Warriors and battle an evil monster. She'd seen Ruwach in his true glory vanquishing their enemy. She still didn't know what to make of it all, but she'd seen too much to still be the same Mary Stanton she'd been before.

"How's Mr. J. Ar?" she asked as Manuel set up his display of plants. "We really miss him here."

"Just saw him this morning," said Manuel. "He seems to be doing better."

"That's a relief. Do you think he'll ever come back to the Rec?"

"I hope so."

Once Manuel's display was ready, Mary gathered up a group of kids to sit on rugs in front of the table. They squirmed around a lot, as little kids do, not paying much attention to Manuel, too busy sticking their fingers in each other's ears. Manuel stood before them and cleared his throat.

"Hey, guys. Did you know there are some plants that kill bugs and eat them?" he said to start things off. The kids turned to him, suddenly interested. Manuel nodded. "It's true. These plants are meat eaters. We refer to them as *carnivorous*. Here are some different ways they do it." Manuel held up the pitcher plant, which looked like its leaves were all rolled up. "The pitcher plant creates a basin that fills up with rainwater, which mixes with a special stew of poisonous toxins the plant secretes. When an unsuspecting bug comes along for a drink of water"—Manuel held up a plastic fly and waved it in the air with his other hand, making the kids laugh—"it lands on the edge of the leaf and dips into the water"—Manuel demonstrated—"then falls in, and wham! It can't get out. Then it slowly dissolves and gets digested."

The kids made noises of disgust and delight. Manuel picked up another plant.

"This one is called a butterwort." Just as he predicted, the kids laughed at the name. "It looks like a harmless tropical flower. But its leaves secrete a shiny liquid that looks like water, so when a bug lands on the leaf for a drink, it sticks. Like flypaper. And then the butterwort secretes another toxin that digests the stuck bug. Basically, dissolves it while it's still alive." Manuel pretended to be a bug being digested by the plant. The kids laughed and clapped.

As a grand finale, Manuel demonstrated his Venus flytrap. He placed a flake of fish food in the spiky jaw of the plant; the kids gasped in amazement as the jaw snapped shut. Afterward, Manuel allowed them to come up for a closer look and to "feed" the plants themselves. As he watched the kids and the plants, Manuel suddenly thought of the flower bulb Ruwach had given him. The water lily.

He began to wonder if that bulb might be useful in the battle that was still to come.

"That was awesome, Manuel," Mary said when he was done. "You sure had their attention."

"Thanks," said Manuel. He starting packing up his plants. "Nothing like carnivorous plants to make kids take an interest in botany."

"So true . . . I was just wondering, have you been back there lately?"

"Where?"

"You know. Ahoratos."

Manuel glanced up at Mary, pushing up his glasses. "Well, yes."

"Really? Can you tell me about it?"

"Well, there was this battle, and it didn't go so well, and Ponéros—you remember Viktor?—he took the Mountain of Rhema, and so we need to get it back."

Mary's eyes got big. "He took a whole mountain?"

"Yes. It's not the best news. We think he's probably making plans to take more territory too. To take over all of Ahoratos."

"That's terrible. What are you going to do?"

"We don't know yet." Manuel put on his coat. "I think my dad is here." He started to leave. Mary stopped him.

"Hey Manuel—do you think it would be possible for me to, you know, go there sometime?"

Manuel turned back and looked at her. His mouth fell open. "You want to go to Ahoratos?"

She nodded.

"Why?"

"Because. Well. I'm not sure. After what happened . . . I was so scared, I didn't think I wanted anything to do with that place. But I can't get it out of my mind. What I saw." She paused. "How do you get there?"

"Well, you have to be called. I think. That's what happened to me anyway."

"You were called?"

"Yeah. The Crest just appeared. It was like an invitation that I could either accept or reject. It was a choice."

"I see." Mary's eyebrows knitted together. "Well, the next time you're there, could you, like, tell that friend of yours that I'm interested?"

Manuel thought about this. "Are you sure you'd really want to do that? Because if you are, I'm pretty sure the call will come."

Mary broke into a smile. "Really?"

"Yeah." Manuel turned around to leave again, but something made him stop. A voice. Not a loud voice. A whisper. So small he was surprised he had heard it at all. It told him to do something surprising.

He reached into his backpack and pulled out the Prince Warrior book, the book given to him by his mother before she died. He always carried it with him, just in case. He turned back to Mary. "Read this. I'll let you keep it for a little while. It will help you . . . understand."

He handed Mary the book. She took it, holding it in both hands like it was a precious treasure, gazing in awe at the shiny image of the Crest on the cover. "Thanks, Manuel."

"Sure. No problem. But I should warn you . . . Opening that book might actually change your life." He grinned. "Have a nice day!"

CHAPTER 23

The Rock

Evan walked down to the pond and sat on the dock, dangling his legs over the side. He had never seen the pond frozen before. It looked like a giant skating rink. He was tempted to try it out, but his mom had forbidden him to step on the ice. It wasn't safe, she said.

He remembered the time he was scared of jumping into this pond because of the sea monster he was certain lived under the water. That was more than two years ago. Before he had ridden a dragon through the skies of Ahoratos. Before he had helped save a prisoner from Skot'os and saved the rec center from an Ent invasion and all the other things he had done that were pretty cool.

And yet everyone thought his idea about capturing the Olethron was stupid. They wouldn't even listen to him. His own brother just made fun of him.

And Ruwach had given him a plain old rock.

Evan took the rock out of his pocket and looked at it for a long time. He had hoped by now it would have turned into something else, like the Krÿs that changed into a sword or the seed that turned into a shield. He'd tried throwing it in the air and rolling it on the ground. He'd put it underwater and even held it to a candle flame to see if he could make out invisible messages.

Yet this rock was still just a rock.

Maybe I'm just as useless as this rock, he thought. *Just like Xavier said.* Evan was tempted to throw it away. He wondered what would happen if he threw it at the icy pond. Would it break right through and sink? But he had done that with the seed, when he thought it was good for nothing. That turned out to be the wrong move.

He turned the rock over in his hand.

There had to be *something* that made it special.

The rock was very smooth; it fit into his palm perfectly. In fact, it was kind of nice to hold. He gripped it tightly; it felt warm in his hand, which was getting pretty cold. He should have worn mittens.

Evan shivered. He got up and headed back to the house, putting the rock in his pocket. He walked through the fresh snow so he could make new tracks and was surprised at how deep it was. With each step his feet sank almost to his knees. He had to jump to make any progress.

Suddenly he felt something behind him and stopped, frozen. He spun around to face the woods at the edge of his yard. There was nothing there. But the nothing felt real to him, a nothing that was more than nothing. He could smell it too, that scent of something rotting. It was there.

The Empty.

Evan gripped the rock in his pocket and trudged toward the woods. He had to see this thing, whatever it was, or *wasn't*. For some reason, he didn't feel scared, only curious.

He walked into the wooded area and stopped to look around. The snow wasn't as deep here, as much of it had fallen in the trees above. Sunlight filtered in from the branches, casting strange shadows on the snow. But none of those shadows was *the* shadow. Maybe he'd been mistaken. Maybe the Empty was really empty, after all.

A branch above his head rustled. He looked up and saw a large white bird sitting there. He almost gasped out loud. It was the exact same bird he'd seen in the scary forest in the In-Between. It had to be. The majestic bird sat very still and stared at him, as if waiting for him to make a move.

Evan felt his heart beating wildly. He took a step toward the bird. It suddenly spread its wings and took off, nearly knocking him over with surprise. It flew a short distance and then settled on another tree branch. Just like before, Evan had the distinct impression he was supposed to follow it.

He took a few steps toward the bird, and it took off again, landing a little farther way. It was going deeper into the woods. Evan got worried. What if he got lost? But he continued to plod through the snow, following the bird.

And then he heard a sound.

It was a very small sound. A tiny squeak, coming from farther ahead in the woods. Like an animal in trouble.

The bird took off again, flying a little farther. As Evan raced to catch up, he heard the animal noise even louder. A crying, whining sound.

The bird flew out the other side of the trees and into an open area, which was actually the backyard of a house. The whining noise was even more pronounced. Evan started to run, leaping through the snow; his heart pounded a million miles a minute, his chest tightened, making it harder to breathe.

He ran toward the small ranch house sitting on a little rise in the distance. Snow was piled up high all around the house. He couldn't see any movement, but he could still hear the whining. As he approached the house, the snow was so deep he practically had to tunnel through it.

Finally, Evan saw a tiny furry head appear from the top of the snow at the bottom of a deck at the back of the house. He took a breath, somewhat relieved. The little dog must be stuck. And no one could hear his cries for help.

But who would let a tiny dog like that out all alone?

The dog saw Evan and started to yip frantically. Evan trudged toward it, calling out, "Take it easy. I'm coming," as he went.

Then he saw something pink in the snow.

Pink was not a color that belonged in snow.

He took a few more steps and stopped, gasping. An elderly woman was lying half-buried, wearing a pink robe and slippers. Evan rushed toward her.

"Ma'am, ma'am!" he shouted. "Are you okay?"

He brushed the snow off the woman and shook her shoulders. She started to move a little, moaning. Evan was thankful she was alive. The dog barked like crazy, its high-pitched yap making Evan's ears hurt.

Evan wasn't sure what to do. Go and get help? But if the lady lay out here in the cold any longer, she might die. He summoned all his strength, grabbed her under her arms, and dragged her, inch by inch, toward the porch steps, all the while talking to her: "I've got you, ma'am. Don't worry."

He managed to get her only halfway out of the snow, lying across the porch steps. He stopped, exhausted, took off his coat, and threw it over her body.

"I'm going to go inside the house and call my parents, okay? Don't worry; everything will be fine." The woman moaned a reply.

Evan stumbled into the house, saw the old-fashioned corded phone on the wall, and picked up the receiver. His hands were shaking so badly from cold and fear that it took him a while to dial his house number. His mom answered. The words rushed out of Evan's mouth in an unbroken stream.

"Mommomanoldladyfellinthesnowandsheshalffrozen andIcantgetheroutpleasecomeandhelp!"

"Evan, slow down. Who is it?"

"I don't know. Other side of the woods . . . she has a little dog . . . I heard it crying . . ."

"Oh no. It must be Mrs. Johnson. I'll call 911. You stay with her and try to keep her warm until we get there!"

Evan hung up, grabbed some old afghans from the living room sofa, and rushed back outside again. He brushed the snow off Mrs. Johnson and wrapped her as best he could in the blankets. She was shivering; her lips were blue. The dog lay down at her side, whining and licking her hand.

"They're coming, Mrs. Johnson. They're coming. Don't worry." Evan spoke the words over and over. Then he thought of the rock. He pulled it out of his pocket and looked at it. Suddenly he recalled Ruwach's words: *stone of remembrance*.

"Ruwach," he said aloud, holding on to the rock. "Please help. Make Mrs. Johnson okay." The rock was really warm from having been in his pocket. He placed the rock in the old lady's hand under the blanket. He closed her fingers over it. As he did, her shivering subsided, and she stopped moaning. She opened her eyes and looked at him. Her lips moved slightly, mouthing the words *thank you*.

An ambulance and a police car arrived a few minutes later, along with his mom. The paramedics lifted the old lady onto a stretcher and brought her into the house, where they proceeded to check her vitals and warm her up. They announced that she was okay, no broken bones. They were pretty sure she didn't have any frostbite either.

"Good thing you found her when you did," one of them told Evan. "If she'd lain out there any longer, we might have lost her."

Mrs. Johnson managed to tell them that she had taken her little dog, Bentley, out to do his business but missed her footing and fell off the deck into the snow. She couldn't get up because it was so deep.

"How is Bentley?" she asked in a thin trickle of a voice.

"He's okay," said Evan, who had wrapped the dog in two blankets.

"Thank goodness," she said. "Thank goodness you came when you did. How did you know to find me?"

"How *did* you find her?" his mom asked. "Her house is over a half mile from ours."

"I . . . heard the dog crying," Evan said with a shrug. "He's got a pretty loud cry."

His mom looked at him, her eyes narrowing slightly. But she just smiled and hugged him. "I'm proud of you, Evan."

"We'll need to take you to the hospital for observation," one of the paramedics said.

"My Bentley!"

"Don't worry, Mrs. Johnson. We'll take care of him until you're well again," said Evan's mom. Evan glanced up at her and smiled.

"Oh, thank you. His food is under the sink. He takes a half a cup in the morning and evening, mixed with a little applesauce. For his digestion." Mrs. Johnson was already sounding better. "And make sure to take his favorite pillow. He won't sleep at night without his pillow."

"Got it," said Evan, cuddling the little dog so the old lady would know he would take good care of him.

Before the paramedics rolled her out to the ambulance, Mrs. Johnson held out her hand to Evan. It contained the rock.

"Thank you," she whispered.

Evan took the rock, smiling at her.

"What is that?" asked his mom.

"Oh, just a rock," said Evan.

But he was pretty sure now that this little rock wasn't *just* a rock after all.

CHAPTER 24

On the Bench

Day 30

Xavier struggled to pull his books from his locker while leaning on his crutches. His knee throbbed. Sweat broke out on his forehead. It was his first day back at school since his surgery. He had never imagined how hard it would be to deal with the ordinary tasks of life. The doctor had warned him not to put any weight on his bad knee for at least two weeks. He'd even told Xavier he should use a wheelchair. Xavier had refused. Now he wasn't sure he'd made the right choice. He didn't know how he would manage two weeks of this.

"Hey, can I help you with those?"

He glanced around and found himself looking into the eyes of Cassie Cavanaugh. He felt the heat rise in his cheeks and shook his head.

"No, I got it," he said.

"No you don't," she said. She took the books from his locker and put them in his backpack for him. "I broke my arm once. Fell off a horse at camp. It's no fun." She smiled. Xavier looked quickly away from her and put the backpack over his shoulder. Then he situated his crutches again.

"Where's your next class?"

"Uh . . . just at the end of the hall."

"Great. It's on my way."

They started to walk together through the crowd of kids, Cassie slowing to match his pace. Xavier saw a lot of kids stop and stare at him; he wondered what they were thinking.

"So," said Cassie, "I meant to tell you that was a really great game until . . . well, you got hurt."

"Oh. Yeah." Xavier didn't like to be reminded about the game. Not that he could ever stop thinking about it.

"Does it still hurt?"

"Yeah." *It hurts*, he thought. *And not just physically*. "Not as much as before." He paused. "I should have quit after I fell the first time. Then it might not have been so bad." It felt good to tell her this, to unburden himself of this nagging thought. What if he had just sat out the rest of the game, iced his knee, put his pride aside? Then maybe he would still be playing. He was hounded by what-ifs these days. What if he had sat out the game? What if he had not gone over that bridge?

"Are you going to the game tonight?"

Xavier glanced at her, startled. "I wasn't planning to."

"Why not?"

"Well, because . . . I can't play. So what's the point?"

"So what if you can't play? I think you should still be there. You're part of the team, right? My dad always says that. When you're on the team, you're on the team, no matter what."

"I guess you're right."

They had reached Xavier's classroom. Cassie turned to look directly into his eyes. "So, I'll see you at the game?"

"I . . . guess so."

"Good." She gave him another smile and walked away.

Xavier didn't know what to make of Cassie Cavanaugh. He felt all mixed up inside whenever he talked to her. He sat through math class, thinking about what she had said. As much as he hated going to that game and sitting on the bench, he knew Cassie probably had a point. It was the same thing Mr. J. Ar had tried to tell him over the weekend. He still had a job to do. He was still on the team. Even if it was from the sidelines.

Besides, she would be there.

So when his mom picked him up from school, he asked her if she would take him to the game that night.

"I thought you said you didn't want to go to the games," his mom said as she drove home.

"I changed my mind."

His mom didn't respond. She only smiled to herself.

Xavier, wearing his team jacket, arrived in the locker room that night as the other players were getting into their uniforms. They gave him high fives and fist bumps. Coach Cavanaugh came in for the pep talk just before the team was to go out to the court. He saw Xavier and nodded.

Xavier made his way into the gym with the team and took his place on the bench, setting his crutches underneath. The rest of the team went out on the court for warm-ups. Xavier rubbed his hands together, feeling awkward and lost. He had no idea what to do. He glanced up at the stands, searching for familiar faces. He saw his parents and Evan and gave a little wave. His dad raised one hand and pointed a finger at him. Xavier pointed back. He had told them not to bother to come since he wasn't playing. But they hadn't listened to him. He was kind of glad.

He looked up to the top of the bleachers, where Cassie was sitting with her friends. She smiled and waved. He smiled and turned around quickly, sure that his face was already bright red.

He watched as the team gathered around the coach for one last pep talk. As the players broke up to start the game, the coach came over to him and patted his shoulder.

"I'm glad you're here, Blake," he said.

"Thanks, Coach."

Once the game started, it got easier. Xavier was soon absorbed in the battle on the court, watching everything the players did, noting the habits and strategies of the other team. He began to shout suggestions and encouragements, cheering when they made baskets. He was surprised at how different the game looked when he wasn't thinking about playing. He could see the bigger picture. He could read the plays before they happened and see when players weren't in their zones.

At halftime, the team gathered for a huddle. They had been playing pretty hard but were down seven points. Coach Cavanaugh talked about ways to put up a stronger defense against the other team's superior shooting ability. Then he turned to Xavier.

"What do you think, Blake?" he asked.

Xavier swallowed hard, surprised the coach was asking for his opinion. He was only a sophomore, after all.

"Try more bounce passes," he said finally. "They've got some tall guys, and there's been a lot of steals because you're trying to pass over their heads. So go under, or around, or even between them. They're all up in the air, so you have to go low. Keep them guessing."

Coach Cav smiled. "Good idea," he said.

The Lions made a comeback in the second half and won the game by three points. The crowd in the stands went wild. Even though he hadn't played a single minute, Xavier felt like he'd had the best game of his life.

His family came down to greet him.

"Congratulations, son," said Mr. Blake, giving him a hug. "I'm proud of you."

"I didn't even play," he said.

"I think you know what I mean. Mr. J. Ar would be proud of you too. He'd hoped to come, but he just wasn't up to it. Maybe you could call him and tell him what happened."

"Sure," said Xavier.

When he got home, Xavier called Mr. J. Ar and told him about the game. "Good job, Xavier," was all Mr. J. Ar said. But those three words meant so much to him.

While he was trying to fall asleep that night, Xavier noticed a bright shaft of moonlight fall across the room and illuminate the stick he'd gotten from Ruwach. He'd almost forgotten about that stick. He got up and hopped over to it. He took hold of it in both hands. It didn't seem so much like a crutch to him now.

Maybe it was meant for something else.

Then he noticed a tiny Crest, engraved into the stick just above where his hands held it. He stared as the Crest seemed to lift off the stick and hover in the air before him, glowing golden, like a tiny star. He reached out and touched it.

CHAPTER 25

Common Ground

Xavier thought at first that the floor under his feet had disappeared.

He was falling, the world around him going by so fast he could see only swirls of color and then nothing but darkness. He clung to the stick with both hands as if it alone could stop his rapid descent.

Gradually, the falling sensation slowed until he felt as though he were just floating gently, like taking a ride on a Ferris wheel. By the time he touched the ground, he was barely moving at all.

He could see the ground around his feet. He couldn't see anything else. It was completely dark.

Got to find the Water, he thought. But he couldn't see a thing. He took a tentative step in one direction, sliding his foot along to make sure there were no pitfalls. Then he slid the other foot. He realized then that his bad leg wasn't hurting at all. It was holding his weight. *Of course*, he thought. In Ahoratos, he wasn't injured.

But that didn't mean he was out of danger. This was the In-Between, and he didn't have his armor. The darkness was so complete that he began to feel disoriented. He had no idea which way to go. Panic rose up in his chest. He fought to push it back down.

Then he noticed that the stick had started to glow very faintly. He held it up, hoping it would illuminate the space around him. But all he saw was more darkness.

He wondered if there was some other way to make the stick "work."

"Show me the way," he said to the stick. He felt a little foolish, talking to a stick.

The stick did not respond to the request.

Xavier sighed. "A lot of help you are." He tried to use the stick like a flashlight, pointing it in various ways to see if it would illuminate any obstacles or pitfalls around him. Still, he couldn't see anything.

"This is so weird," he said aloud. "It's never been like this before."

Ahoratos was always showing him something new, something more challenging than the last time.

Suddenly a speck of light appeared before his eyes, growing brighter, turning into a shape.

A bird.

A large regal bird, pure white, like snow.

It was sitting on something, but Xavier couldn't tell what. And then it suddenly spread its wings and flew at Xavier's face.

Xavier swung the stick at the bird, covering his face with his other hand. His heart raced, but the swinging stick didn't hit anything. It felt different, however— softer and slippery . . . and it was *moving*!

Xavier uncovered his eyes and gasped, dropping the stick, which writhed around on the ground like a snake.

It *was* a snake! Xavier struggled to make sense of this. A bird had flown at him. He'd swung the stick, and it had turned into a snake. And now the bird was gone, and the glowing snake was slithering away from him.

He couldn't lose that stick. He charged after it as it veered left and right, always just out of reach. Then, without warning, the snake disappeared. First the head, then all the way to the tail. It was gone.

It couldn't just disappear, Xavier thought. *It must have gone somewhere*. He slid one foot forward, in the direction of where he had last seen the snake. He felt something wet soaking into his sneaker.

Then the Crest appeared before him, lying flat and rippling, as if it were resting on the surface of a moving object. The Water. This must have been where the snake went. Without further hesitation, Xavier stepped forward, putting both feet into the Water. He kept going until it was completely over his head.

The next thing he knew, he was in the Cave, wearing his armor. His clothes, instead of the usual gray, were snow white. The stick was lying on the ground. It was no longer a snake, but an ordinary stick again. He reached down to pick it up.

He looked around and saw the Sparks floating around him, the bluish rock formations of the Cave pulsing with inner light. The last time he had been here, the Cave had been chock-full of Warriors. Now, he was alone.

"Xavier."

He whirled to see Levi coming toward him, all in white as he was. He felt a stab of nervousness.

"Hey," Xavier said, trying his best to make his voice sound casual.

"Hey." Levi gave him a curt nod.

"Are the others here too?"

"I don't think so." Levi looked around. "Just us."

"Oh."

They stood awkwardly, in silence. Xavier wanted to say something, to apologize for what he'd done at the battle, even to say how sorry he was that Mr. J. Ar was so sick. But the words stuck in his throat. He stole a glance at Levi, who avoided his gaze, apparently absorbed in watching the Sparks flicker around their heads.

"Warriors."

They both turned to see Ruwach standing before them, his hands hidden inside his purple sleeves. Xavier was thankful he was there, breaking the awful silence.

"Ru," he said, "what's going on? Where is everyone?"

"You are enough," Ruwach replied. "But you must work together."

Xavier glanced at Levi, who frowned and looked at the ground.

"Can you do that?" Ruwach asked.

"Sure," said Xavier.

"Yeah," said Levi.

"This mission will be difficult," Ruwach went on. "Do you have the Glass, Levi?"

"Yeah." Levi dug into his pocket and produced the Glimmer Glass. Xavier peered at it, wondering what it was.

"And you have the Staff, I see," said Ruwach, turning to Xavier.

"Staff?" Xavier said. "I thought it was a crutch."

"What is the difference? It has helped you move forward."

"Yeah I guess . . . but you could have warned me about the snake thing."

"The what?" said Levi.

Ruwach interrupted. "Then you are ready."

"For what?" asked Xavier.

"To go up the mountain."

Both boys looked at Ruwach as if they hadn't heard him right.

"Excuse me?" said Levi. "*Up* the mountain?"

"By ourselves?" said Xavier. "We can't attack the fortress by ourselves."

"I did not say you should attack," said Ruwach. "Just go to the top and see what you can see."

"How do we get up there?" asked Levi. "Will Tannyn take us?"

"You will know," said Ruwach.

"How will we know?" asked Xavier.

"As you always do. Fear not, Warriors. I am always with you."

Before either of them could ask another question, Ruwach took his hands from his sleeves; they glowed a brilliant white. He raised them to the boys, covering them in his light, so they thought they were staring into the sun.

CHAPTER 26

The Right Track

When the light subsided, Levi and Xavier found themselves covered by a thick cloud. The air was cold. Their boots were sunk in deep snow. Wind whipped against their faces.

"I can't see a thing," said Xavier.

Their breastplates began to blink rapidly. Both boys turned until the light beamed steadily.

"Guess we need to go that way," Xavier said. Levi nodded.

The two trudged in the direction the breastplates pointed. They still had no idea where they were because of the heavy cloud that seemed to rest upon them.

"Must be Ru," Xavier said.

"What?"

"The cloud. He said he would be with us."

"Oh. Yeah."

The cloud suddenly disappeared just before the boys collided with two boulders sticking out of the snow. The rocks were tall and narrow, shaped like triangles that came to sharp points at the top.

"That's weird," said Xavier. They went up to the rocks to investigate and found a narrow opening between them, a path that cut deep into the snowy mountainside.

Levi checked his breastplate. It was beaming steadily when he faced up the hill. "I guess that's the path we're looking for," he said.

They gazed at the steep path with consternation. Ice and snow covered the slope, which rose up to a thick, dark cloud that encircled the peak. There was one sky-pod visible from where they stood. But they knew there were Bone Breakers up there with very keen eyesight.

"Our cloud is gone," Xavier said. "What if those birds see us?"

"Let's hope they aren't looking this way." Levi was glad their clothing and armor were all white, so they would blend in with the snow.

Xavier was about to start up the path when he stopped and turned to Levi. "Sorry. You can go first," he said. "If you want."

Levi shook his head. "That's okay."

Xavier nodded, planted his stick in the snow, and took a step onto the path. His boot instantly sprouted sharp cleats that dug into the ice, giving him secure footing. The same thing happened for Levi. They began their trek up the steep path, neither of them speaking, concentrating on their footsteps. The path twisted and turned and sometimes required them to use their hands to climb from ledge to ledge, but they made steady progress upward. Occasionally Xavier would stop to look up to the skypod, watching for movement, any sign they had been spotted. But all remained quiet.

They reached a wider ledge, and Xavier stopped. "Let's take a break," he said.

"I don't need a break," said Levi.

"Well . . . I do." Xavier sat down on the ledge, setting his stick aside. Levi sighed and sat down beside him.

"I'd love a bacon burger about now," Xavier said.

Levi knew he was trying to get him to say something like, "I could go for two bacon burgers and cheese fries and a chocolate shake." But he didn't say anything. He heard Xavier sigh.

"Look, I know you're mad at me. And I just wanted to say . . . I'm sorry."

Levi glanced at Xavier, surprised. "It's okay."

"No, it's not okay. I let you down. I thought I was . . . well, I guess I was just showing off, maybe. It was wrong."

Levi felt something hard inside of him get a little bit softer. "I wasn't much help," he said. "I was too busy thinking about my dad."

"I get that. We're all thinking about him."

Another silence. Then Xavier looked up toward the dark cloud that ringed the top of the mountain, which was much closer now.

"I guess we can go as far as that cloud," he said. "The crater can't be too much farther beyond that."

"Yeah," Levi said. "The cloud will give us some cover, and maybe we'll be able to see what's up there."

They started up the mountain again. Levi felt lighter, as if a weight had been taken off his shoulders. Maybe it was Xavier's apology, or his own admission that he might have contributed to the problem. Maybe it was that the heavy silence between them didn't feel quite as heavy anymore.

In a few minutes they reached the edge of the dark cloud that rimmed the crater. The noxious fumes of the cloud made their throats burn. They held their breath as they continued up, gasping for air once their heads cleared the cloud layer.

To their surprise, brilliant sunshine greeted them. They could see to the rim of the crater, where lava flowed down the side of the mountain, turning to steam when it hit the snow and ice.

But it was what they saw above the crater that shocked them to stillness. The tip of a mammoth pyramid rose from the top of the mountain. It looked like it was made of some very smooth black stone that shone in the sunlight. A column of thick smoke rose from the very tip of the pyramid, forming a dark cloud overhead.

"Is that the fortress?" asked Xavier, shocked at what he saw. "That pyramid?"

"Must be," said Levi. He didn't want to say out loud what they both were thinking: that this fortress looked indestructible. He pulled the Glimmer Glass from his pocket.

"So that's your gift?" Xavier asked.

"Yeah."

"What's it do?"

"It helps me see things." Levi held it up to his eye and stared up at the fortress.

"Could I try it?" Xavier asked, as he watched Levi studying the fortress through the Glass. Levi glanced at him, uncertain.

"I'm not sure. . . ."

"Never mind. Ruwach gave it to you. Not me."

Levi nodded and turned back to the Glass. "I see Forgers. But not regular Forgers. They look as though they are made of rock. There's hundreds. Maybe a thousand. They're building catapults, I think. Maybe to hurl lava fireballs down the mountain."

"What about the Askalons? Do you see them?" Xavier asked.

Levi shook his head.

"They must be somewhere," Xavier said. "Maybe they're inside."

"No, they aren't."

Xavier looked at Levi. "You can see inside?"

"Yeah. But only partially. I need to get up higher. I think there's something going on in there."

"That's not a good idea," said Xavier. "It's too dangerous. You might be seen if you go any farther up." Xavier glanced nervously at the skypod directly across from the fortress. The Bone Breakers would have them in their direct line of sight.

"I'm going," said Levi. "Stay here and warn me if you see the birds coming."

"I think I should come with you."

"No." Levi glared at Xavier, who backed down.

"Okay," he said. "Just . . . hurry."

Levi tucked the Glass back in his pocket and started to climb farther up, above the cloud that ringed the mountain. He climbed all the way to the edge of the ice. Beyond that was crusty black lava, all the way up to the crater. He lay on his belly and held the Glass to his eye once more.

"See anything?" Xavier called up.

Levi didn't answer. He strained to make out the shapes that were moving about inside the pyramid. The vast space was mostly empty except for a huge, roiling pit of lava in the middle. A set of stairs led to a throne where Thayne himself was sitting. Three creepy-looking figures were stirring the lava with long sticks . . . or were they bones? Suddenly something started to emerge from the lava—a giant figure that seemed to harden into rock. It looked like the creatures on the ramparts. *So that was where they came from.*

"He's making new soldiers from the lava," Levi called down to Xavier. "They're coming out of a pit."

"Lava Forgers," said Xavier.

"Yeah." Levi was about to lower the Glass when something moved at the corner of his vision. He noticed then a figure at the foot of the stairs, like a person. But he was half-metal. Levi gasped. It was a prisoner. Not fully metallized yet. Something like what Rook had looked like when they had seen him in Ponéros's prison the first time.

The prisoner was on his knees. Levi couldn't hear his words but had the impression that the prisoner was begging for his life. Then Thayne raised his huge hammer and pointed the glowing end at him. It looked like a pronouncement of judgment. The prisoner threw himself to the floor as a Forger that was standing guard went over and touched him, just a small touch. The prisoner screamed in terror as the metal parts of him began to melt, his flesh burning, turning to ash.

Levi jerked backward in horror, the arm holding the Glass flying up so that it glinted in the sunlight.

"Levi! What's wrong?" Xavier called from below.

"Nothing," Levi said, recovering his shock. "I'm fine. I'm coming down—"

"Bone Breakers!"

A second later, Levi heard an ear-shattering screech.

"Levi! Come down! Now!"

Levi looked up to see two Bone Breakers hurtling toward him. His heart hammering, he started to scramble down the slope, still clutching the Glass. But he missed his footing and began to slide, trying to grasp something solid with his free hand to stop his momentum. The screeching of the birds grew louder. He yelled out a strangled "Help!"

He slammed hard into something solid that stopped his sliding. Xavier stood over him, his staff firmly planted in his path. Levi grabbed hold of the staff just as one of the birds snatched at him, its powerful talons gripping his arm. He saw the bird's beak opening, lunging for the Glass in his hand.

Xavier swung his sword at the bird, knocking it off Levi's arm. The other Bone Breaker flew in to attack. Levi shoved the Glass in his pocket and grabbed his Krÿs. He swiped at the bird just as the blade extended, catching it by surprise. The bird flew off with a scream while Xavier swung his sword down on the first bird, silencing it for good. It instantly turned to ash that blew away on the wind.

Once free of the birds, the two boys wasted no time scrambling down to the dark cloud, where they would be out of sight in case other Bone Breakers were on their way. They took cover and lay still, gasping for breath.

"That was . . . close," Levi said after a long moment.

"Yeah." Xavier paused. "The Glass was shining. That's how they saw you."

Levi pulled the Glass from his pocket and looked at it. "I wondered. Thanks. For . . . helping me."

"Sure. Did you see anything up there?"

Levi took a deep breath and told Xavier about the prisoner burned up by the touch of a Lava Forger. "Ruwach said I would see things . . . that I didn't want to see." He glanced at Xavier, who was staring at him wide-eyed with shock. "You're lucky you got a stick." He smirked.

"I'm not so sure. This thing turns into a snake when you least expect it."

"Seriously? That's kind of—cool."

Xavier grinned. Then he sat up and glanced down the mountain. "It's going to be as hard going down as it was going up," he said.

"Then we should get started," Levi said. "I think we've seen enough for one day."

"You can say that again."

CHAPTER 27

Mary

Day 32

Mary sat at her desk in the Cedar Creek Recreation Center, staring at the book.

It had been four days since Manuel had given it to her, but she hadn't yet had the nerve to open it. She knew it was silly, but she half-worried that something might pop out, like a dragon or a snake or . . . Viktor. She still shuddered whenever she thought of that malevolent boy who turned out not to be a boy at all.

She took a courage-enhancing sip of her chai latte and set down the cup. The Crest—the funny-shaped symbol that looked like an *N*—seemed to shimmer on the cover. She gripped the edge and pulled it open.

Nothing happened. She let out a breath. But as she stared at the first page, she was astonished to see a single word engraved in the center.

MARY.

She gasped to herself, wondering how her name had gotten into Manuel's book. But then again, Mary was a common name. Maybe the original owner had been named Mary, and she had written her own name in the book, long ago. But in such a beautiful script? Well, that was how people wrote stuff in the old days.

Still, it was unnerving. She shut the book quickly, too nervous to turn another page. But as she stared at the shimmering Crest, it seemed to rise up from the book and hover in the air right before her eyes. Wow, this was some crazy book. She blinked, wondering if she was imagining things.

She was suddenly overcome with the urge to touch it. Just to see if it was really there. It floated so enticingly before her eyes, rotating slowly, so real and solid and yet . . . unreal too. She lifted her hand, reaching toward it . . .

"Miss Stanton!"

Her hand slammed back down on the desk. The Crest disappeared. Mary looked up at the girl in the doorway of her office, covered in paint.

"What happened?" she asked, alarmed.

"Joey squirted paint all over me!" The little girl started to cry.

"Oh dear. Don't worry; I'll help you clean up!"

Once Mary had washed the paint off the girl's clothes as best she could, called Joey's parents to inform them of his infraction, and gotten everything else settled down again, it was nearly time for the rec center to close. Mary waited until the last child had gone home before she gathered her things and headed out the door.

That's when she remembered the book. She went back into her office to retrieve it. Maybe she'd look at it again at home, figure out what that crest was all about.

It lay there on her desk. The Crest glowed brilliantly in the darkened office. As she watched, it rose up to a vertical position, as it had earlier, growing larger and more solid. She sensed, though she wasn't sure how, that the Crest was demanding something of her.

"Oh, sorry," she said to the Crest. "I can't do this now. Whatever this is. I've got a date tonight. Maybe tomorrow. Okay?"

The Crest continued to grow, filling the office, touching the walls. It was so bright it blinded her so she couldn't even find the door to get out.

"Okay, okay!" she said. The Crest was inches from her face now. She reached out with one hand, putting her palm against it. Her palm went right through.

As did the rest of her.

"Hello?"

Mary Stanton turned in a slow circle, staring. Nothing but moss-covered rocks as far as she could see. She had felt as though she'd been pulled through a suction tunnel, but the sensation had been so brief it was over almost before it had started. Now she stood alone on a barren field of rocks. The sky above her was inky black. It was as if she had landed on the moon.

"Hello? Anybody?" She was scared. She wondered what had happened. Maybe she had slipped in her office and hit her head. Maybe this is what it felt like to be unconscious, trapped in your own mind, an infinite field of nothing. "Help me!" She started to panic. "Please! Help me!"

And then she saw something. A black dot on the horizon, growing larger. A big lumpy thing. Like a boulder. Rolling right toward her.

She moved away, out of its path, though it was difficult to walk on the moss-covered rocks. When she looked up again, she was astonished to see that the boulder, too, had changed direction. It was still heading for her. She turned and started to run away from it, her feet slipping and sliding on the rocks. She fell and got up again and kept trying to run. But the more she ran, the slower she seemed to get.

Then she saw to her horror that another boulder was rolling toward her from the front as well. She stopped, panting.

"What's going on?" she demanded. The boulders didn't answer; they just kept rolling. They were huge, as big as buildings. She would be crushed under them.

Desperate, she tried a third direction. Maybe the two boulders would slam into each other. But once again, the rolling boulders changed direction and continued to roll straight at her. In despair, she dropped to her knees, out of breath, out of hope. The rumble of the boulders was loud in her ears. In a few seconds, it would be over. She would be dead. Flat as a pancake. She started to cry.

Then she heard another sound, the sound a bathtub makes when it starts to drain. She opened her eyes and saw to her amazement that bubbles were coming up from the rocky ground in front of her. Suddenly, the bubbles turned into a geyser, knocking her backward and soaking her completely. She gasped, wondering if this could get any worse. But when she managed to look behind her, the boulders had stopped moving, remaining just at the edge of the pool of water the geyser had created.

The geyser suddenly stopped shooting, but the pool of water remained. And there, on the surface of the murky water, Mary saw the Crest, rippling slightly, as if it floated just underneath. Before she could even wonder what all this was about, the pool began to dry up, sinking back into the rocky ground.

"No, don't leave me!" she said to the water, sensing that if the water went away, the boulders would start moving again. "Come back!" She flung herself at the rapidly disappearing pool. It was deeper than she thought, for she felt her whole body sink all the way in.

The next thing she knew, she was standing in a dark cave, perfectly dry, wearing a plain white shirt and smooth, leatherlike pants. Rock formations glowed blue all around her, and tiny flickering puffs like snowflakes floated in the air.

"This is a really bad dream," she said aloud. "Will someone wake me up?"

Then she heard a voice, deep and resonant, that might have been inside her own head.

"Welcome to Ahoratos."

CHAPTER 28

Rescue Mission

Brianna had just gotten through the Water and landed in the Cave when she found herself staring into the eyes of someone she would never have expected to see.

"Miss Stanton?" Brianna blinked several times to make sure it was really her. Mary Stanton stood proudly next to Ruwach. She was wearing armor: a breastplate, belt, and boots. She smiled broadly and waved.

"Hi Brianna! Fancy meeting you here."

"What are you doing here?" Brianna asked. She saw Ruwach raise an arm toward her and added: "I mean . . . wow. You came to Ahoratos. That's . . . amazing."

"I saw the Crest and just grabbed it," said Mary with a little laugh.

"The Crest?"

"From the book. Manuel's book. He gave me that book about the Prince Warrior to look at." She paused. "That is *quite* a book."

"Yeah, it is." Brianna smiled, relaxing. "So, what do you think, so far?"

"This is really different," Mary said. "I wasn't too sure about the outfit, but I can't wait to try it out."

"Great," said Brianna. She looked around, hoping the others would be showing up soon. "Is anyone else coming?"

"No," Ruwach said. "Just you."

"Just me?" Brianna looked confused. "But usually there's a bunch of us."

"Did you bring your gift with you?" Ruwach asked.

"Oh, yeah." Brianna pulled the root from her pocket. "Are you going to tell me what it's for?"

"You will see soon enough." Ruwach's hood nodded, and Brianna had the impression he was smiling, even though she couldn't see his face.

"So what's the mission?" Brianna asked.

"This is a rescue mission," Ruwach replied.

"A rescue? You mean, a prisoner?"

"Not exactly."

"Then who?"

"You will see."

"Can't you tell us, just this once? After all, Miss Stanton is new here, and I'm not so sure I can handle a rescue mission without the others—"

"Remember, you have everything you need." Ruwach turned and glided away.

"Wow. Does he always do that?" asked Mary.

"Kind of," said Brianna with a sigh.

"So, how do we get out of here?" Mary looked around. "Should we take one of these tunnels?"

"Probably." Brianna turned in a slow circle, watching her breastplate, which began to blink slowly. Finally, it stopped blinking and beamed steadily. "This one." Brianna headed toward the tunnel directly in front of her. She stopped and turned to Mary. "Are you coming?"

"Oh, okay," said Mary, hopping a little before following.

As soon as the girls passed into the tunnel, the Cave itself disappeared. They found themselves in a snowy landscape under a stormy sky.

"Where are we now?" said Mary. She sounded exasperated, as if she were getting tired of the scenery changing every five minutes.

"Somewhere in Ahoratos," Brianna said. "But I don't recognize it. It's all so snowy." All she could see were huge mounds of snow everywhere she looked. There was no sign of the Mountain of Rhema or the enemy fortress. She wondered where this prisoner they were supposed to rescue could be.

"It's so cold here," said Mary. "I always thought Ahoratos would be warmer."

"It used to be warm," said Brianna. "But it's winter here now."

"Winter? Yuck. I've had enough of winter already. Couldn't that little guy Ruwach have given us some fur coats or something?"

"We always have everything we need," Brianna said. "I guess we'll have to figure out who needs rescuing on our own. Let's go."

"Go where?"

"Not sure. We'll just follow the breastplates and see where they lead."

"Oh." Mary looked around worriedly. "I don't like this. I don't really think I want to do this after all."

Brianna could see Mary was scared. She felt a little sorry for her. "It'll be okay. Promise."

"How do you know?"

"I just do. You came through the Water, right?"

"Oh, yes. That was awful."

"Yeah, I remember the first time. I almost got eaten by a sand grobel."

"A what?"

"You don't want to know. But if you got this far, well, you can go the rest of the way. Trust me."

"If you say so."

Brianna led Mary through the snow, around the huge snow piles. She made sure her breastplate wasn't blinking, which would indicate she'd taken a wrong turn. But still she saw nothing new. Nothing resembling an enemy stronghold with prisoners. Just more snow piles.

After a while, they both began to get tired.

"This seems pretty pointless," said Mary. She was panting. "I think we should go back."

"We can't go back," Brianna said. "The breastplates point this way."

"We're walking in circles!" Mary was starting to panic. "We'll never get out of here! This was a terrible mistake!"

"Just stay calm, Miss Stanton—"

"But I can't!" Mary yelled. "I wish I'd never come here. I want to go home!" Mary spun around and headed back the way she'd come.

"Don't do it!" Brianna said. Before she had even finished saying the words, Mary let out a little scream and . . . disappeared.

It was as if she just vanished into the snow.

Brianna stood still, not knowing what to do. Then she saw a hand shoot up from the snow, Mary's hand, fingers outstretched, reaching for something. She realized that Mary was under the snow, and she was really stuck. She wouldn't be able to get out on her own. But Brianna couldn't move from where she was. If she went backward, she would probably fall into the snow trap as well.

The hand clenched and unclenched, fingers splayed. Mary was running out of air. Brianna had to act fast.

She extended her sword and reached out with it toward the hand, leaning over as far as she could. But her sword wasn't long enough. She still couldn't reach. She pulled it back.

Maybe the belt, she thought. It might reach Mary. She was about to take off her belt when she remembered the root in her pocket.

She took it out, staring at it. *A rescue mission*, Ruwach had said. It suddenly occurred to her that the person she was supposed to rescue was . . . Mary Stanton.

She gripped the root in one hand and extended her arm out as far as it would go toward Mary's hand. To her amazement, the root started to grow, new shoots appearing and lengthening, some of them digging down into the snow around Brianna's feet and others reaching toward Mary's hand. The shoots coiled around Mary's wrist several times. Brianna tugged on the root with both hands, feeling the shoots around her feet hold her steady, giving her more strength than she knew she had. She kept pulling, drawing the buried root slowly from the ground. Soon Mary's arm appeared, and then her shoulder, then her head. Mary's mouth opened in a wail.

"Stay calm, Miss Stanton!" Brianna cried out to her. "I've got you! I promise!"

Finally, the rest of Mary emerged from the snow. Brianna didn't stop pulling until she had gotten Mary all the way to safety at her side. Then she bent over and helped the frightened woman to her feet, brushing the snow off her. The root untangled itself and then retracted itself back into the small, ordinary root it had been in the first place.

"I almost *died*!" Mary exclaimed when she could speak actual words. "That snow was trying to kill me!"

"Now you know why I was serious about staying on course," Brianna said.

"Brianna, you saved me." Mary's wide eyes rested on Brianna in amazement.

Brianna realized it was true. She had done something she never could have done in her own strength. It was the root, Ruwach's gift, that had enabled her to help Mary get out of the snow. Brianna reached into her pocket to make sure it was still there.

"We'd better keep going," Brianna said. "Don't worry, Miss Stanton. Everything is going to be okay."

Before the words were even out of her mouth, a tremendous noise erupted from somewhere beyond the snowbank in front of them.

"What is that?" Mary said. "Sounds like a truck with no muffler."

Just then an Askalon came into view, headed straight for them.

"What is that thing?" Mary screamed.

"It saw us! Over here! Quick!" Brianna dashed behind one of the snow piles nearby. Mary didn't move a muscle. Brianna grabbed her arm and pulled her into the hiding place.

"Shhh. Stay still. Don't make a sound."

The Askalon drove directly toward them and stopped. Its engine rumbled and then went quiet. Brianna held her breath and peeked around the snow pile. Suddenly, the top hatch of the Askalon opened, and a huge, helmeted figure climbed out. Its heavy armor seemed to be made of knife blades, and it had thick spikes sticking up from its helmet. But the eyeholes were completely blank. Like there was nothing inside.

Brianna felt her throat close.

It was Thayne.

He carried a giant hammer with a red-hot tip in one massive fist. He took a few steps and stopped. The helmet turned in a complete rotation, surveying the landscape.

Brianna ducked back behind the snow pile as Thayne started to walk in their direction. He must have seen them. Now he would find them hiding, take them prisoner perhaps. Or even kill them. Thayne was so close, she could hear the creaking of his metal arm as he raised and lowered the hammer.

Maybe they could run. Thayne didn't look like he would be a very fast runner. Too much armor. But the Askalon would catch them. It would roll over the snow piles easily. They had no choice but to stay still.

Brianna waited, holding her breath. Mary was so paralyzed with fear she couldn't breathe either.

After an agonizing moment, the crunching, creaking sound of Thayne's heavy footsteps receded. Brianna peeked out again to see the massive armored enemy climb into the hatch. It closed shut over him. The Askalon roared to life. It started to plow toward them, but instead of rolling over the snow pile, it swerved around it, continuing its search. Brianna waited until the Askalon had disappeared from view before daring to let out a breath.

"I'm ready to go home now, if you don't mind," Mary said in a trembling voice.

"Me too," said Brianna. "Hopefully the breastplates will lead us back to the Cave."

"Is this what you usually do? Just traipse around looking for trouble?"

Brianna almost laughed. "No. We don't have to look for it. It always finds us."

CHAPTER 29

Turn for the Worse

Day 39

Levi was in math class, listening to Mrs. Brayburn's monotonous commentary on the isosceles triangle, when the principal, Mrs. Loomis, appeared in the doorway.

Everyone stopped what they were doing and sat straight up in their chairs. The principal had that sort of effect on kids. Her towering height, her severe hairdo, and her thick glasses that masked her eyes made even the toughest bully quiver. They all wondered which of them had done something to incur her wrath today.

"I'm sorry to interrupt," Mrs. Loomis said to the math teacher in a tone that didn't convey any sort of sorry-ness. Then the principal turned her attention to the classroom.

"Levi Arthur, can you come to the office, please? Bring your things with you."

Levi felt his heart drop into his stomach. All the other kids turned to stare at him, some with sympathy in their eyes, others with relief. He stuffed his math book in his backpack, got up, and walked slowly to the front of the room until he was within a few feet of Mrs. Loomis. Without really looking at him, Mrs. Loomis turned and walked out of the classroom. Levi followed.

She stayed in front of him for the long and terrifying walk to the office. All the while, Levi wondered what he had done to deserve this.

Mrs. Loomis was probably the most unfriendly principal of any school in the universe. Levi wondered why she had even gone into a career in education in the first place, because she really seemed to dislike kids. She was always making announcements on the public address system, denouncing the students' behavior, and imposing new and stricter rules. Her latest was to make everyone, even seventh and eighth graders, walk in single file on the "brown line" to the cafeteria, like a bunch of kindergarteners. She'd even had a brown line painted on the floor, and she instructed the hall monitors to send anyone who veered from the line to her office for detention. In fact, you could get detention for even the smallest infraction, like being thirty seconds late for class or failing to turn in homework on time. Levi had been late a few times, and lately he had not been able to finish all his homework. Was that why Mrs. Loomis had called him out of class?

Mrs. Loomis opened the main office door and waited for Levi to go in first. He could feel her eyes following him as he did. Then she breezed past the secretaries and led him into her private office. She shut the door behind him.

Levi took a quick look around. The office was dominated by a large desk that was swept clean of everything except a computer and a can of pencils. There were two chairs in front of the desk and one on the other side. A large fern, half-dead, sat in a planter by the window.

Beside it was a goldfish bowl with the biggest, ugliest goldfish Levi had ever seen swimming around inside. A bookcase covered one wall, filled with books but with no family pictures like most people's offices. Levi suspected Mrs. Loomis didn't have a family at all. Maybe she ate them.

"Sit down, Levi," she said. Levi went to sit in one of the two chairs. To his surprise, instead of going to the other side of the desk, Mrs. Loomis sat down right next to him. Levi flinched slightly at her being so near. He kept his backpack on his lap, as if in defense.

"Your mother is coming to pick you up. I'm afraid your father has had a setback and had to be taken back to the hospital."

"What?" Levi thought he might faint; the room seemed to spin. Mrs. Loomis took off her glasses, which were attached to a chain around her neck. Levi was surprised to see that her eyes were brown and almost . . . kind.

"I'm very sorry, Levi. I've notified the attendance office that you might need some time off in the next few weeks. They will help you keep up with your schoolwork." She paused. "If there is anything I can do to help, please let me know."

Levi nodded. "Thank you," he said.

"You should probably go and get your coat from your locker. Your mom will be here soon. And Levi, I am really very sorry."

Levi nodded and did as he was told. Mrs. Loomis was waiting for him at the front counter when he returned. She'd put her glasses back on.

"I'll walk you out," she said in a gentle voice.

Levi walked beside the principal to the outside door. Before he went out, he turned to the principal. "Thank you."

"You're welcome."

Levi raced down the steps to his mom's car. As soon as he opened the door, he knew she'd been crying. He got in the passenger seat and closed the door, trying to quell the rising panic in his chest. "What happened?"

"I had to call an ambulance. Your father was . . . unresponsive when I tried to wake him up this morning."

"Unre—what? But I thought he was getting better!"

"Me too. Levi, they had to put him on a respirator."

"A what?"

"It's a machine that helps him breathe."

Levi's mom drove like a NASCAR racer to the hospital. Mr. J. Ar was still in the emergency room when they got there. Levi approached his dad's bed, noticing that a tube had been put in his mouth; his face was taped up, and a big machine was next to him. The breathing machine, he thought. Levi wanted to cry and scream and throw himself on the floor. He was so angry, though he didn't know who to be angry with. His mom went to talk to the nurse. Levi put his hand on his father's chest, feeling it rising and falling rhythmically with the machine.

"Wake up," he whispered. *Don't leave me. I need you.*

Mr. J. Ar didn't respond. Didn't open his eyes.

Help me, Ruwach, Levi pleaded silently. *Help him. Make him well again.*

He waited for an answer. For his father to wake up. Nothing happened.

He glanced through the curtains and saw that a man in a white coat had joined his mother and the nurse. His expression was grim. Levi heard snatches of their words, including the word *coma*.

Coma. Another word Levi didn't like. He turned back to his father and bent close to his ear.

"I won't leave you," he whispered. "I'll be right here until you wake up."

Dr. Arthur returned to the bedside. "They're going to move him to the ICU," she told Levi. "That's the intensive care unit."

"I can go too, can't I?"

"Sure, Levi." His mom went over to him and hugged him. Levi saw that her eyes were wet with tears.

Orderlies came to move his dad to the ICU. Levi stayed at his side. A nurse brought chairs for him and his mom. Levi stared at his father, wanting to be there the moment he woke up. He even refused to go to the cafeteria for supper. His mom brought him a sandwich from a vending machine.

Levi was eventually lulled to sleep by the rhythmic gasps of the respirator and the beeping monitors. He dreamt he was in Ahoratos, climbing that mountain with Xavier again, only this time neither one of them could keep their footing, and with every step they slid farther and farther down the mountain and then fell into a dark, cold, bottomless river.

The sensation of sinking into that river jolted him awake. It was the middle of the night. The ICU was dark, the only light coming from the machines and monitors around the patient beds. His mom was asleep in the chair on the other side.

Levi got up and went over to his father's side, putting his hand over his father's hand. The hand was warm. He stared at the closed eyes of Mr. J. Ar, willing them to open, to look at him, to assure him he was all right.

Then he felt a warmth on the back of his neck and turned. There, hovering in the air before him, was the Crest, glowing golden as a star.

No. He shook his head. *I'm not leaving my dad. Go away.*

He turned back to his father. But the Crest appeared in front of him. "Go away!" he said aloud. The Crest continued to hover, growing larger, so that he couldn't avoid it no matter which way he looked.

"Ugh. Okay. Fine." He took his father's hand and held it between his own. "I'll be back soon. Wait for me." Then he reached out and touched the Crest.

CHAPTER 30

The Nameless King

Levi found himself back in the same barren field filled with square yellow buildings, just like the last time he had come to Ahoratos. That was weird. He couldn't remember ever having returned to the same place twice. Ahoratos always had new surprises for him, new challenges. But since he'd been here before, he knew that all he had to do was walk to the other side and kneel before the dry lake bed and the Water would appear.

Levi started walking straight down the first row. But then he stopped, remembering the one building that had been open, and the voice that had spoken to him. He wondered if that voice was still there. He went to the door and tried the knob. It turned, unlocked.

I shouldn't go in, he thought to himself. *I should just get to the Water*. But his curiosity got the better of him—he wanted to know who—or what—that voice really was. If it was still there.

He opened the door. It was as dark as it had been the last time, the light from outside failing to penetrate it. He stepped inside, keeping one hand on the doorknob, in case he had to leave quickly. The smell of dead worms filled his nostrils.

"Hello?" he said into the blackness. "Anyone there?"

"You're back," said the voice. It sounded amused.

"Yeah." Levi paused, at a loss for what to say next.

"Why are you here, Levi?" said the voice.

"You know my name?"

"Of course."

"I want . . . to know who you are."

"No, you don't."

Levi took a deep breath. "I want to see you. I want to see . . . your face."

"Close the door."

Levi hesitated. Then he slowly closed the door. To his surprise, the room brightened, a pale light rising up from the dusty floor. Levi gasped at what he saw.

The building was littered with what appeared to be broken toys: deflated balls, dolls with no heads or arms, stuffed animals—lions, bears, dogs—with the stuffing bursting from their sides, toy train cars and pieces of track thrown into tall piles. It was like a Christmas morning nightmare.

In the center of the room, sitting on a very large pile of broken toys, was a small, aged figure with a gaunt, yellowish face and wisps of white hair that sprouted from the top of his head. His deep-set, droopy eyes were pure white with no irises. Levi realized that the man must be blind. He was dressed in a tattered robe that looked as though it had once been the royal garment of a king. The velvet lining was worn off, the fur trim matted and clumped.

The oddest thing was that even though the man was small, he cast a very long shadow that reached all the way to the corner of the room. Levi couldn't see any light source that would have created such a shadow. He wondered how that was possible.

Lying on the floor at the bottom of the junk pile was a crown. It was large and appeared to have been magnificent once, but now it was discolored and bent, and all the jewels were missing.

The man opened his mouth, which contained no teeth. "Now you see me."

"Who are you?" Levi asked.

"I was once a king. But now I am here."

"Did Ruwach put you here?"

The man nodded slowly.

"Why? What did you do?"

"I didn't do. I simply was. And still am. Though I am not."

"That doesn't make sense."

"Not to you, I suppose."

"Do you have a name?"

"I once had a name. But no more. You can call me Nameless."

"Nameless. So . . . you just sit here, all the time?"

"Not always. I get out once in a while." The strange man smiled a toothless smile. "I've been out quite a bit lately. Because it is Winter."

"Did you bring the Winter?" Levi asked.

"No. The Winter brought me."

"I don't understand."

"Yes. That is for the best. It was nice of you to stop by, Levi. I don't get many visitors." Nameless let out a long sigh. "Most who come through here don't even try to open the doors. They don't want to know what's behind them."

"Why not? Are they afraid?"

"I suppose they are. With good reason."

"Are you dangerous?"

"To some, I am. But not to you." Nameless paused. "Or your father."

"My father? You know about my father?"

"Of course."

"Are you the one who . . ."

Levi didn't finish. He studied the withered face of the person before him, feeling as though all the questions in his mind were coming together, falling into place like pieces of a puzzle. He suddenly knew exactly who this worn-out king really was. "You can't have him," he said, his voice rising in fury. "I won't let you take my dad!"

"That is not for you or me to decide," said the old king wearily. "You should go now. The dark is soon to come. You do not want to be caught here in the dark."

Nameless rose slowly and stepped down from his throne of broken things. He unfolded his arms from his robe and reached down with crooked fingers to the crown lying on the floor. He put it on his head, but it was too big and fell over his blank, unseeing eyes and rested on his nose. He opened his mouth and laughed. It started as a wheeze but grew into something shrill and terrifying, like a maniacal clown.

Levi rushed for the door, threw it open, and ran outside, slamming it hard after him. He paused, breathing hard, his heart racing. He could feel the shadow coming as it had before, rushing over the rooftops toward him. He ran with all he had to the dry lake bed and dropped to his knees. Instantly the lake bed filled with water—the Water. He held his breath and dove in without looking back, disappearing as the water began to turn red and close in around him.

CHAPTER 31

Back in the Cave

Levi was still shaking when he "landed" in the Cave. His friends were already there—Xavier with his tall staff, Evan, Manuel, Brianna, Ivy, and Finn. They all had on the white clothes and armor, as he did. Many other Prince Warriors were present too, but not nearly as many as the first time they had gathered in the Cave that Winter.

"There you are," said Brianna. "We were getting worried about you. Is everything okay?"

Levi swallowed hard. "My dad . . . my dad is back in the hospital. They hooked him up to a machine that breathes for him. And I heard the doctor say the word *coma*."

"What?" Brianna gasped. "When did that happen?"

"Just before I came here. They aren't sure what happened. He seemed to be doing fine, and then he just . . ." For the first time since his father had become sick, Levi fell to his knees, put his hands to his face, and cried.

The others just stared, not knowing what to do. Then Brianna moved toward him and, kneeling beside him, carefully put her hand on his shoulder. She closed her eyes, blinking away tears. Following her lead, Ivy knelt and put her hands on both their shoulders. Manuel, Xavier, and Evan followed suit, linking them all together. Then Finn, whose arms were long enough to wrap around all of them. They knelt together in the midst of the great gathering of Warriors, holding on to each other and their friend in pain.

"Warriors."

The kids looked up to see Ruwach standing before them. But no one else in the Cave seemed able to see him; they continued to shuffle about and talk to each other as if nothing were happening. Ruwach was surrounded in Sparks, so he shone very brightly, as he had that day in the rec center when confronting Viktor. The sounds of chatter in the Cave had dimmed as well, as if someone had hit a mute button.

Ruwach glided toward Levi, the others moving out of the way. Then Ruwach, too, placed his glowing hand on Levi's shoulder. Levi felt his whole body grow warm and light, as if he could float up into the air. As if he could fly. His tears dried, leaving no trails on his cheeks. He glanced around and saw that his friends had experienced the same thing, as they were all connected to each other—it was as if Ruwach had placed himself inside their hearts, taking up all the empty spaces, crowding out even the memory of their present sadness.

"There is a time for everything," Ruwach said, in the softest voice they had ever heard him use. "A time for laughter. A time for tears. A time for peace. A time . . . for war."

Levi rose to his feet, as did the others. He stood straight, his eyes steady on Ruwach, and he bowed.

"I'm ready," he said. "But my father . . ."

"You will see him again," said Ruwach. Levi sucked in a breath at this news. He managed a small smile.

Ruwach then turned to Xavier. "You must lead the Warriors today," he said.

"Me?" said Xavier. "But I . . ." He paused, knowing the others were staring at him, either in shock or dismay. "Why me?"

"Because I gave you the Staff," said Ruwach, pointing one glowing hand at Xavier's stick.

Xavier nodded, swallowing hard.

"You have the armor," Ruwach said, addressing all of them. "Use it. And use every gift I have given you, and every word I have spoken. You will need them this day."

The mute button went off, and the sounds of many Warriors in the Cave filled their ears again. Ruwach was no longer standing before them. He reappeared in the air high above all their heads, surrounded by Sparks, who created a nimbus of light around him.

"Warriors!" Ruwach spoke, his voice once again like music, but not a gentle trill—this time it was a crashing symphony. "You have been given a task. To defeat the renegade general Thayne and take back the Mountain of Rhema. This will not be an easy day. You are likely to see and hear things you don't understand at first. You are likely to be afraid. Remember your mission. Know I will be with you. You need only to do your part. And remember this above all: you have everything you need."

The Warriors cheered wildly, raising their arms high in the air as music burst over them like a tidal wave, drowning out the walls of the Cave, so that everything was light and sound. The Warriors hushed, thrown for a moment into a blinding radiance, and then in a flash it was gone again.

PART 4

A Time for War

CHAPTER 32

Hiding Out

When the light subsided, the Warriors found themselves at the edge of the bleak forest, near the bottom of the Mountain of Rhema. The mountain was covered in ice, with a dark cloud rimming the summit, obscuring the view of the fortress itself. Skypods hovered all around the mountain. The sky was stormy, and icy snow fell, clinging to their cheeks. The wind howled forlornly through the barren trees.

"What are we supposed to do?" asked Evan.

Xavier glanced at his breastplate. There was no light telling him which way to go.

"Wait," he said.

"We should attack!" yelled someone from the ranks of Warriors around them. More voices joined the chorus. "Attack! Attack!"

"No!" Xavier shouted back. He raised his staff and set it on the ground before him. "Don't attack!"

"But Ruwach said . . ." someone replied.

"Not yet," Xavier countered. He wasn't going to rush into anything without knowing what they were about to face. He glanced at Finn. "You're a football player, right?"

"Yeah," said Finn.

"Throw a snowball."

Finn looked at him, his eyes narrowing. "What for?"

"Can you throw a snowball all the way to the base of the mountain?"

Finn looked out, gauging the distance. "I think so."

"Do it."

Finn bent down, scooped up some snow, and formed it into a ball. Then he aimed, took a breath, and threw the snowball as hard as he could. The snowball sailed toward the mountain and landed directly on top of one of the snow drifts.

It was as if Finn had thrown a bomb. The mound of snow exploded into life, revealing what lay underneath. An Askalon. Its awakening triggered a chain reaction; soon all the snow mounds encircling the mountain were shaken apart, uncovering more Askalons that roared and sputtered, belching out streams of ice as they thundered toward the Prince Warriors.

"Take cover!" someone shouted. The Warriors broke ranks and began to run back to the forest to escape the charging Askalons. Ice-snakes burst from the giant machines, coiling around their legs. Ice-webs snatched Warriors in mid-stride.

"Stay still!" Brianna said, turning to her friends. "Don't move!"

"What?" said Evan. "Haven't you seen what those things can do?"

"Yeah, I know. But I know what I'm talking about! Stand still!"

Everyone looked at Xavier. A flash of uncertainty crossed his face, but then he nodded. "Do what she says," he said.

The seven Warriors stood perfectly still as the Askalons bore down on them.

"Finn," Brianna said. "Throw another snowball. Now."

"Where?"

"Anywhere."

Finn quickly formed and threw another snowball off to one side. The Askalon immediately swerved to follow the movement, rolling right past them and continuing into the woods, spurting out ice-snakes and ice-webs. Several Warriors had already been caught, the rest scrambling to find hiding places.

"It didn't see us," said Ivy, her voice full of wonder. She turned to Brianna. "How did you know?"

"I ran into one of those the last time I was here."

"You were here? Alone?"

"I wasn't exactly alone. I was with Mary Stanton."

All the Warriors' mouths gaped open at the same time.

"Miss Stanton?" said Evan.

"Yeah. Long story. One of those things saw us and came straight at us, but we hid behind a snow bank." She paused. "I saw Thayne. He got out of the Askalon and started looking for us. He was like ten feet tall and covered in spiky armor."

"He didn't find you?" Manuel said.

"Nope. Maybe we just blended in with the snow bank. And then the Askalon drove past us, but I don't think it can see behind, because it didn't stop."

"So the Askalons can only see movement?" Manuel asked.

"Exactly," said Brianna.

"But we can't stay here forever," said Finn. "What are we going to do now?"

Xavier scanned the area. "There," he said, pointing to a hollow in the snow at the base of the mountain where the Askalons had been hiding. "We can hide in there while the Askalons are patrolling the woods. Quick!"

He picked up his staff and began to run toward the base of the mountain. He dove through the opening and scrambled in as far as he could to make room for the others. It was very cramped once they all got in, under the cover of an overhanging ice shelf. They could still hear the icy belches of the Askalons roving back and forth, plowing through the woods, searching for more Warriors to trap.

"Did you know they were hiding in the snow?" Ivy asked Xavier.

"No. But there was something suspicious about those big snow drifts." Xavier shrugged, a little embarrassed. "It seemed like something Thayne would do—try to trick us. Just like his boss, Ponéros."

"What if the Askalons come back here?" Evan whispered.

"I think they will stay out there and patrol, to keep the Warriors in hiding so we can't attack," Xavier answered.

"So we're stuck here," said Ivy.

"Talk about being caught between a rock and a hard place," muttered Manuel.

"I sure wish Ruwach had given us one of those chariot things," said Evan. "Would have come in handy."

"We have everything we need," said Levi. Then he added, almost to himself: "The way up is down."

"What?" said Xavier.

"Oh, nothing. Just something someone told me once."

"Who?"

"He . . . didn't have a name."

Xavier sighed. "The way up is down," he repeated, hoping it was a clue.

"We're definitely down," said Evan.

"No place to go but up," said Finn with a grin.

"We need a plan," said Brianna.

"Right," said Xavier. "What have we got? Our forces are cut off and scattered. The Askalons are patrolling all around the mountain and through the forest, which will make it harder for us to communicate with the others. If we try to organize an assault up the mountain, the Bone Breakers will see us coming, and they'll start hitting us with those catapults."

"What catapults?" asked Finn.

Xavier turned to Levi. "Tell them what you saw with that glass thing."

"What glass thing?" said Evan.

"It's called a Glimmer Glass," said Levi. He took the Glass out of his pocket to show them. "It helps me see things."

"Things? And people too?"

"Yeah, maybe. I saw inside the fortress. I saw the Lava Forgers coming out of a giant lava pit. And I saw them on the ramparts, building catapults. So they can fling balls of lava at us."

"Fireballs," said Ivy with a sigh. "Just like the Olethron."

"Right. The whole fortress is surrounded by a lava moat. So even if we got to the crater, we'd have to figure out a way to cross the moat and get past the Forgers. They can turn a person to ash and bones with one touch." Levi shivered at the memory.

"Wait a minute. . . . The Forgers are made of lava?" said Manuel.

"Yes," Levi said. "Their outer shells are hard like rock. But I could see the molten lava running through them like . . . blood."

"Lava Forgers," said Manuel. He scratched his chin. "That could be an advantage for us."

"How's that?" asked Xavier.

"Yeah, turning a person to ash seems like a pretty big advantage," said Evan with a snort.

"Lava cools the farther it gets from the source," said Manuel. "And with all this snow, it would cool even faster. Perhaps that will make the Forgers slower, or at least less hot, when they come down the mountain."

"What if they don't come down the mountain?" asked Ivy. "What if they just stay up there and shoot fireballs down on us?"

"Ponéros only has the mountain right now," said Xavier. "If he wants to take over all of Ahoratos, he needs to move out of the fortress. He needs to attack us. He wants us to go up there. But what if we didn't? What if we stayed here and forced him to send his army down?"

"How do we do that?" asked Brianna.

"We could . . . destroy the fortress," said Xavier. Everyone looked at him.

"Okaaay," said Evan. "So . . . let's destroy an indestructible fortress. And then maybe we can take a quick trip to the moon."

"What does the fortress look like?" asked Manuel, ignoring Evan.

"It's shaped like a pyramid," said Levi. "No windows, only one door, and a hole in the very top. I saw smoke coming out."

"What is it made of?"

"Stone, I think. A really smooth, shiny black stone."

"Obsidian!" said Manuel excitedly, pointing one finger in the air. "It's actually a glass that forms when lava cools very quickly. It's very hard and sharp but also very brittle."

"So what does that mean?" asked Brianna.

"We might be able to create some sort of explosion that would collapse the fortress," Manuel said. "That might compel Thayne to attack, to send his army down the mountain."

"Yeah! Let's blow it up!" said Evan.

"We don't have any dynamite or anything," said Ivy.

"Yes, but . . . didn't you say the pool you found under the mountain had a funny smell?" Manuel asked.

"Rotten eggs," said Finn.

"Right. That smell indicates the presence of sulfur. Sulfur is highly explosive. Water by itself could create an eruption, because the lava would cause the water to rapidly boil and expand. But that explosion might not be enough. With the sulfur added, however, that might just do it."

"How much of that water would we need?" Finn asked.

"Well, it depends on the concentration, I suppose," said Manuel. "But in general I would say as much as you can carry."

"So you're saying we'd have to go back to that pool, get some stinky water, find something to carry it in, never mind the leviathans that will attack us, and somehow get past the Askalons and the Bone Breakers and get up to the top of the mountain and pour it in the moat," said Ivy, all in one breath. "Seriously?"

"Piece of cake," said Evan with a smirk.

"I'll do it," said Levi. "I mean, I'll take it up the mountain. I know the way. Xavier and I went there before."

"I'll go with you," said Xavier.

"No, Xavier, you need to stay here," Levi said. "Once that explosion happens, you'll need to lead the rest of the Warriors in the attack."

"I'll go with you," said Brianna, looking at Levi. He seemed about to refuse, but then he nodded.

"Okay," he said.

"How are Levi and Brianna gonna get out of there in time?" Evan asked. "Won't they get blown up too?"

"I hadn't thought of that," said Manuel, his brow furrowing.

"Well, let's not get ahead of ourselves," Ivy said. "We don't even have the water yet."

"Okay, so Phase One, Ivy and Finn will go and get the water," Xavier said.

"What's Phase Two?" asked Evan.

"We'll work on that while they carry out Phase One."

CHAPTER 33

Whack-a-Mole

Ivy and Finn crept along the edge of the mountain in search of the spring they had found the last time they had come to Ahoratos. They were constantly on the lookout for Askalon patrols and ice-snakes that might be hiding in the snow. But they saw no trickles of water flowing under the ice. Everything was frozen solid.

"Maybe it's gone," Ivy said. "Maybe the water's all frozen and the spring is sealed up."

"Then we're in trouble," said Finn.

Ivy put her hands on her hips. "You're supposed to say, 'Of course it's here somewhere! Just keep looking. We'll find it.'"

"Huh?" Finn said, straightening to look at her.

She sighed. "Never mind. I just needed some encouragement, that's all."

The roar of an Askalon suddenly filled their ears. They crouched down and froze, holding their breath. The Askalon came into view and lumbered past them. Then it stopped, and the engine went quiet, like it had turned itself off.

"What's it doing?" Ivy murmured.

"Waiting for something to move," Finn said.

"Great. We'll be stuck here until it goes away."

"Maybe. But if Thayne's in that thing, we might be able to end this war before it starts."

"What do you mean?"

But Finn was moving, crouched low, to the back of the Askalon. He suddenly rose up from the snow and jumped on top of the machine, climbing his way to the top hatch. Ivy stifled a scream. Finn extended his sword and pulled open the hatch. He stared down, puzzled. Then he looked over at Ivy.

"It's empty," he called. The Askalon came to life, spinning its tracks and throwing out ice-webs. Finn jumped down from the back of the chariot and ran like the wind, barely getting away in time.

"Run!" he cried. The Askalon had started to turn to come after them. Ivy and Finn ran toward a snowbank and dove in headfirst. The Askalon kept coming, skirting the snowbank and continuing on its way.

Ivy let out a breath. "What did you think you were doing?" she said, annoyed.

"It was empty. There was no driver."

"Yeah? So?"

"So how is it moving at all?"

Ivy thought about it. "Maybe remote control? Like a drone?"

"Yeah. That's what I'm thinking too."

"You could have gotten us killed." Ivy glared at him.

"Oh. Sorry. Well, we'd better find that spring before that thing comes back."

"Tell me something I don't know," Ivy huffed.

"Hey." Finn put his hands up in mock surrender. "Don't bite my head off."

"Sorry. I'm just . . . freaked out right now."

"Makes two of us."

They kept going, keeping their heads down, their bodies as low to the ground as possible to mask their movements. Ivy wondered where Kristian and Kalle were right then. Probably hiding out in the woods, with the other Warriors, while the Askalons patrolled all around them.

"I think we've walked around the entire mountain now," Ivy said in a frustrated voice. "I give up."

"Can't do that," said Finn. Then he gave her a huge smile. "I'll bet it's right around the corner. Come on. One more step."

"Very funny," said Ivy.

Just then, Finn took a step, and his foot fell right through the snow. The rest of Finn followed, disappearing in a puff of snowflakes. Ivy gasped, ran to the edge of the hole, and fell to her knees, peering into the darkness below.

"Finn! Finn! Where are you?"

"Here," came the weak, echoing reply. Ivy couldn't see him.

"You're okay?"

"Yeah, I'm okay."

"What's down there?"

"It's a tunnel," said Finn.

"You mean like the last time?"

"There's no water. Only ice. Green ice."

"Green ice? Hang on. I'm coming down," Ivy said. She threw her legs over the edge of the hole, took a breath, held it, and jumped. *Land on your feet*, she thought to herself all the way down, which was farther than she had expected. And yet she did.

Ivy had once been to a big city where they had subway tunnels underground to get from one place to another. This tunnel looked like that, except it was made of ice. Curvy waves of glowing green ice, like an upside-down ocean on a windy day.

"Whoa," she said, staring around her.

"It doesn't look like the tunnel we were in the last time. But it might still lead to the pool," said Finn. "I think we should follow it."

Ivy looked both ways. They were exactly the same. "Which way?" As if in answer, her breastplate began to blink. She turned until it glowed steadily. She pointed. "Looks like we're going this way."

They walked side by side, their boots sprouting cleats that gripped the smooth ice under their feet.

"This ice used to be a stream," Ivy said. "Everything is getting more frozen."

"Winter is spreading," Finn added. "The pool might be all frozen too."

"What happened to being encouraging?" Ivy asked.

"Oh, right. Well, if it's all ice, at least it won't spill as easily." Finn grinned. Ivy rolled her eyes. "Wasn't that encouraging?" Ivy shook her head and turned away.

All around them were strange groans and creaks, the ice above them shifting and cracking.

"What's going on?" Ivy asked, gazing up in consternation at the tunnel ceiling.

"I don't know, but I don't think it's good," Finn said. Then he checked himself. "Oh, it's probably nothing. Just the ice moving and shifting over our heads."

The farther they walked, the darker it got, until they could no longer see the green ice over their heads.

"We're going under the mountain now," Ivy whispered.

"Well, at least that's the right direction," said Finn. He was trying hard to be positive.

In time, their only light came from the glow of their breastplates.

Suddenly Finn stopped. "Do you hear that?"

"I think it's my stomach growling," said Ivy.

"No it's . . . water." Finn grinned. "For real. I can even smell it."

"Me too," said Ivy, wrinkling her nose against the sulfur fumes that had started to waft in the air around them. "I hope this is really it."

They continued, feeling their way along the tunnel as the rotten-egg smell got steadily stronger. Finally, they saw it. The pool. The water lapped gently against the edge of the tunnel walls, steam rising from the surface. It looked quite inviting. Like a backyard swimming pool or a giant hot tub.

"We made it," she said, letting out a breath of relief.

"Yeah," said Finn. "So, we found the pool. But how are we going to carry out the water?"

"Good question." Ivy looked all around. "I don't see anything useful," she said. "Just a bunch of rocks."

"Maybe we could use our helmets," Finn said.

Ivy considered it. "Maybe, but then how will we protect our heads?"

"Good point. I really wish Ruwach had given us something to carry water with when he gave us those gifts," said Finn, discouraged. "Instead of just making our hands glow."

"Wait." Ivy thought back to that day when Ruwach had put something in their hands. It had looked at the time like nothing. Just a flash of light. But when she had said she couldn't see anything, Ruwach had said something she only now remembered.

She looked down at her hands. She took a breath and held them together straight out in front of her, palms up.

"What are you doing?" Finn asked.

Ivy didn't answer. She waited. Then she felt a warmth in her palm, a tingling, and a glow rose up from her skin, as it had that day Ruwach had touched her hands. And then, to her surprise, she saw something.

A small clay pot with a rounded handle and a tapered neck with a stopper. In her hand.

Finn gasped. "How did you do that?"

"I didn't do it," Ivy said aloud. "Remember what Ru said when I told him I couldn't see anything?"

"You will in time," Finn said, repeating the words he now remembered. "Let me try that." He too held out his hands, and they were instantly filled with another pot. The pots looked very old-fashioned, like they'd been sculpted by hand long ago, in another age.

"But they're so small," said Finn. "They aren't going to hold much."

"This is all we've got," said Ivy. "It has to be enough." She glanced at the water. "Do you see anything swimming around down there?"

Finn bent over to look. "No."

"Good. Then maybe we can just fill our pots and get out of here." She pulled the stopper out of the pot and bent down at the edge of the pool. Holding the pot by the handle, she carefully dipped it into the water.

Before the pot even touched the water, a huge splash knocked her backward. A leviathan rose up from the depths, its jaws snapping just inches away. Ivy fell backward, gasping, the little pot flying from her hand. Suddenly the pool was filled with dark, circling shadows, twisting and turning around each other.

"Where did they come from?" she sputtered, getting back up. To her dismay, she saw that her pot was now floating in the pool, rocked by the waves of the breaching leviathans. "Oh no, now I've lost it!"

"It's okay," said Finn. "We still have mine."

"We need both. Ruwach gave us each one. I have to get it back."

"But the leviathans . . ."

Ivy shoved the stopper in her pocket and took out her small red seed-shield. "Should have done this the first time," she said. "I'm going out there to get the pot." She thrust her arm out straight, the seed tight in her fist. The shield deployed, a net of tiny red seed-lights all around her.

"I'm coming with you," Finn said. He took out his Krÿs and extended it to its full length. "No more hands for the shield," he said.

"I've got you covered," Ivy said.

Finn stood back to back with Ivy, close enough that they were both covered by the shield.

"On three, ready? One, two . . . three."

They stepped out onto the pool together, bracing themselves. Their boots held them above the water, which rocked violently with the sudden reappearance of the leviathans, breaching full force straight into the air, opening their wide jaws to display rows of sharp teeth. As soon as they hit the shield, they fell away, repelled by the force field the shield created. But they continued to badger Ivy and Finn as they struggled to keep their footing on the rolling waves, which pushed the clay pot farther and farther away from them. Finn would slam his sword on their heads, which made them fall back into the water but otherwise did them no damage. And for each one he managed to strike down, two rose up in its place. Ivy struggled to keep her shield deployed in the rocking waves as she bent to grab at the pot, which continually rolled away from her just before she grasped it.

"It's like playing an endless game of Whack-a-Mole," Finn said breathlessly. "They keep coming back. More and more of them."

"Stay with me! I need to get that pot!" Ivy said. A strong wave had suddenly pushed it toward her. "Almost got it! Hang on!"

She bent forward, bracing herself to keep her balance, her fingers just touching the handle of the pot before she was knocked backward by another mountainous wave. She fell into Finn, who grabbed her before she hit the water. Both of them stared in amazement as a monstrous leviathan rose out of the pool, twice as large as the others, slitted yellow eyes fixed on them.

Ivy had only one thought: there was no escaping this thing.

CHAPTER 34

Sybylla

The mammoth creature rested on its coiled snake body, its small flippers suddenly growing into elongated arms with sharp claws. It was quite different from the other leviathans Ivy and Finn had seen before, with a more streamlined body and large, winglike gills of green and gold. Its head was sort of triangular, with long, almond-shaped yellow eyes. It opened its mouth, revealing gleaming teeth. *This is it,* Ivy thought. *We're dead.*

Then, to her utter surprise, the creature began to speak.

"Why do you attack my children?"

Its voice had a strange, soft, almost feminine quality. Ivy and Finn stared, openmouthed. The creature made no move to attack, yet the Warriors could feel its menace, its danger, right through their armor into their skin.

"We meant—your children—no harm," Ivy said in a trembling voice. She lowered her shield and nudged Finn to put away his sword. He did so, reluctantly. "We just needed a little water."

"Why do you take my water?"

"To help our friends," Ivy said. "And it's not your water. Technically. It belongs to the mountain."

"It belongs to me!" The creature's voice rose to a high pitch. The yellow eyes flashed like lightning. Ivy gasped softly; Finn put one arm around her. "You took my water. You injure my children. Now you will never leave this place." The creature ruffled its giant gills in a very threatening manner. Then it said, more softly, "Unless you help me."

Ivy and Finn, who had been searching frantically for some kind of escape, glanced at each other.

"Help you?" Finn said cautiously.

"To free my children."

"Free your *children*?" Ivy asked, speaking slowly, as if she didn't understand.

"My children and I once roamed a wide, beautiful sea, filled with fishes, with mighty waves. But Ponéros caught us in his nets with promises of an even wider, more beautiful sea. Then he brought us to this place. A tiny pool under the mountain. My children are all crammed together, unable to play as they used to. They long to go back to the sea. But I cannot find the way." The creature's voice had become almost forlorn.

"Ponéros says he will keep his promise, once this war is won. But I don't believe him anymore. He is a liar."

"That's true," said Ivy. She suddenly began to feel sorry for this creature. "What's your name?" Finn nudged her, nervous. She ignored him.

"Sybylla," said the creature.

"Sybylla," repeated Ivy. The name sounded familiar. "Well, I'm sorry about what happened to you and your children. We can't help you find your way to the sea. But with this little pot of water"—she pointed to the pot floating a few feet from her—"we will be able to destroy Ponéros's fortress. Maybe then, you will be free again. And you can find your way home."

"Don't tell her that," whispered Finn. "She's probably a spy for Ponéros."

"You humans think you will destroy Ponéros's fortress?" Sybylla let out a strange, hissing laugh. "That is not possible. You are too small. Too young."

"We're Prince Warriors," said Finn.

The name had a strange effect on Sybylla. She drew back, her eyes closing, as if she had been hit by a sudden gust of wind. "No, you are much too young and weak to be Prince Warriors," she whispered.

"We are not," said Ivy, drawing herself up to be as tall as she possibly could. "Let us take our pots of water and go, and we will prove it to you. Or, you can keep us here forever, and you will be here forever too. You *and* your children."

Sybylla seemed to think about this for a long time. Then she slowly uncoiled her snake tail and slithered toward them. Ivy and Finn froze, pressing together slightly. Ivy's heartbeat slowed to a dull thud; she could feel the giant creature's rancid breath on her own skin. She still held the seed in her fist, ready to raise it if necessary. But she was afraid to make even the smallest move.

"Two children," said the creature, her burning yellow eyes roving over them, "and two measly pots of water will bring down Ponéros?"

"Yes," Ivy whispered, swallowing the lump in her throat. "They will. *We* will."

Sybylla closed her eyes and drew back her head, cobra-like. Then she reached out with one graceful arm and plucked the pot from the water. She held it up a moment, examining it. Then she dropped it into Ivy's hand.

"Thank you," Ivy murmured, her fingers closing around the pot. "Thank you—Sybylla."

Sybylla regarded Ivy a long moment and tilted her head ever so slightly, as if she were trying to understand something. Then she rose up, her body unfurling, and flung herself headfirst back into the pool again.

The water went still.

CHAPTER 35

Phase Two

The Warriors waiting in the snow bunker had just begun to give up hope when Ivy and Finn appeared, carrying two small pots of water.

"That's it?" said Evan, staring at the tiny vessels in disappointment.

"I know it doesn't look like much," said Ivy. "But these were the containers Ruwach gave us, so they must be enough."

"Technically speaking, that small amount will only produce enough of an explosion to maybe singe a few eyebrows," said Manuel. "Assuming the Lava Forgers have eyebrows."

"Well, this is what we've got," said Finn. "We almost didn't get out of there at all. If it wasn't for Sybylla, we'd still be in there."

"Sybylla? Who's that?" asked Levi.

"The leviathan," said Ivy. "But she was bigger. I think she was the mother of the others. She called them her children. She looked pretty scary. But she actually helped us."

"Sybylla is her name?" Levi asked.

Ivy nodded.

"That's . . . interesting," Levi murmured to himself.

"She wants us to help free her children from Ponéros," said Ivy.

Evan was bewildered, "How in the world are we going to do that?"

"No idea," said Ivy. "But we told her we would destroy the fortress, so she helped us get out of there. After scaring us half to death."

"We'd better get moving then," said Xavier. "Time for Phase Two."

"So you now have a Phase Two?" Ivy asked.

"Yes. Well, sort of. First we need to find the path Levi and I used the last time. Then Levi and Brianna will carry the water up the mountain to the fortress. In the meantime, we'll need to gather the rest of the Warriors and take over one of those skypods."

"You're going to take over a skypod?" Finn asked, lifting one eyebrow.

"Yeah. That way we can see what's going on in the fortress and let the Warriors on the ground know when the attack is coming."

"Okeydokey." Ivy shrugged, then she and Finn handed their pots of water to Levi and Brianna.

"You sure you don't need help carrying them up?" asked Ivy.

"We'll be okay," said Brianna. "Thanks. And . . . good work. I knew you could do it." She smiled at Ivy, who smiled back.

"Thanks," she said.

"So, how do we find the path?" Brianna asked.

"There were these two big rocks that marked it," said Levi. "We'll need to find them." He stuck his head out of the snow bunker and glanced up at the sky. It had stopped snowing, and the sun was out, shining brightly, though the top of the mountain was still shrouded in the dark poisonous cloud. "It'll be easier going now, but we need to keep a lookout for Askalon patrols."

"That reminds me," said Finn. "We ran into one of those too."

"An Askalon?" said Evan, wide-eyed.

"Yeah. Finn jumped up on it and opened the hatch. And it was empty," said Ivy.

"He did *what*?"

"Came at it from the back," Finn said. "Like Brianna said, it can't see behind. But there was no one inside. We think they are being operated remotely."

"Of course!" said Manuel. "They are programmed to attack movement!"

"Okay. Let's do this." Impulsively, Xavier stretched his arm straight out into their midst, his hand out flat. One by one, they all put their hands over each other's. The orbs in the center of their breastplates began to spin, churning out words that hovered in the air over them. Words they'd heard before but were glad to be reminded of again:

Be strong and courageous.

Do not be discouraged.

You are never alone.

Xavier got out of the bunker and stood straight, waiting. As if sensing his humility, his breastplate began to pulse softly. He turned around until the pulsing changed to a steady glow.

"This way," he said.

"Better than a compass," said Manuel.

As soon as the others stepped out of the bunker, a cloud descended upon them, materializing out of the air, draping over them like a soft blanket.

"Ruwach," whispered Evan with a smile.

They walked in single file with Xavier leading the way. The cloud hovered over their heads, masking their movement. Their boots were able to glide quickly and silently over the snow, just like skis. They could hear the growling engines of the Askalons patrolling through the forest, churning out webs of ice.

"How much longer?" asked Evan.

"Stop asking," said Xavier. It was difficult to see too far ahead, because the cloud blocked their view as well as the view from above. It was like walking in their own personal fog.

Finally, they nearly collided with a large rock jutting out from the side of the mountain, through the snow.

"This is it," said Levi, relieved. As they got closer, they could see the identical rock right next to it, with a narrow space between them. But the path between the rocks was covered by fresh snow. "It's hard to see the path though."

"It looks slippery," said Brianna. "And steep."

Levi put his boot in the space between the rocks, where the path was supposed to be. He instantly felt his foot shiver as long cleats burst from the bottom of the boot. "We'll be okay," he said.

"Wait," said Xavier. "That skypod overhead is the only one that has a clear view of the path you're taking.

We need to get rid of the Bone Breakers up there first. You remember what happened last time."

Levi nodded. "Right."

"What happened last time?" asked Evan.

"The birds attacked us," said Levi. "They were attracted by the Glimmer Glass; it was shining in the sun. So probably now they'll be looking for us."

"How are you going to get rid of the Bone Breakers?" asked Brianna.

"Hmmm," Manuel scratched his chin thoughtfully. "I think I have an idea." He dug into his pocket and pulled out the flower bulb Ruwach had given him in the Garden of Red.

"A flower bulb?" Evan said, arching an eyebrow. "What are you doing to do with that?"

"Plant it, of course." Manuel smiled crookedly. He took several deep breaths. Then, softly counting to himself, he began to creep out into the snow. He tiptoed like a super spy, stopping often to check his position and look around furtively. His movements were a little comical, and Evan started to giggle. Xavier nudged him.

When finally Manuel had found the spot he was looking for, he bent down and started digging furiously into the snow. He had to stop every so often to blow warm air into his hands and shake them out. But he kept digging until he was down so low he practically disappeared.

"Is he seriously trying to plant a bulb in the middle of Winter?" said Ivy.

"This is Ahoratos," said Xavier. "Anything can happen."

Manuel finally resurfaced and low-crawled back to the others under the shelter of the cloud. His hands were red and stiff with cold, and his fingers were covered in dirt. A broad grin carved his face.

"All set."

"What's supposed to happen?" said Finn.

"Well, I'm not exactly sure. But I have an idea why Ruwach gave that flower bulb to me."

The Warriors waited, staring at the hole that Manuel had dug. Nothing happened.

"Are you sure . . ." Evan began, but Xavier nudged him to be quiet.

After what seemed like an eternity, something started to poke up from the hole. A greenish stalk, easily seen against the backdrop of white. It grew taller and then split into several stalks that spread out over the snow and unfolded into purplish-white petals. Flower petals. The petals grew to almost the size of a small car, and then they started to curl upward, forming a large bowl.

"A flower?" said Ivy, sounding skeptical.

"A big flower," said Evan.

"That's cool, but how's that going to help?" asked Brianna.

Before Manuel could answer, the cloud that had been protecting the Warriors moved until it was directly over the huge flower. Then, to everyone's surprise, it started to rain.

"Ruwach is watering the flower," said Brianna.

"It didn't look like it needed watering," said Evan.

The cloud dissipated as the rain filled the flower. Then it disappeared altogether. The rain stopped.

"The cloud's gone," Brianna said. Her shoulders dropped. The Warriors crouched lower, pressing toward the cover of the rock to hide themselves. "Why did Ru leave us? He said he would never leave."

All of a sudden, the Bone Breakers on the skypod far above began to screech, the sound echoing off the mountain. The Warriors huddled together, fearful that they had been seen, that the Bone Breakers were raising an alarm. The birds spread their wings and dove right at them, still screeching.

"They saw us!" Brianna cried.

Two by two, the Bone Breakers crashed into the water of the giant flower. They screamed in alarm as the flower petals snapped shut, trapping them inside. The Warriors could hear their desperate cries and see the bulges in the petal walls as the birds struggled to get out. But the flower held them fast.

"Sweeeet!" said Evan. The others echoed his exclamation.

"Why did they dive into the water?" Finn asked. "Were they that thirsty?"

"Levi said the Bone Breakers were attracted to the Glass because it was shiny," said Manuel, excited now that his experiment had actually worked. "This worked just like my pitcher plant. The sun shining on the water made it sparkle. The birds fell for it!"

"Awesome, Manuel," said Xavier, giving him a high five. "But now we need to move fast. Before Thayne figures out what happened. Levi, you and Brianna start going up now. We'll get to the skypod and keep a look-out for the explosion."

"Okay." Levi turned to Brianna. "You ready, Bean?"

She smiled. He hadn't called her that in quite a while. "Sure thing."

Levi went first. He tucked the pot of water inside his belt and stepped onto the icy path. Brianna did the same with her pot and stepped up beside him. Her boots also sprouted cleats. She turned and gave her friends a thumbs-up.

"See you guys soon!" she said brightly.

"You bet you will," said Ivy, giving Brianna another thumbs-up.

Xavier waited until they were far enough up the mountain that he couldn't see them anymore. Then he took a deep breath and turned to his friends.

"Ivy and Finn, once things start happening here, you need to run into the forest and find the other Warriors who are hiding. Gather them for the attack."

"But how will we know when the attack happens?" asked Ivy. "We can't see the fortress from here."

"We'll signal you from the skypod," said Xavier. "Just keep an eye on the skypod. Got it?"

"Got it," said Ivy. Finn nodded.

"Cool." Xavier turned to Manuel and Evan. "You guys will come with me. You ready?" Evan gave him a thumbs-up. Manuel just nodded nervously. Xavier walked away from the rock and raised his staff high over his head.

"Tannyn!" he cried.

CHAPTER 36

Great Balls of Fire

The huge green dragon appeared in the sky almost instantly, making a wide circle in plain view of the fortress before folding his wings and diving for Xavier and his friends.

"Run!" Xavier said to Ivy and Finn, who took off for the woods just as Tannyn made a crash landing, sending up an explosion of snow.

"Now, jump on!" Xavier leapt on the panting dragon before the snow had time to settle. Evan jumped up behind him. Manuel couldn't leap that high, but Xavier bent down, grabbed his hand, and pulled him aboard right behind him. Manuel threw both arms around a spike on Tannyn's back. They all braced themselves as the dragon took off again, shooting straight into the air.

"Lava cannons!" Evan shouted. Fiery balls of molten lava rocketed toward them from the fortress. Tannyn managed to twist and dip to avoid the onslaught, sometimes flipping into somersaults.

"I think I'm going to be sick!" Manuel said in a strangled voice, hugging the dragon's spike in terror.

"Gorp!" Tannyn warbled his battle cry as he flew in corkscrew circles and tumbled into a landing on the skypod. Tannyn could fly like an eagle, but he landed more like a one-legged gooney bird, flopping on his face and skidding almost to the very edge.

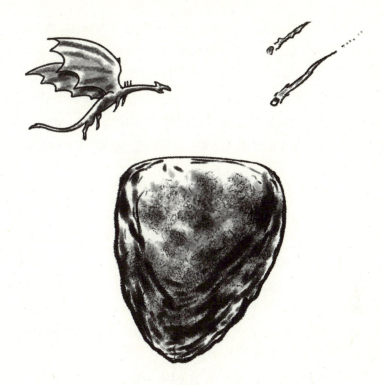

Xavier drew a breath of relief and turned to check on the other passengers. "Everyone okay?"

"Great," said Evan, who slid down the dragon's belly and went over to give him a pat on the head. Manuel was searching the skies wildly, looking green from the unexpected thrill ride.

"What about the catapults?" he croaked.

"They're not aimed at the skypod," Xavier said. "Not yet anyway."

"That's a relief," said Manuel. Rather than sliding down the dragon's belly, he inched his way down the neck, going from spike to spike to keep from falling. Tannyn kept his head low, patiently waiting.

Xavier went to the edge of the skypod, which was almost level with the rim of the crater. From there he could see the gleaming fortress, the lava moat, and the Forgers frantically launching fireballs from their catapults. Dark smoke billowed from the top of the pyramid and spread across the sky, casting a long shadow over the fortress.

"We're safe for the moment," Xavier announced. "But as soon as Thayne figures out what happened, they're going to re-aim those catapults at this skypod."

"That sounds bad," said Manuel.

"No, it's actually good," said Xavier. "We will be like a diversion. Take the attention off Levi and Brianna."

"And what if we get polarized by fireballs?" said Evan.

"Pulverized," said Manuel under his breath.

Xavier didn't answer right away. "We have everything we need," he said finally.

CHAPTER 37

Stand Firm

Finn and Ivy had just ventured into the open to see if Xavier and the others had made it to the skypod when the horrible noise of the Askalons reached their ears. They quickly hid behind trees. But the chariots weren't looking for them; they were headed toward the flower that contained the squawking Bone Breakers. The two Warriors watched as the Askalons launched ice-webs and snakes at the flower in an effort to make it give up its prisoners. But their efforts only succeeded in freezing the flower and the birds inside.

While the Askalons were occupied, Ivy and Finn stole back into the woods.

"That was close," Ivy said.

"Yeah. Looks like Xavier made it up there okay. Phase Two accomplished."

"Right. Now for Phase Three. Find the rest of the Prince Warriors who went into hiding when the Askalons attacked."

"So where are they?"

Ivy glanced at the snow. She could see tracks—many sets of boot prints leading deeper into the woods.

"We could follow those tracks," she said.

They set off, following the footprints in the snow until they came to two huge ruts that ran straight across their route.

"Askalons," Finn said. "See how the Askalon tracks go around the big trees and the boulders?"

"Yeah, I see that," said Ivy. "So they must have some sort of radar system that helps them avoid obstacles."

"Right."

On the other side of the Askalon tracks were large ice-webs hanging between trees, blocking the Warriors' way. Ivy pulled out her sword and slashed at the web, shattering it. The sound awakened an ice-snake that had been lying under the snow; it reared up and lunged for Ivy, coiling around her boots. Finn quickly drew his sword and smashed it to pieces.

"Thanks," said Ivy.

"No problem," said Finn. "Gotta watch out for those snakes. They make a little cracking noise before they strike, like ice cubes in a glass of water."

"Great," said Ivy with a sigh.

"Hey, if we're prepared, and we know how they operate, it won't be as big of a problem."

"You're right. I know."

They moved as silently as possible, staying with the human tracks and avoiding the Askalon tracks. Whenever they heard the rumble of an Askalon, they crouched down or hid behind a tree until it passed by. But they didn't see any other Warriors.

"Maybe we should call out," Ivy said.

"That might alert the Askalons," said Finn.

"We'll never find anyone at this rate." Ivy stopped walking and leaned against a tree. "Where are they?"

"Ivy? Is that you?"

The voice sounded familiar. Ivy and Finn looked all around, wondering where the voice was coming from.

"Up here!"

They looked up to see two young Warriors high in the tree.

"Kalle? Kristian?" Ivy said.

"Yes, it's us!" Ivy wasn't sure which one of them was speaking.

"Come down!" Ivy demanded.

The twins scrambled down from the tree. Kalle—Ivy was pretty sure it was Kalle—spoke first. He was the more talkative one. "What are you doing walking around in the open?"

"We need to gather the Warriors," Ivy said. "Xavier stole a skypod, and Levi and Brianna are headed up the mountain to blow up the fortress."

"What? Blow up?" said Kalle.

"What do you mean 'stole a skypod'?" asked Kristian.

"Well, kind of. He's up there now. He's going to let us know when they start attacking."

"Who?"

"The Lava Forgers."

The twins looked at each other and then back at Ivy.

"Lava Forgers?"

"Yeah, Forgers made of lava. Long story. We got rid of the Bone Breakers, and then Tannyn took the guys up there. He's a dragon."

"We saw the dragon," said Kalle. "We thought it was an enemy dragon."

"No, he's actually a friend of ours," said Ivy with a grin.

"How are your friends going to blow up the fortress?"

"That's another long story. Right now we need to gather the others," said Finn impatiently. "Do you know where they are?"

"No idea," said Kalle. "We went up into the tree, and that's the last we saw of anyone."

"We can take down as many of these webs as possible and clear the way," said Ivy.

"But the Askalons . . ."

"They only see movement, we think," said Ivy. "We should be able to avoid them."

"Oh," said Kalle with a grin.

"Better if we split up," said Finn. "You guys go that way. We'll go this way."

"Watch out for snakes," said Ivy.

———————

Far above them, Levi and Brianna continued on their slow, cautious trek up the icy mountain, searching for the path that was still mostly buried in snow. If it weren't for their breastplates, they would have been totally lost by now.

Levi had not spoken five words to Brianna, other than "Watch your step" and "Be careful." He was not in the mood to talk. He had turned his fear and worry for his dad into determination and grit.

Occasionally a huge ball of fire would pass over their heads, forcing them to take cover. Bursts of steam hissed above them, the effects of the hot lava escaping from the crater hitting the snow and ice. It was an angry sound, Brianna thought, as if the lava itself were filled with fury. But the cloud ringing the mountain helped mask their movements as they got closer to the top.

"How much farther?" Brianna asked.

"Not far to the lava part," said Levi. "Xavier and I didn't go any farther than that the last time. But getting all the way to the rim—not so sure about that."

"Do you think we can . . . stop for a second?"

Levi glanced down at her, then shrugged. "If you want."

Brianna sat down on a small ledge in the ice. Levi sat beside her.

"Thanks," she said, catching her breath.

"Sure."

Brianna pulled the clay pot from her belt to check on the contents. Levi did the same.

"All good?" Levi asked.

"Stellar." She smacked her lips together softly. "This cold makes my lips so dry. I could really use my lip gloss about now."

She grinned, but Levi didn't return her smile. She thought for a moment about what to say.

"I was sad when my mom left," she said finally. "It was hard. I felt like I had done something wrong." She waited, but Levi didn't look at her or respond. He was staring at his pot of water. "But it wasn't because of me, or my sisters. It wasn't anyone's fault. Bad things happen sometimes. We don't always know why. We're supposed to help each other through these things. But you won't let anyone help you."

"How can you help me?" Levi asked. "Can you make my father better?"

"No," said Brianna. "But I can tell you that I'm your friend, and I am here for you. We all are. And Ruwach especially. And if you want to cry or scream, I will do that with you. Only I wouldn't recommend screaming right now."

Levi cracked a smile. "I keep thinking that if I can take down that fortress, my dad will get better. The Winter will be gone, and everything will go back to the way it was. But now I'm wondering, what if that doesn't happen? What if we destroy the fortress and it's still Winter? And Nameless gets my dad . . ."

"Nameless? Who's that?"

Levi let out a breath. "This guy I met, in the In-Between. Turns out he's the one we were smelling. You know . . . that dead worm smell?"

"The Empty," Brianna murmured.

"Right. The Empty. Anyway, this guy said he was a king who had lost his kingdom and all his power. His crown was all rusted, and his robe was all ripped. I asked him his name, and he said to call him Nameless. But I think I know his real name." He paused, then said in a low whisper: "It's . . . Death."

Brianna's face went still. "Death?"

"Yeah."

"Wow. And he comes with the Winter in Ahoratos?"

"Yeah. I guess."

Brianna was silent for a while. "You know, in the winter, the trees and the grass and everything look dead, but they aren't. They come back to life again."

Levi looked at her. "What are you saying?"

"I'm saying that what might look like death to you and me . . . really isn't. Not in Ahoratos anyway."

Levi's eyes brightened for a moment. "Yeah, maybe." He looked up the mountain, to where they were headed. "My dad told me the battle is already won. I just don't know if I really believe that."

"Well, I believe it," Brianna said. "We just might not know what victory looks like yet. In this battle, or in any of them. But whatever happens, Levi, I'm right here with you. Like always."

Levi looked at her and cracked a smile. "Thanks." His gaze wandered to the skypod. "Guess we need to keep going then, don't we?"

Brianna nodded and stood up, brushing snow off her clothes. "I'm ready when you are."

CHAPTER 38

Out of Hiding

Ivy and Finn walked through the woods, searching for more Prince Warriors. They were getting tired from all the exertion of shattering ice-webs and slashing at snakes and dodging Askalons. Now the sun was starting to sink, and the forest was getting darker.

"Prince Warriors!" Ivy called softly as they walked. "Come out. We need to get ready for battle!"

There was no answer. Suddenly Finn stopped and turned toward a large tree with a deep split in the trunk. "Did you hear that?"

"I didn't hear anything," said Ivy.

Finn stepped closer to the tree, picked up a stick from the ground, and gently poked inside the trunk. A small squeaking noise erupted.

"Was that human?" Ivy asked. She drew her sword and approached the tree. Finn did the same on the other side. "Come out of there!"

"Okay! Okay! Don't shoot!" came the high-pitched reply. Slowly an arm and then a helmeted head popped out of the tree trunk.

Ivy gasped. "Miss Stanton?"

Mary Stanton smiled sheepishly. "Hey, guys. Fancy meeting you here."

"What are you doing in there?"

"Well . . . I'm kinda . . . stuck at the moment."

Finn helped Mary climb out of the tree, which was a tight space, even for her.

"Thanks, Finn. I don't know what I would have done if you hadn't come along. I was afraid to call out because of those tank things. They are all over the place!" She looked around to make sure none of the "tank things" were lurking nearby. "Honestly, I'm not even sure I'm supposed to be here at all. I was just in my office—Mr. J. Ar's office, I mean—at the Rec when that Crest thing appeared on my phone. I just swiped it and . . . well, you know the rest." She looked up thoughtfully. "I hope everything is okay there without me."

"Oh, don't worry," Ivy said. "They probably don't even know you're gone."

"Oh?" Mary looked confused, as if she wasn't sure if that was a good thing or not. "Well, anyway, this is only my second time here. The first time I was here with Brianna. I fell into some sort of snow trap, and she pulled me out, and then we ran into one of those tank things, and that was pretty scary, and so when I saw them today, I just sort of freaked out. I'm thinking maybe I'm not cut out for this kind of work. I think I'm pretty much of a failure."

Ivy smiled. "If Ruwach sent you here, then you are supposed to be here."

"Really?" Mary's expression brightened. "Well, I don't even have a sword yet—"

"You can come with us," Ivy said, cutting her off from another monologue. "We're looking for the others."

"But what about the tank?"

"Don't worry. We'll protect you," said Finn.

"Let's go," Ivy said. "Watch out for snakes."

"Snakes?" said Mary. She jumped a little as her foot brushed a twig on the ground.

"Ice-snakes," said Finn. He swung his sword and smashed through a web. Mary jumped again.

They walked through the tangle of woods, following the human boot tracks, as the sun sank and the shadows of the trees lengthened. Mary tripped a lot and jumped often when she was sure she was being attacked by a snake, but usually it was just a tree branch grazing her leg. Ivy and Finn knocked down more webs as they went.

They came upon an Askalon unexpectedly and froze, waiting for it to pass by. But it wasn't moving even though steam rose from its vents. Finn motioned for the girls to get back.

"What's it doing?" Mary asked.

"It's waiting," said Finn. "For something to chase."

"Why isn't it chasing us?"

"We're behind it. It can't see us."

"I don't know. . . . The last time, this big monster man got out and came looking for us." Mary started to hide behind Finn.

"You mean Thayne," said Ivy.

"Well, Thayne could be in there," said Finn. Let's see for sure. Don't move until I say so." He slowly reached down and picked up a stick from the ground, then threw it with all his might. The Askalon came to life, chasing after the stick.

"Now! Run!" Finn said. He darted out behind the Askalon and raced to another large tree. Mary and Ivy followed. They watched the Askalon continue to roll away from them.

"Whew! That was amazing," said Mary breathlessly. "How did you know it would do that?"

"Practice," said Finn. "Let's keep moving."

They continued to follow the boot tracks, which led them to a deep ravine.

"Dead end," said Ivy.

"There they are!" Mary said, pointing down. "Hello down there!" she called out. "We come in peace!" Ivy looked down into the ravine and saw dozens of Prince Warriors staring back up at her.

"Good hiding place. Askalons can't go into the ravine," said Finn. The three of them slid down into the ravine as the Prince Warriors gathered around. They quickly introduced themselves.

"Hey guys. I'm Ivy, and this is Finn," said Ivy. "And this is our friend Mary Stanton. We've been looking all over for you."

"Pleased to meet you," said a thin, pretty girl with a bright smile. She came forward. "I am Bupe. I come from Zambia."

"Is that near Cedar Creek?" asked Mary.

The girl laughed. "It is in Africa. This is Banji. And Luki." She indicated a boy and girl on either side of her. Their armor was slightly different from the other Prince Warriors; their helmets were more conical, and there was an intricate design engraved in gold on their breastplates.

"Nice to meet you," said Ivy. She put out her hand to shake. Bupe took it. Then she switched to a hand clasp, then back to a regular shake. But she still wasn't done. She grasped Ivy's fingertips in her own and clicked their thumbs together as she put her hand over her heart. She finished with a little bow.

"That is how we shake hands in our country," said Bupe.

"Wow," said Ivy. "That was cool."

"I love secret handshakes! Let me try," said Mary. She went through the ritual with Luki and laughed with delight. "That was so fun! I can't wait to show the kids at the rec center."

"What is a rec center?" Bupe asked.

Soon all the Warriors were introducing themselves. Ivy met two boys from India named Ravi and Ninad, who bowed with their hands together. Their breastplates and boots had elaborate scrolling, and their helmets came to a point at the top of their heads. There were Prince Warriors from many other countries too.

"We want to fight," said Ravi. "This ravine offered us a safe place to regroup and come up with a plan."

Ivy and Finn told them how they and their friends had learned to avoid Askalons, as well as their plans to blow up the fortress.

"Don't be afraid," said Ivy. "We must gather and prepare for the battle. We need all of you. I'm not saying it isn't dangerous. But I am saying that if we stand together, we will have victory." She pulled out her Krÿs and extended it to its full length. "So, are you with us?"

"Yes! Yes!" The Warriors all chimed in. They too raised their swords.

They climbed out of the ravine and followed Ivy, Finn, and Mary back through the woods to the meeting place. The sun had set, and it was getting darker by the minute.

Finn halted the column when he came upon an Askalon. He raised a fist for everyone to be quiet. He waited, but the Askalon didn't move or make any noise.

"Maybe they don't operate at night," Ivy remarked.

"Let's see," said Finn. He threw a snowball right in front of the Askalon. It didn't move.

"I don't think they can see in the dark," said Bupe.

"I have an idea," said Ravi. "Gather some sticks. We can put them in the spokes of the wheels and keep them from moving."

As the Warriors moved through the forest, they gathered tree branches and stuffed them into the wheels of all the Askalons they saw.

"By the way," Ravi asked Ivy as they worked. "How did your friend get up to the skypod?"

"Tannyn flew him. He's a dragon. A friend of ours."

"You have a friend who is a dragon?"

"Doesn't everyone?"

CHAPTER 39

The Red Dragon

High up on the skypod, Xavier lay flat at the edge and kept his eyes on the mountain, waiting for some sign that Levi and Brianna had made it to the top. *They have to be there by now, he thought. What was taking so long? Maybe they got stuck. Maybe they gave up.* Too many possibilities. It was getting dark, and soon he might not be able to see anything at all.

"Come on, guys," he whispered, as if Levi and Brianna could hear. "Where are you?" He looked down to the tree line. He couldn't see any Warriors; he hoped they were there, that Ivy and Finn had managed to assemble them. His palms began to sweat; his breath felt stuck in his chest. The longer they waited, the more time they gave Thayne to redirect his catapults toward the skypod.

"Evan," he called out. There was no answer. "Evan!" Still no answer. Xavier finally turned around. He saw Evan and Manuel lying against Tannyn's big belly. They were both asleep. Annoyed, Xavier got up and walked over to them. He kicked the bottoms of their boots.

"Wake up!" he said. "You're supposed to be keeping watch."

"What? Sorry!" Evan said. "I'm just so tired."

"Yeah, me too," said Manuel, rubbing his eyes.

"I can't believe you fell asleep!" Xavier said. "We're in the middle of a war here."

"It's kind of a boring war," Evan said with a yawn. "When's something going to happen?"

As soon as the words were out of his mouth, the ground in front of him burst into flame.

Evan and Manuel both screamed at the same time. Tannyn gorped and spread his wings, flopping over to one side. Xavier dove under the cover of the wings with the two boys, grabbing his seed-shield from his pocket.

"Dragon!" he yelled. Evan and Manuel fumbled for their seeds.

The dark shadow of a giant red dragon loomed over the skypod. It roared and blasted them with its fire breath just as Xavier threw up his shield. Manuel followed his lead. Tannyn bellowed and took off after the red dragon. The two dragons grappled in the air above the skypod, and random blasts of flame landed all around the Warriors.

"My seed!" Evan shouted. He'd pulled his seed out of his pocket too hastily. It flew out of his hands and landed several feet away.

"Get it!" Xavier shouted.

Evan started to crawl toward the seed. He was about to grab it when a Bone Breaker flew in out of nowhere and snatched it in its beak.

"No!" Evan yelled as the Bone Breaker flew away. "Nooooooo!"

———————

Levi and Brianna cautiously poked their heads above the dark cloud that encircled the mountain and took deep breaths. The noxious fumes of the cloud had made them feel dizzy and disoriented, so they took a moment to rest and gaze up at the daunting journey that still lay before them.

The terrain around the crater looked like a carpet of blackened blobs folded all around each other. In between the blobs ran red spidery rivers of hot lava that occasionally erupted into fires.

"It's worse than the last time I was here," said Levi.

"It's going to be like walking on hot coals," Brianna said. "Well, at least it's warmer up here." It was so warm, in fact, that both of them had broken into a sweat.

Levi took out his Glimmer Glass and raised it up to the fortress high above them. He saw masses of Lava Forgers gathering on the ramparts. They looked as though they were getting ready to begin another fireball assault, and several of the catapults had already been repositioned to face the skypod Xavier had captured.

"They're going to attack the skypod," he told Brianna. "They must know Xavier is there. We've got to get up there before that happens."

"Can we actually walk on this stuff?" Brianna reached down to touch the blackened rock. Steam rose up around her finger. "It feels kind of crinkly. And soft. And it's still hot. We might sink. And there's fire everywhere."

"Our boots will get us through."

"What if someone sees us? The Bone Breakers or the Forgers or Thayne?"

"Seems like they're more interested in the skypod right now," Levi responded. "Keep your shield ready, just in case."

Grasping their seed-shields in their fists, the two Warriors started to make their way to the rim. As soon as Levi put his foot on the black, crusty rock, he felt his boot heat up and vibrate slightly. He looked down and saw something silvery emerge from the bottom. At first he thought that the lava was burning through his boot and was about to pull it away. But as the silvery substance worked its way up the boot, he realized it was some sort of lining for protection.

His eyes widened. "Our boots are fireproof," he whispered.

They climbed slowly, their silver-lined boots leaving deep impressions in the burning rock.

Suddenly they heard a violent screech and a sound like a blast furnace firing up. They swiveled to see a huge red dragon engaged in a midair battle with Tannyn over the top of the skypod. The two dragons attacked each other viciously, spewing fire everywhere.

"It's Tannyn," Brianna whispered. "And—"

"Just keep going," Levi said. "Don't look at them."

It took all Levi's concentration to continue the steady trek up the mountain, especially with the dragon battle going on and the sense that, despite what he had told Brianna, he had a strong feeling they *were* being watched. Maybe by the Bone Breakers. Or maybe by that broken-down king who called himself Nameless. Someone knew they were there and wasn't about to let them get away unscathed.

CHAPTER 40

Dragon Fight

Evan huddled under Xavier's shield to avoid the flaming jets of the two dragons fighting like crazy above them. And now there were Bone Breakers all around them, squawking and flapping their wings. The Warriors took in their blood-dipped feathers, their long, sharp talons, their thick, bone-breaking beaks.

"What are we going to do, Xavi?" Evan whispered, hoping his big brother had a plan.

"Just stay calm," Xavier said.

"That bird ate my seed!"

"Yeah, I know. Just stay cool, little brother. Manuel and I have got you covered. Okay? Listen. Don't worry about the Bone Breakers. Think of them like seagulls on the beach. You remember, Evan?"

"Yeah, that time a seagull took a peanut butter sandwich right out of my hand."

"Right. These Bone Breakers are just like that. Don't be afraid of them. Now, we're going to move together to the edge of the skypod so we can see what's happening at the fortress before it gets too dark. We'll stay together, keep the shields up. Evan, just stay between us." He paused. "Manuel, you with us, man?"

"Uh . . . uh . . ." Manuel seemed unable to speak, his eyes darting from the squawking birds to the fighting dragons, taking in the chaos all around them. Instead, he started to count, which was what he did when he was getting fearful. "One, two, three, four . . ."

"Stay with me now. Just listen to my voice, okay? When I say go, stand up, back-to-back. Ready? Go."

The three boys rose together slowly, pressing their backs against each other. Evan stayed squashed between them, covered by Xavier's and Manuel's shields.

"Good. Now. Walk with me. Easy does it."

They moved as a single unit toward the edge of the skypod. The Bone Breakers flapped around and scolded them with their revolting screeches. Xavier knew they wouldn't attack, especially with their shields deployed. The Bone Breakers wanted to instill fear, and they were doing a pretty good job of that. Xavier focused on his goal—to get to the edge of the pod.

"Far enough," said Xavier, stopping their trek. He glanced over to make sure Evan and Manuel were okay. Then he turned to face the mountain. He thought he saw two more specks of white against the dark top of the mountain, reflected by the setting sun.

"They're pretty close to the top," Xavier said. "It shouldn't be too long now."

"Can you see below? Is the army ready?" asked Manuel in a shaking voice.

"I can't tell. It's too dark now."

"I hope they're ready. I've had enough of these stupid birds," Evan said. He slashed out at the closest Bone Breaker with his sword. It shrieked and skittered away. "That's probably the one that ate my seed. I hope it chokes."

Suddenly the two dragons crashed down on the sky-pod, both of them badly wounded, with large burned spots on their bodies. Tannyn had a broken wing and was gorping loudly. They continued to fight on the surface of the skypod, jets of fire and smoke shooting in all directions. Then the Bone Breakers swooped onto Tannyn, glomming onto his head and pecking at his eyes with their powerful beaks. Tannyn cried out in agony, thrashing around to shake them off.

"They're going after Tannyn!" Without waiting for the others, Evan raised his sword and charged at the attacking birds, leaving the cover of the shields.

"Evan!" Xavier shouted, but Evan didn't hear. He let out a warrior cry and leapt on top of Tannyn's back, slashing left and right at the Bone Breakers, screaming at them to leave his dragon friend alone. Xavier ran after him, putting away his own shield and extending his sword. The red dragon swung his great head in Evan's direction, opening his mouth to incinerate him with a fresh blast of his fire breath.

Xavier saw only one way to help his brother. Dropping his staff, he charged up Tannyn's swishing tail and threw himself onto the top of the enemy dragon's head. He grabbed hold of a spike right between the dragon's eyes and held on with one hand. The dragon swung its head to shake him off, then opened its mouth. Xavier cried out as he thrust his sword into the dragon's gaping mouth. He felt his whole arm shudder with the impact, and the searing pain as the dragon's fire breath raced up his arm. He gritted his teeth and hung on as the dragon screamed and tipped over backward, crashing to the ground. Xavier was thrown clear and rolled all the way to the edge of the sky-pod. He couldn't stop his momentum; he was certain he would keep rolling right over the edge and fall. With one last gasp he swung out his sword, still in his burned hand, and dug it into the edge of the skypod as his legs dipped over the edge. He threw up his other hand and grabbed the sword, the rest of his body dangling helplessly.

"Xavier!" Evan shouted. "Manuel! Help!" Both boys went running to Xavier, skidding to their knees and grabbing hold of his arms.

"Hang on, Xavi!" They heaved with all their might and gradually managed to pull Xavier up over the edge.

"Xavi! Are you okay?" Evan leaned over his brother, his eyes wide with worry. Xavier's arm looked really bad, his sleeve burned off, the skin red and puffing up already. The sword dropped from his hand, the outline of its hilt imprinted in his palm.

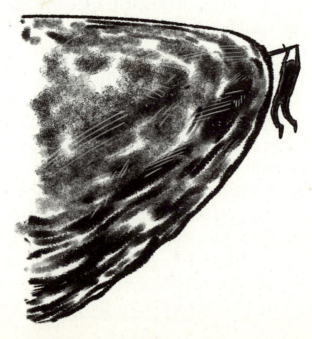

"I . . . don't . . . know . . ." Xavier's head felt jarred from the impact, and the fire in his arm seemed to be moving through his entire body.

"Man, that was awesome," Evan said, once he was sure Xavier was alive.

"Is it . . . dead?"

"I don't know. Maybe. It fell off the skypod. Not bad, big brother."

"Thanks."

"But your arm . . . does it hurt?"

"Not that much," Xavier lied. He sat up slowly, cradling his arm. "How's Tannyn?"

As if hearing his name, Tannyn cried out sorrowfully.

"He's alive, but his eyes . . ." Evan couldn't finish the sentence.

"At least the Bone Breakers are gone," said Manuel. "As soon as the red dragon went over, they just flew away."

"They must have been scared," Evan said.

"Yeah," Xavier said. "But not of us. They just don't want to get hit by the fireballs."

At nearly the same moment, the lava fireballs began to fall, exploding all around them. They slammed into the skypod, creating fiery craters from which blasts of smoke erupted.

Only this smoke fluttered with a thousand metallic wings.

Ents.

CHAPTER 41

Through the Night

The Warriors on the ground couldn't see what had happened to the two dragons, only that they disappeared from the sky. The fortress had renewed its attack with the lava catapults; huge fireballs streamed into the night sky and smashed into the skypod, causing a shower of burning rock to fall all around them, setting trees on fire. With every strike, Ivy wondered if Xavier, Manuel, and Evan were okay. She wished she could see them, but she just had to hope that Ruwach was taking care of them.

Ivy and Finn reunited with Kalle and Kristian, who had rounded up another forty Prince Warriors. They now totaled about one hundred all together. A fraction of their number from the battle at the Bridge.

Ivy tried not to let her discouragement show. She rallied the Warriors to prepare themselves for the battle, assuring them that victory was theirs as long as they stayed strong and stayed together. She hoped she was convincing; she was having a difficult time convincing herself.

It was dark and cold. And to make matters worse, a storm had rolled in, bringing fierce winds and snow that whipped through the trees and cut into the Warriors' exposed faces.

"At least it's putting the fires out," said Finn, still trying to stay positive.

"We'll need lookouts," said Kalle. "To keep an eye on the skypod, in case there is a signal. Or to see if the fortress blows."

"How can we see anything in this weather?" asked Ivy. Still, she agreed to the plan. Several Warriors volunteered to climb the taller trees and take turns keeping watch. Ivy told the rest to take turns sleeping if they could but to keep their shields and swords ready, just in case. There were still snakes around.

The remaining Prince Warriors huddled together for warmth, raising their shields to buffer the wind. Between the rumbling of the storm and the fireballs hitting the skypod, it was going to be hard for anyone to get any sleep. They all knew it was going to be a long, cold, uncomfortable, and possibly dangerous night.

Finn put his arm around Ivy. "You okay, little sis?"

She glanced up at his big, goofy smile, unable to help smiling back. "Not bad. You?"

"Hanging in there."

"Thanks," she said.

"For what?"

"For . . . just being there."

Finn grinned again and gave her a thumbs-up. "You got it."

Glancing over, Ivy saw Mary Stanton, sitting all alone, crying softly. Ivy got up and went over, sitting down beside her. And then, without knowing why, she started to sing.

She had never sung in front of other people before. But now, in this cold and dark place, it felt right.

Mary looked at her and smiled gratefully. She picked up the melody, humming and then mouthing the words. Soon others joined in, singing softly at first, but rising in strength. The wind and the storm seemed to get quieter as the voices grew louder, filling the dark night with music.

———————

Levi's legs felt like lead. The effort of lifting them from the thick, spongy rock and placing them down again was getting to him; it was like slogging through thick mud, except that with every step a little burst of flame erupted from under his feet.

"Not . . . much . . . farther," Brianna said for the fifteenth time. She seemed to be having an easier time than he was, or at least she was pretending to be full of energy still.

Then they heard the sound of a catapult being launched and the first ball of lava hurled at the skypod on which their friends were standing. It slammed into the side of the pod, emitting a torrent of nasty Ents.

"Not those things again," Levi muttered under his breath. He'd had just about enough of Ents, those evil-looking metallic butterflies with their deadly stingers. In fact, he'd had enough of this whole expedition. What were he and Brianna doing anyway? Climbing a mountain so they could throw a thimbleful of sulfurous water into a giant lava pit. As if that would do any good. As if there were any way they could topple that huge fortress all by themselves.

"We should stop now," Levi said. "It's getting too dark."

"No, we can't stop," Brianna said. He saw that she was looking at him squarely, as if reading his thoughts. "We have to keep going."

"Through the night?"

"Yes. Through the night."

Levi sighed and nodded. He knew she was right. But the thrill of entering a real battle had drained out of him long ago. He was a good swordsman—he'd even defeated Ponéros when that monster had been disguised as a human—but this trudging through crusty lava up a mountain was not, in his mind, a valiant fight. It was a hopeless waste of time.

You're so right, said a voice in his head. *It doesn't matter what you do. I will win, in the end.*

The warped, distorted voice droned on, saying the same thing over and over, thudding in Levi's ears. His steps became slower and slower. Brianna turned suddenly and put her hands on her hips, glaring at him.

"Levi, use your helmet."

Levi looked up at her, annoyed. "What do you mean?"

"Remember how you begged me once to put on my helmet? That day under the tree—and I kept refusing? You almost died trying to get me to put it on."

"Yeah, so? I'm wearing my helmet."

"Well, you may be wearing it, but you aren't *using* it."

Levi thought about this. He wasn't sure he knew what she meant.

"You need to listen!" Brianna said.

Levi slowly put his hands on either side of the helmet and pressed it closer to his ears. The voice sounded different suddenly. No longer tired, but strong and resonant.

It matters what you do. I will win. In fact, I already have.

It was unmistakably Ruwach's voice. The words seeped slowly into Levi's brain and trickled down to his arms, his back, his aching legs. He took another step, suddenly realizing that it wasn't as hard as he had thought it was at first. The soft rock felt springy, as if it pushed his foot back up for another step.

As the morning dawned, Levi and Brianna found themselves just below the rim of the crater. They had made good progress during the night, but they were both near exhaustion. It was suffocatingly hot, so hot they felt their skin would be seared right off. As tired as they were, they dared not try to sit for fear of being burned. Only their boots seemed to be fireproof.

"Stay here. I need to go up farther to see what's happening," Levi said. The rim dropped steeply toward the lava moat that encircled the tall obsidian pyramid, whose point seemed to pierce the red-and-black sky. Lava Forgers crowded the steep slope leading up to the fortress, working the catapults. Levi could see now that there was barely anything left of Xavier's skypod at all. Above them the Bone Breakers circled in pairs, gliding on their huge wings, buffeted by the warm air rising.

Levi contemplated what to do. The lava moat was very far below the fortress—much too far, he thought, to do any damage to the fortress itself. If he wanted to bring down the fortress, he'd have to get the water pots into the lava pit inside. That was going to be trickier.

To get into the fortress, they would have to cross the moat. But if they used the obsidian bridge, they would be seen by the Lava Forgers and the Bone Breakers. They'd never make it.

"Okay, Ru," he said to himself, "show me how to get in there."

Levi held up the Glimmer Glass. As he peered through, something began to appear—a fizzy, shimmery light. Sparks? The light took on shape, a walkway of sorts, a bridge that led from the rim of the crater and went up at a diagonal all the way to the tip of the pyramid. Over the heads of the Forgers with their cannons.

He knew there was a hole at the top. And that hole was directly over the lava pit.

Levi slid back down to join Brianna. "We need to get to the top of the fortress. We can drop the pots in the hole up there. And Ruwach's given us a bridge."

"Won't the Bone Breakers see us?"

"Maybe. I'm not sure. But the bridge is . . . invisible."

"Invisible?"

"You can only see it with this." Levi held up the Glimmer Glass. "Maybe when we're on it, we'll be invisible too."

"Okay," Brianna said, still uncertain. "But Levi, if we drop the pots . . . what then?"

Levi took a breath and shrugged. "I'm not sure. We'll cross that bridge when we get to it." He chuckled at his own joke.

Brianna smiled, although there was fear behind her eyes. "Stellar."

"You might not be able to see the bridge either, so just stay with me."

"Here." Brianna pulled the root from her pocket. It seemed to stretch, elongating. She wrapped one end around her wrist and handed him the other end. Levi took it. "That way I won't fall off or something."

Levi nodded and wrapped the end of the root twice around his palm. Somehow being connected to Brianna this way made him feel more secure. He led the way to the rim, climbed up, and quickly jumped onto the invisible bridge. It held him, even though he could see all the way down to the sloping rampart and the ledges where the Lava Forgers were working the catapults. Brianna hesitated, but when she saw Levi was being supported by virtually nothing, she jumped up after him.

"Seems like we've done this before," she said with a little laugh. She stayed close to Levi as he sprinted up the walkway toward the sheer dark wall of the fortress.

CHAPTER 42

Breaking Point

Day 40

"This . . . is . . . not . . . good," Manuel said.

Throughout the night, Xavier, Evan, and Manuel had been under assault by Ents, which had been released as the skypod had started breaking apart. The boys had climbed on top of Tannyn with their shields to protect him from the fireballs and to give him as much comfort as they could. Tannyn continued to moan, the sound echoing mournfully in the darkness.

Now it was nearly dawn, and yet the swarming Ents created a cloud so dense it blocked the rising sun. There were now more holes in the skypod than there was actual skypod. Only the spot on which Tannyn rested remained intact. They knew it was only a matter of time before the entire pod collapsed.

None of them had been able to get any sleep, between the constant buzzing of the Ents and the crashing fireballs. Evan could hear Xavier breathing heavily, fighting against the pain in his burned arm. Manuel was now the only one who was able to raise his shield. He kept his arm outstretched, resting on Evan's shoulder, with his fist closed. Evan often heard him counting during the night. He was up to four hundred twenty-nine. When he needed to rest, Xavier would take a turn, raising his seed-shield in his good arm for a time, with Evan's help.

They needed to get off the skypod before it collapsed. But Tannyn's eyes were badly damaged and his wing was broken, so there was no way he could fly them out. Evan couldn't see any other way they could be rescued.

Manuel was right. This was not good.

Evan closed his eyes and rested his head against one of Tannyn's spikes. He reached into his pocket for the hundredth time, hoping to feel the seed there, as if it would miraculously reappear. Instead, he felt the rock. It was warm from being in his pocket for so long. He wrapped his fingers around it.

Remember.

The voice seemed to come from inside his head. Remember . . . what? Something Ru had said. *I am with you. You have everything you need.*

Ruwach was here, somewhere, even if Evan couldn't see him.

"Okay Ru," Evan said to himself. "Give me what we need."

Put your hand on your brother's arm.

Evan's eyes flew open. He was certain Ruwach was right in front of him, speaking to him. He looked around but didn't see the little guide anywhere.

Put your hand on your brother's arm.

Evan hesitated, glancing at his brother, who was leaning forward on one of Tannyn's spikes with his eyes closed. *He's going to freak out.*

Just do it.

Evan reached toward his brother and carefully laid his hand on the wounded arm. Xavier jerked upright, gasping.

"Hey!"

"Sorry," Evan said out loud.

Xavier tried to jerk away, but he didn't have the strength. "What are you—?"

"Just hold it."

Xavier went still, staring at his arm. Evan closed his eyes and focused on the words Ru had spoken to him. *You have everything you need.* When he opened his eyes again, Xavier had twisted around to stare at him. His face was filled with surprise, but Evan could tell that he felt better. The reddened skin of Xavier's arm looked less angry, and the swelling in his fingers had gone down. Xavier raised his arm to stare at it, then wiggled his fingers.

"It doesn't hurt anymore," he said. "How did you—?"

"Not me," said Evan. "Ru did it."

"But he's not even here."

"Yes he is." Evan felt calmer. Even though they were still under intense attack, he knew that Ru was with them.

"It's a . . . miracle," Manuel said.

"Thanks, little brother." Xavier looked at Evan and smiled. Evan beamed back. Finally, Xavier really *saw* him. Even though the Ents were still swarming and the fireballs were still falling, Evan was happy.

Levi and Brianna sprinted over the bridge until they could touch the side of the pyramid. The bridge ended several feet below the very top of the pyramid. Levi stood on tiptoes, but he couldn't reach the opening above him.

"We're still too low," he said. The pinnacle was smooth as glass and very narrow.

"I'll climb up," Brianna said. "There's only room for one anyway. Give me your pot." Levi handed over his water pot. She stuck it in her belt with the other one. "So, hopefully once I do this, we can escape down the bridge before . . ."

"Yeah," said Levi. He glanced down at the shimmering bridge they stood upon. That would be their escape route.

Brianna nodded and set her foot on the glass wall. Her boot stuck to it like a suction cup. She took another step, holding her hands out for balance. When she was as close to the top as she could get, she grabbed one of the pots from her belt and stretched her arm toward the opening. When the pot was in the right spot, she took a breath and dropped it.

The Bone Breakers started to caw loudly. They'd spotted her.

"Hurry!" Levi said. "Drop it!"

"I did," Brianna said, puzzled. "But nothing happened. Maybe I missed."

"Throw the other one!" Levi shouted. He could hear the birds sending signals to each other all around them.

Brianna took the second pot from her pocket and threw it down into the opening.

Still nothing.

"I don't get it," said Brianna. "Why isn't there an explosion?"

The cawing of the Bone Breakers filled Levi's ears. "Come down! We need to get out of here!"

Brianna turned to climb back down. Levi put one foot on the pyramid to help her. Just then two huge Bone Breakers swooped upon them. Levi went for his shield, but it was too late. Brianna screamed. The birds snatched the two Warriors in their talons as if they were nothing more than a pile of bones.

CHAPTER 43

Heart's Desire

"What have you brought me, Nesher?"

Thayne, sitting high atop his throne of gleaming obsidian, stared down at the two Warriors sprawled on the floor where the Bone Breakers had dropped them. The bird spoke in a series of strange squawks that Thayne seemed to understand.

"Spies," Thayne said. "Prince Warrior spies." Thayne's voice sounded like gears grinding in an old truck. It was worse than even the squawking of the Bone Breakers.

The birds took their places on high perches to the right and left of the throne. They folded their wings and ruffled their feathers, pleased with themselves.

Levi, lying flat on his stomach, stole a glance at Brianna to make sure she was okay. She lay on her side, her eyes open and wide with fear. But she didn't look injured as far as he could tell.

His mind raced through what had just happened. They had been captured by Bone Breakers, carried into the fortress, and deposited on the floor before Thayne's throne. At least, that's what he thought happened. The flight had been so breathtakingly fast he could hardly catch up to his own memory.

Levi slowly raised his eyes to Thayne. Up close, he was even bigger than Levi had imagined.

Thayne stepped down from his high throne and approached the two Warriors. He held his war hammer in one hand, with its spiked tip glowing red-hot.

"What were you doing on top of my fortress?"

"Uh . . . watching the sunrise?" Levi said.

Thayne chuckled, though the sound was more like a death rattle. He bent and opened his other fist.

"Looking for these?"

Levi saw to his dismay that the two little pots of water lay in Thayne's massive, metal palm.

"Did you think we could not see you? We have been tracking your movements all the way up this mountain. I could have destroyed you at any time, but I was curious to see what you were up to. Tiny little children, armed only with tiny little pots. It was quite amusing."

Thayne tossed the pots away. They rolled on the shiny floor, just out of reach. Levi glanced at Brianna. She was keeping her face hidden, but he could tell she was watching those pots as well.

"I'm glad you liked it," Levi was stalling for time, his mind racing. He glanced at the smoking lava pit behind them. Beyond that was the doorway, guarded by two massive Lava Forgers. They had to be at least ten feet tall and almost as wide. More Forgers were probably standing guard outside the door. He knew he and Brianna wouldn't have a chance getting out that way.

He got up slowly and helped Brianna to her feet. She looked okay to him, just still very scared. He slowly reached into his belt, grasping his Krÿs. She followed his lead.

Thayne raised the hammer and began to tap the handle against his other hand slowly. The sound was like the ticking of a loud, clanging clock. "So what shall I do with you? I could throw you into the fire. Then we will see if you burst into flame or just incinerate slowly as the lava consumes you. That will be very entertaining. But there is another way for you."

"There is?" asked Levi.

"Join forces with me."

Levi's mouth dropped open. "*Join* you?"

"It is the only way you will live. Bow down to me. Serve the great Ponéros, who will soon be Master of all Ahoratos."

"Ruwach is the Master of Ahoratos," said Brianna. "Not Ponéros. He will never be."

"Silence!" Thayne thundered.

"I think she means, no thank you," said Levi evenly. "We aren't interested."

"You would rather be burned alive in a pit of lava?"

"Yes. There is no way we are going to bow down and serve you."

Thayne seemed to consider this. "What if I told you that I could give you anything your heart desires? What do you desire, little Prince Warrior? A fortress of your own? More riches than you could ever imagine? Power beyond your wildest dreams? I can give you what Ruwach would never give you."

"I don't want anything you can give me."

"No?" Thayne bent forward, so his empty-eyed helmet hovered close to Levi's face.

"Not even . . . your father?"

Levi froze.

He was suddenly aware of a familiar smell: dead worms. He thought it must be coming from Thayne, who was so close, but then he caught a movement and looked up at the throne. Seated there was the blind king in tattered robes.

Nameless was here. In this fortress. Did that mean that Nameless—Death—was under the power of Thayne? Or Ponéros? If that was so, then Thayne might actually be able to give him his father back.

Levi hesitated, unable to answer.

"He's lying," Brianna whispered. "Don't listen to him."

Still, Levi couldn't speak. He stared into the blank eyeholes of the helmet looming before him.

All he wanted was his father restored. Healthy. Alive.

He would do anything . . .

Suddenly, he felt something grab his hand. He glanced down to see that Brianna had slipped her root around his wrist. He closed his eyes, fighting tears. Even if . . . even if it were true. Even if Thayne *could* give him back his father . . .

"Never," Levi said, drawing himself up as tall as he could. "I will never bow down to you. Or your master."

"Me neither," said Brianna.

Thayne let out a horrendous bellow and raised his hammer up over Levi's head, as if to strike him down. Levi braced himself, pushing away his fear. He reached over and grabbed Brianna's hand and held it tight.

Don't be afraid. I am with you. Even now.

The hammer did not fall. Levi glanced up at the mighty being standing before him, the hammer still poised over his head. But then Thayne lowered the weapon, as if he had changed his mind.

"Very well. You will die. But first, you will watch your friends die."

Thayne returned to his high throne. The blind king was not there anymore. Levi looked all around but didn't see him anywhere. Maybe he had just been imagining things.

"He was lying, you know," Brianna whispered.

"I know."

Thayne sat down, resting the hammer on his knees. Levi and Brianna watched him, curious. He sat very still, and yet his massive armored body began to vibrate as if charged with electricity. The empty eyeholes in his helmet lit up, streaming bright lights that flashed on and off like strobes. The Bone Breakers began to squawk in excitement, flapping their huge wings.

"What's going on?" whispered Brianna.

"I don't know. . . ." Levi pulled out his Glimmer Glass and stared through it. The walls of the fortress became transparent, revealing the massive Lava Forger army charging over the obsidian bridge and heading down the mountain, their horrible voices rising to a roar.

Levi turned to Brianna. "I think the battle has begun."

"What's that noise?" Evan asked. The boys strained to see through the cloud of Ents. They caught glimpses of something spilling over the rim of the crater.

"It's the Lava Forgers," Xavier said. "They're attacking."

"But the fortress hasn't blown up yet!" Evan shouted.

"We need to signal them below," said Xavier. He patted Tannyn's hide. "Tannyn!"

The dragon moaned softly.

"Come on. I know you're hurting. Just give me three short blasts."

"You can do it, Tannyn!" Evan shouted. All three boys began to pat the dragon's back and encourage him.

Finally, Tannyn raised his head, stretching his long neck as far out as he could. He summoned all his strength and blew three bursts of flame. The Ents scattered.

"Again!" Xavier shouted.

Tannyn blew three more bursts.

"Do it again!" Over and over, Xavier commanded, and Tannyn obeyed.

Xavier hoped the Prince Warriors on the ground were watching.

CHAPTER 44

Ask

"There it is!" Bupe shouted. "The signal!"

Bupe, sitting in the top of a tree, saw three bursts of flame come from the tiny remnant of the skypod. She scrambled down and raced to Ivy and Finn, shouting all the while. "The signal! The signal! They are coming!"

Ivy jumped to her feet, her heart racing. Finn looked at her. She gave him a shaky smile.

"It's time." Finn nodded.

"Prince Warriors!" Ivy shouted, pulling her seed-shield from her pocket. "Assemble!"

"What's going on?" Mary Stanton, the only one who had actually fallen asleep, sat up and looked around blearily.

"Come on, Miss Stanton," Ivy said. "Get up. It's time."

"Time for what?"

The forest burst with commotion as the Warriors jumped up, putting on helmets and heading for the battle zone. As they emerged from the woods into the open area, bright flashes erupted from the dark cloud that hovered around the summit.

"Fireballs!" Ivy shouted. She threw up her shield. The other Warriors did the same. They hurried to get into position, forming a single, unbroken line.

All around them the fiery balls of lava began to fall. The Warriors pressed themselves closer together so their individual shields formed one large covering, a sparkling net of red seeds over all of them. Fireballs of lava fell all around them, creating smoking craters in the snow. There was so much steam it was difficult to see anything at all.

"Stand!" Ivy shouted, the command carried down the line by others. It was all they could do.

Finally, after what seemed like an eternity, the attack from above stopped. The only sound was the hiss of lava turning to steam and the heavy breathing of the Prince Warriors.

"They've given up!" said Mary, her voice filled with hope. "So it's over, right? 'Cause they know it's not going to work?"

"It's not over," Ivy said in a stern voice. She shouted to the rest of them. "Don't move! Keep your shields up!"

The Prince Warriors continued to stand firm with their shields raised.

New noises arose, the sound of engines churning. The Askalons, most of which were still in the woods behind them, were starting up. But instead of the familiar roar, they were sputtering and straining, as if unable to get going.

"They're stuck," Finn said.

"What if they manage to break through the sticks in their wheels?" Ivy said.

Just then a huge fireball crashed into a tree, and it burst into flames. More fireballs followed. Soon the entire forest would be on fire.

"Maybe the fires will hold them off," Finn said.

Ivy turned back to the mountain. She hoped Finn was right. Because now she could plainly see a dark wave descending from the cloud that rimmed the crater, rippling down the slope.

The Lava Forgers were coming.

———

"We need to get off this rock," Xavier said. The boys could see the Lava Forger army streaming down the mountain. But the fireballs were still falling all around them, and the Ents were still attacking. They were trapped.

Ask.

The words bubbled up from some distant memory. The Cave. The Book. The letters dancing in the air. *Ask and you will receive.* Xavier turned around and looked at his little brother.

"Evan, do you think if you asked Ru, he would fix Tannyn?"

"I . . . don't know if it works on dragons. But I'll try." Evan slid down from Tannyn's back. There was barely any room to stand. He inched his way over to Tannyn's head and put one hand on his nose. The dragon moaned out soft gorps. His eyes were closed. His broken wing was outstretched, for he couldn't even fold it properly.

"Hey, big guy," Evan said softly. "It's okay." Evan placed his hand over one of Tannyn's eyes. Tannyn yelped a little, smoke steaming from his nostrils. "Just relax." He reached into his pocket with the other hand and gripped the rock tightly, remembering Ruwach's words to him. He spoke aloud. "Ruwach, I know you're here. I know you can hear me. Please, make Tannyn's eyes all better."

Evan waited, but he didn't feel the familiar heat from the rock. He heard the answer clearly, as if Ruwach had spoken aloud.

No.

No? Evan's heart sank. He closed his eyes in despair. *The wing.*

Evan's eyes flew open. He turned and inched over to Tannyn's broken wing. He put his hand on it. Suddenly he could see Ruwach, see him as clear as day, standing right in front of him, reaching out one of his glowing hands and putting it over his own. He felt the warmth of that hand filling his body, radiating into the broken wing. He saw the wing begin to straighten, the bones knitting together, the torn flesh sewn up. He smiled and bowed low and thanked Ruwach for healing his friend.

"Gorp!"

Evan's eyes flew open as the giant wing under his palm flapped once, nearly knocking him over. The wing had straightened, the burned-out skin returned to its normal green. Tannyn flapped it again and gorped loudly. Evan made sure to duck that time.

"He did it," Manuel said, in awe.

Evan saw Xavier's staff still on the ground, where he had dropped it during the dragon fight. He picked it up and handed it to Xavier and then climbed onto Tannyn's back.

"He still can't see," he said. "How's he going to fly?"

"We can guide him," said Xavier.

The skypod shuddered as another big chunk fell off.

"Let's get out of here!" Evan shouted.

Holding his staff in one hand, Xavier inched along Tannyn's neck until he was straddling him right behind his head. "Okay, boy, I'll tell you where to go. You just fly."

Tannyn flapped his wings, sent a blast of fire into the cloud of Ents, and took off into the sky. He wobbled and almost did a somersault, but Xavier steadied him, clinging to his neck.

"Hang on, guys!" Xavier shouted to Evan and Manuel. He glanced back and saw the last remnant of the skypod crumble, releasing another cloud of Ents.

"Four hundred seventy-three, four hundred seventy-four . . ." Manuel whispered.

"Let's get down to the battle!" Evan cried.

Xavier looked at the battle below, where the Lava Forgers were barreling down the mountain, headed straight for the Prince Warriors. He was about to guide Tannyn that way when he saw something the Warriors on the ground couldn't see.

"Hang on, guys," Xavier said. "There's something we need to do first."

CHAPTER 45

Stand Firm

Ivy and Finn and the rest of the Warriors braced themselves for the onslaught of the Lava Forgers.

We are so few, Ivy thought. Their line didn't extend very far. The Forgers would easily be able to overrun them.

She heard a familiar trumpet call and saw Tannyn flying overhead. She couldn't tell if the boys were with him. Tannyn didn't fly down to the battleground. He kept going, over the treetops, and disappeared from sight.

"They're gone," Ivy said, a thick knot of sorrow building up in her stomach.

"How do you know?"

"Tannyn just flew away."

Finn sighed and put a hand on her shoulder. "We can do this, Ivy."

She looked up at him, blinking back tears. She would not let him see her cry. "But Xavier . . ."

"You'll lead. You've been doing it all along."

Ivy gasped at the realization. She *had* been leading them. Without even really thinking about it.

"Warriors," she shouted so everyone could hear. She had to put Xavier and the others out of her mind. "Stand firm, no matter what happens! We have everything we need!"

The next moment, Ivy's line of vision filled with the shocking sight of a thousand monstrous Lava Forgers smashing into their shields.

Ruwach! Ivy screamed his name in her mind as she felt the impact of the attack shake her very bones. The Forgers smashed their rock-hard bodies against the shields over and over. They roared like out-of-control blast furnaces. Ivy longed to fight back, to pull out her sword and thrust it into those molten cores. But it was all any of them could do just to keep their shields raised.

The sky overhead darkened suddenly, and Ivy looked up to see the air fill with Bone Breakers and Ents that had been released from the fallen skypod. They swooped down over the Prince Warriors, their terrible shrieks joining the roars of the Forgers. The Bone Breakers dove at the seed-shields as if trying to peck at the sparkling lights while the Ents released a torrent of poisonous darts.

"We need more help," Ivy said aloud. She tried not to let the panic in her heart reach her voice. She gripped her Krÿs, wondering if she should pull it out. She wanted to fight, but she knew the time had not come for that.

Then Ivy heard someone singing. She turned to Mary, but it wasn't her. Mary looked too terrified to speak. Ivy looked all around, but she couldn't figure out where the voice was coming from.

Then more voices joined in. Beautiful voices, whispering at first, then rising to a hum. And then white puffs like snowflakes began to swirl all around them, filling the air with music and light.

Ivy glanced at Finn, who looked back at her and smiled.

"They're here," he said.

Xavier saw the Lava Forgers slam into the Warriors' shield wall as he directed Tannyn to fly over the battle. Then he saw the Ents and the Bone Breakers descend on the army. He longed to be there with them. But he had something else he had to do first.

Tannyn soared over the vast forest until he came to the open plain before the Bridge of Tears. There stood hundreds of Prince Warriors, scattered over the field and locked in frozen poses, just as they had been ever since the first battle.

"They're still frozen!" Evan shouted. "How are we going to unfreeze them?"

"Come on, boy," Xavier said, patting Tannyn's head. "Just enough to melt some ice, okay?"

Xavier steered Tannyn over the frozen Warriors and signaled him to let loose with small bursts of fire over their heads. They made several passes, Xavier directing Tannyn's fire breath while Evan shouted encouragements and Manuel called out a progress report. By the fourth pass, the Warriors had melted enough that they could move their heads and release their arms. They wriggled out of their ice prisons and gazed around in wonderment at where they were.

Some saw the dragon circling above them and drew their swords as if preparing for an attack.

"Don't be afraid!" Xavier shouted down to them. "We've come to help you!"

The Warriors gaped in awe at the sight of three boys mounted on the back of a dragon. Xavier directed Tannyn to land. The Warriors saw what was coming and scattered quickly as Tannyn did his usual belly-flop landing. Xavier slid down the side of Tannyn's belly and set his staff on the ground before them.

"There's a battle at the mountain. We need your help."

Murmurs rose up from the Warriors, who were still somewhat confused by what was going on. One of them, an older boy, stepped toward him. He was even taller than Xavier.

"Aren't you the one who led your friends into a trap?" he asked. "We will not follow you!"

"You have to!" Evan shouted, coming to stand beside his brother. "Xavier is right this time! Look—he has Ruwach's staff!"

Xavier held up the staff for them all to see.

"That's just an ordinary stick," said the tall boy. "I'll prove it to you!" He reached out and grabbed the staff from Xavier's hand. Instantly, the staff began to wiggle and hiss—like a snake. The boy screamed and let go. The staff fell to the ground, an ordinary staff once again.

"That thing's alive!" the tall boy cried.

Xavier bent down and calmly picked the staff up again. The jaws of all those watching dropped. Some of them started to snicker.

"How'd you do that?" asked the tall boy. "Is that some sort of trick?"

"I think he's telling the truth," said another boy.

"It's just a trick," said the first boy.

"I know you don't trust me," Xavier said. "You have good reason to doubt me. But you have to believe me when I tell you that dozens of Prince Warriors are battling right now at the foot of the mountain, and everything is at stake. If you don't come to stand with us . . . then we will find another way. But if you want to stand against Ponéros and his army, if you want to defeat Thayne and rid this land of his dark schemes, you need to come now."

The Warriors were silent a moment. Then they broke into low murmurs, discussing the situation with each other.

"Come on, people!" shouted Evan. "We don't have time for this! We've got to go NOW!"

"I'm with you." One of the Warriors stepped forward and presented his sword.

"Me too," said another. Soon, all the Warriors were committed to the fight, including the tall one who had grabbed the staff.

"What are we waiting for?" shouted Evan. "Let's get this show on the road!"

———

Levi and Brianna sat on the floor before the throne, staring up at Thayne. His blank eyeholes were now filled with light, projecting an image into the space between him and the kids, like a hologram. It showed the Lava Forgers charging down the mountain and crashing into the Prince Warriors' shields.

The image switched to the forest, where the Askalons were struggling to move. Thayne growled and shot to his feet, clearly agitated.

"The Askalons are stuck," Levi whispered.

Thayne began to rant, making unintelligible noises. The Bone Breakers started squawking and flapping their wings.

"He's pretty mad," said Levi.

"I'm going for the pots," said Brianna. She could see them, discarded on the floor several feet away from where they sat. "It's now or never."

Brianna started to crawl toward the pots very slowly so Thayne or the guards wouldn't notice her. She was just about to grab one of the pots when Nesher flew down and snatched it up in his beak. The other Bone Breaker then made a grab for the second pot. They shrieked in triumph as they flew back to their perches, the pots firmly in their beaks.

"Stupid birds," Brianna muttered.

The movement of the birds caught Thayne's attention. He roared for his guards and pointed to Levi and Brianna.

"Kill them!"

Brianna scrambled back to Levi. They jumped to their feet and pulled out their swords as the Lava Forgers thundered toward them with outstretched arms.

"Don't touch them!" The voice boomed in the fortress, bringing even the Forgers to a standstill.

Ruwach? Levi spun around, searching for the source of the voice.

But it wasn't Ruwach.

It was Levi's father.

CHAPTER 46

Shiny Things

"Dad!" Levi's voice was a mixture of wonder and puzzlement. His father was lying in a coma in a hospital room on earth. Yet here he was in the enemy fortress, standing tall before them, dressed in his full, regal armor, his long, lethal sword prepared for battle.

"Mr. J. Ar!" Brianna gasped.

Mr. J. Ar lunged forward and thrust his sword into a Forger's midsection. "You two okay?" he asked as he spun around to face the other Forger, who was coming at him from behind. He slashed his sword in the Forger's neck; the Forger's head was thrown backward, nearly severed. But it soon recovered, the head fusing to the body once again.

Levi shook himself from his shock as two more Forgers entered from outside the doorway, rushing toward Mr. J. Ar with mighty growls. Levi raced to intercept them, his blade sizzling as it sliced through a Forger's red-hot core. The Forger arched and stumbled sideways, but when Levi withdrew his sword, he saw the wound he had inflicted close, as if it had never even been there.

"Dad, how did you get here?"

"No time to explain right now," said Mr. J. Ar. Thayne was thundering down the steps, wielding his hammer.

"Get the water!" Mr. J. Ar lashed at another Forger and went to meet Thayne.

Two Forgers came at Levi and Brianna.

"They're too big," Brianna whispered.

"Go low," said Levi.

As the Forgers closed in, both kids dropped to the floor and slid across the smooth floor between the Forgers' legs. They were up in a flash, slashing at the rock-hard legs with their swords. The Forgers toppled over, grunting.

"Get the pots," Levi shouted. "I'll handle these guys!"

Brianna saw Mr. J. Ar and Thayne fighting, though Mr. J. Ar couldn't seem to get close enough to the armored leader to get a strike. But he danced and darted this way and that, keeping Thayne occupied.

She turned to the throne. The two birds, still on their perches, were too high for her to reach. How was she going to get those pots away from them? Another Forger lunged at her. Despite their size, they were quite slow. Brianna swung her sword, hitting the monster in the leg. She ran for cover to the other side of the lava pit and searched frantically for something that might attract the birds. Something shiny. She saw nothing but blackened lava rocks and broken bones.

The heat and gases from the lava pit overwhelmed her. Brianna coughed and fell to her knees, her head swimming. She could barely breathe. She reached into her pocket and pulled out her seed. She saw that it was glowing in her palm, sparkling like a tiny red star.

Then she had an idea.

She closed her fingers over the seed and thrust her fist straight out in front of her. The network of sparkling seeds deployed over her head, giving her instant relief from the toxic fumes. She took a few deep breaths to clear her head. Then she stood up straight, hoping that the little seed lights would shine through the smoke.

"Come on, goonies," she called out. "Come and get it!"

Despite the hazy smoke and the two Warriors still fighting Forgers and Thayne on the other side of the pit, the Bone Breakers holding the pots became mesmerized by the sparkling lights of the shield. They spread their wings and flapped slowly, making noises in their throats.

"Come and get the shiny lights," Brianna whispered.

The birds took off from their perches and glided toward her. As they flew over the top of the pit, the birds opened their beaks to snatch the sparkling lights. The pots fell into the pit. They flared and then cracked from the intense heat. The birds closed in on Brianna, but before they hit the shield, the lava pit exploded, unleashing tongues of bright blue flame that shot all the way to the top of the fortress and into the sky above.

———————

Xavier saw the explosion at the fortress as he rode Tannyn through the sky. Blue lava shooting out of the pyramid, tearing the top of it apart. The percussive blast stirred up the air into turbulent waves that rocked Tannyn's whole body, throwing him backward.

"Hang on!" Xavier shouted to Evan and Manuel as Tannyn struggled to recover. The Warriors following on the ground let out gasps of fear. They too knew something had happened, but they weren't sure if it was bad or good.

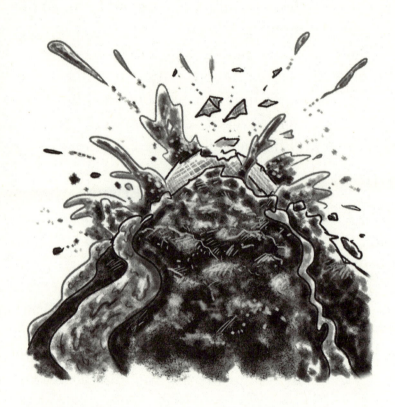

"They did it!" shouted Evan. "They blew up the fortress!"

"I hope they're okay," Manuel said in a shaking voice. "I hope we're okay too! Five hundred sixty, five hundred sixty-one . . ."

The Prince Warriors were standing firm—and singing.

They had been doing this for what seemed like hours, bracing their shields against the enemy attack. The Sparks, who appeared now as bright, shining warriors, took their places on either end of the line so the Lava Forgers could not break through. They were still singing, and the Prince Warriors had joined in the song.

But they were getting tired. Ivy's arm was cramping from holding this position for so long. More and more Lava Forgers were piling up against their shields. The Bone Breakers hadn't relented in their attacks. In the woods behind them, the Askalons were starting to move, breaking through the branches that stopped up their wheels. Ivy wondered how much longer they could last.

Suddenly the sound of an explosion met their ears, and the ground began to quake, knocking both armies off their feet.

"What was that?" Mary cried, falling against Ivy, who fell against Finn.

"The fortress," said Finn.

Ivy's stomach did a flip. *The fortress*. She looked up to the mountain. Above the dense cloud around the summit, blue lava was shooting into the sky.

"They did it," she whispered. *Levi and Brianna . . .*

The Lava Forgers began to act strangely, spinning around in circles and knocking into each other. The Bone Breakers flew back up toward the fortress, shrieking. The Ents seemed to turn to dust right before their eyes.

Ivy knew it was time to fight. She drew her sword and raised it in the air. Finn did the same; he was tall enough that everyone could see him.

"Attack!" she shouted. "Attack!" Finn echoed the command.

The Prince Warriors let out a joyful cheer and raised their swords, slashing at the confused Forgers. Every stroke reduced them to ashes. All along the line, the Forgers were falling.

But then the growling of the Askalons rose up from the woods. Ivy spun around to see the deadly machines once more on the move, churning out ice-webs and snakes as they rumbled through the burned-out trees.

"Askalons coming!" Mary screamed. She looked as though she might faint. Others turned in confusion, unsure of what to do. The Askalons would overrun them at any moment.

"Don't run!" Ivy shouted. "Stand firm!"

The Askalons barreled toward them, picking up speed. Ivy's breath caught in her throat. She kept her shield raised, urging the others to do the same. It was all she could do.

Then she became aware of a noise rising up from somewhere beyond the Askalons. It sounded like a battle cry. She squinted, sure she was seeing things, for coming up behind the Askalons were dozens of figures dressed in white armor, with swords and voices raised.

CHAPTER 47

All Fall Down

The explosion knocked Levi, Mr. J. Ar, and the Forgers across the vast room and slammed them against the walls. Levi landed on the floor, overcome with the blast of heat and smoke that filled the fortress. Gasping, he reached into his pocket and grabbed his shield, thrusting it out before him. He took several deep breaths, filling his lungs.

Huge blocks of obsidian were falling from the top of the fortress. The walls were cracking and breaking apart. Levi couldn't see his father anymore, or Brianna. *Brianna*. Where was she? She must have gotten the pots into the lava pit somehow. But that meant she was probably somewhere near the pit when it erupted. Fear seized his heart. What if she—?

"Bean!" Levi shouted in the smoke. He had to know if she was okay. Fingers of hot lava and small rocks were slamming into his shield. Giant pieces of obsidian fell all around him.

The Forgers, who had been blasted apart by the explosion, were re-forming themselves, though their body parts now seemed to be in all the wrong places. One's head was at the end of its arm; another's leg was sticking out the top of its head. They fumbled around as if they couldn't see where they were going, running into each other. One of them fell into the lava pit.

"You will pay for this!" Thayne's voice boomed. He turned from fighting Mr. J. Ar and lunged at Levi with his hammer raised. The explosion had caused some of Thayne's armor to melt, making his movements jerky and stiff.

Levi saw the hammer coming down on him; it ricocheted off his shield, propelling Thayne backward, into Mr. J. Ar. Both of them fell. Mr. J. Ar was up quickly and slammed his sword into Thayne's midsection.

But the sword seemed to be stopped in midair, repelled by some invisible force. Thayne rose up and smashed his hammer into the center of Mr. J. Ar's breastplate. Mr. J. Ar flew through the air, headed for the lava pit.

"Dad!" Levi shouted. He started to run toward his dad, but he knew he wouldn't make it in time to save him. "Dad!"

A blinding light met his eyes, and Levi fell to the floor. He couldn't see his father anymore. But then the light compressed, taking the form of a person. A tall person, so perfectly white it was as if he were made of light. He was dressed in glittering armor and held a sword that seemed to be on fire. He stood at the edge of the lava pit, stopping Mr. J. Ar's flight and setting him on his feet.

Mr. J. Ar nodded toward the shining warrior.

"Thanks, Gavreel," he said.

"No problem," said the warrior.

Thayne bellowed in rage at the sight of this newcomer. "How dare you enter my fortress!"

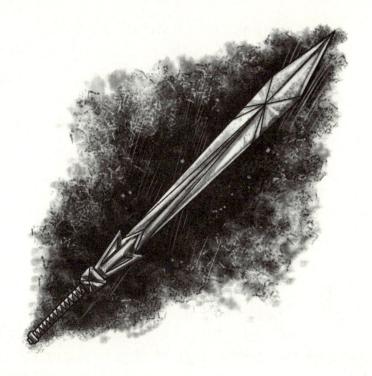

Without a word, Gavreel leapt toward Thayne, covering the distance in a single, effortless jump. The fire sword smashed through Thayne's belt. It broke off and slid to the floor. Mr. J. Ar picked it up and threw it into the lava pit.

Thayne roared again, but Gavreel just disappeared in another flash of light. Levi blinked, wondering where he had gone.

Thayne lunged for Mr. J. Ar, enraged by the loss of his belt. But a weird thing happened. Other pieces of Thayne's armor began to fall off his body, clattering to the floor. It was as if the belt had kept all the other pieces in place. Even stranger: underneath the armor, there seemed to be nothing there at all. Thayne, though he was still fighting, was beginning to disappear.

Mr. J. Ar swung his sword, which worked this time, as it was no longer repelled by the Belt of Lies. The two fought, the sound of their clashing weapons reverberating off the walls, which continued to crack and break and tumble down around them. The Lava Forgers were busy attacking each other now, for they couldn't see who they were supposed to fight.

Levi spun around, searching for Brianna. He called her name, but there was no answer. Then Gavreel suddenly appeared before him, shining through the smoke. His sword was sheathed, no longer on fire. He didn't speak, but he motioned to Levi to follow him. Then he turned and disappeared.

Levi chased after him, keeping his shield raised against the smoke. Glowing blue lava continued to spew straight up into the top of the pyramid. He couldn't see Gavreel anymore, but then he saw, on the other side of the pit, a small figure lying on the floor.

"Bean! Bean! Brianna!" Levi rushed toward her, covering her with his own shield.

She was so still. Levi felt panic well up within him. He shook her. "Bean! Wake up!"

Her eyes fluttered. Then she coughed.

"Bean!" Levi almost cried with gratitude.

"What happened?" she asked, still coughing. She looked around as if she didn't know where she was.

"We need to get out of here," Levi said. "This whole place is about to fall. Can you walk?"

"I don't know . . ."

Still holding his shield, Levi pulled Brianna to her feet. She wobbled and leaned against him then smiled slightly and opened her fist. Her seed was still in her palm. "Stellar."

Levi helped her to the doorway and sat her down outside at the top of the slope. The obsidian bridge was still intact, though the moat was churning and spitting up fire. "Wait here," he said. "I'm going to help my dad. We'll be right back. Keep your shield up."

Brianna nodded weakly and raised her fist.

Levi raced back into the toppling fortress to find his father, who was still locked in mortal combat with Thayne. A large piece of the wall was starting to collapse right on top of them.

"Dad, look out!" Levi yelled. Gavreel appeared suddenly, catching the jagged slab of glass and throwing it off. The shining warrior disappeared again. Levi blinked, not sure he had really seen that happen. Then Mr. J. Ar let out a bellow, spun in a circle, and smashed into Thayne's armored body; Thayne was thrown backward and rammed into the sharp tip of the slab, impaled. He flailed about, struggling to free himself, the black glass sticking out of the middle of his chest.

Levi gasped. Then he threw his arms around his dad, hugging him tightly. It was really him. He was here. He was okay.

"Brianna," said Mr J. Ar.

"She's outside. Come on!" Levi and Mr. J. Ar made a dash for the door, skirting around chunks of glass and rock, dodging falling debris. A huge chunk fell in front of the doorway, blocking their exit. But then Gavreel appeared again, lifting the gigantic stone up in the air so Mr. J. Ar and Levi could pass through.

"Thanks, Gavreel!" Mr. J. Ar said.

"Who is that guy?" said Levi. Mr. J. Ar didn't answer.

Brianna was still seated on the rampart, under the cover of her shield. Mr. J. Ar bent down to give her a hug.

"The bridge!" Levi gasped. He pointed to where the black obsidian bridge over the moat was starting to break apart. "Hurry!"

"I can't . . ." Brianna struggled to stand. Mr J. Ar put away his sword and lifted her in his arms.

"Come on, son!" Mr. J. Ar ran down the slope, headed for the bridge. Levi started to follow when he was suddenly yanked off his feet and flung through the air. He crashed onto the hard floor inside the fortress, the impact jarring him. His whole body screamed with pain.

And Thayne stood over him.

CHAPTER 48

The Turning

"Now you will die!"

Levi struggled to catch his breath, which had been knocked out of him. His back ached. His sword was gone. He tried to rise.

Thayne had broken away from the shard of obsidian that had impaled him, though there was now a gaping hole in the middle of what was left of his chest. Part of his helmet and one arm were gone. But he still had enough of both legs left to stand and move. He raised his hammer over his head.

Levi managed to roll away in time; the hammer smashed into the floor, creating a large crack. Lava bubbled up from the crack, spreading out like a pool of blood. Levi had to keep rolling to get away from the hot lava as the crack lengthened. He saw his sword lying on the floor and crawled toward it. As Thayne reached down to grab him again, Levi flipped over and swung the sword with all his might. The sword caught the hammer and flung it from Thayne's hands. The hammer flew through the air and landed in the lava pit, which exploded again as the metal sizzled and melted. Thayne bellowed in rage. He reached down, ripped Levi's sword from his hands and hurled it into the lava pit, which caused another small eruption. Levi moaned at the loss of his sword.

Thayne grabbed hold of Levi by the neck and lifted him high over his head. Levi twisted in his grip, beating hopelessly on the heavily armored arm. He couldn't breathe, couldn't cry out. Thayne carried him to the lava pit. Levi felt the searing heat of the lava blast his face. He closed his eyes.

"Levi!" It was Mr. J. Ar, calling to him from somewhere near the doorway. "Levi! Son!"

Thayne was about to throw Levi in the pit when a piercing scream filled the air. The sound made Thayne's whole body shake. He spun around, letting go of Levi, who dropped to the floor. Levi gasped, struggling for breath, as a huge reptilian creature with yellow eyes seemed to sail through the air over his head.

Sybylla.

Thayne spun around as the leviathan landed on him, both of them crashing to the floor. Thayne smashed a fist into the creature's head. Sybylla fell sideways then righted herself, her powerful jaws clamping down on Thayne's only remaining arm. She yanked him off the floor and flung him about like a rag doll as she slithered to the lava pit. Thayne hooked his leg around her neck as she tried to dump him into the fire. She whipped her head from side to side but couldn't shake him off.

Then she seemed to pause for a moment, turning to look at Levi. Her yellow eyes peered into his, and she blinked. She dipped her head once, as if she was nodding to him. Then she turned away and leapt into the lava pit, Thayne still locked in her jaws.

Levi stumbled backward, covering his face as the lava splashed and sputtered, engulfing the leviathan queen and her prey in blue fire.

The fire was suddenly quenched, and the lava pit began to steam as if rapidly cooling. Levi moved gingerly to the edge and looked in. He could see no evidence of Sybylla or Thayne in the pitch-black hole. If was as if they had been swallowed up by the fire, just as the fire was now swallowed up by . . . something else.

"Levi!" Mr. J. Ar had managed to climb over the piles of broken wall, hurtling glass shards in all directions.

"Dad," Levi gasped, falling into his father's arms. His legs suddenly felt too weak to hold him up.

"It's okay, son," Mr. J. Ar said softly, holding him close.

"Where's Bean?"

"She's outside."

The floor under them shook violently, as if the whole mountain were gripped by a terrible earthquake. More pieces of glass wall began to tumble down into the lava pit, as if being sucked in by some unknown force.

"Let's get out of here," Mr. J. Ar whispered.

"Best idea I've heard all day."

––––––––––

The whole army cheered as the newly arrived Prince Warriors overtook the Askalons from the rear. Several Warriors jumped up onto the machines, got into the hatches, and began steering them into each other, causing major pileups. Others thrust burning sticks into the side hatches, turning the ice-webs and ice-snakes to harmless water.

Tannyn appeared soon after, crash-landing at the edge of the woods. Ivy screamed with joy when she saw Xavier, Manuel, and Evan jump down from the dragon's back and run to join them, their swords drawn. Xavier still carried his staff.

"Guys! You're alive!" Ivy exclaimed.

"Yeah," said Xavier. "Have you seen Levi and Brianna?"

Ivy shook her head. But there was no time to talk. The five friends joined the rest of the army in finishing off the Lava Forgers, who were still bumbling in all directions, slamming into each other.

"Thayne must be gone," Xavier said. "He was the one controlling them."

"Good! Finish 'em!" Evan shouted. He thrust his sword into a confused Forger, who exploded into ash.

The Bone Breakers came back, but instead of flying, they were just falling from the sky, as if their wings no longer worked. They flopped around on the ground, squawking like mad, creating even more havoc. Evan stop fighting Forgers when he noticed one of the birds choking and sputtering, as if something was caught in its throat. He drew closer to investigate.

"Hey! You took my seed!" Evan cried and rushed toward the bird. He was about to stab it with his sword when it simply fell over as if dead and its beak dropped open. Evan's little red seed rolled out onto the snow, covered in slime. Evan lunged for it, grabbing it away before any other bird got hold of it. "I got it back!" he exclaimed. "Look, Xavier!"

Instead of making some snide remark, Xavier smiled at him. "That's cool, Evan. I knew you would."

As the battle wound down, Xavier began to wonder more and more about Levi and Brianna. Maybe they were still up there, still alive. Maybe it was possible to rescue them. He had to know for sure.

"You keep going here," he said to the others. "I'm going up there." He raced back to Tannyn, positioning himself once more on the dragon's neck. "Let's go, boy," he whispered, and Tannyn took off.

CHAPTER 49

Left Behind

Mr. J. Ar and Levi stumbled out of the fortress just as the entire structure collapsed, raising a thick black cloud of dust and ash. Firecrackers of blue flame were shooting every which way, like a Fourth of July celebration gone haywire. Brianna was still sitting outside; Mr. J. Ar grabbed her hand and pulled her away from the disaster. The three of them half ran, half slid down the sloping rampart toward the fiery moat. But the obsidian bridge had already been destroyed by the roiling lava. Levi looked through the Glimmer Glass, but no other bridge appeared to him. There was no way he could see to get off the mountain. Ash fell upon them like snow, coating them in a layer of gray, so they looked like statues of themselves.

"At least we're out of the fortress," Brianna said, trying to smile. She huddled closer to Mr. J. Ar, who lay on his back, holding both kids close. "We did it, didn't we?"

"Yes, you did," said Mr. J. Ar.

"So who was that guy in there?" Levi asked. "Gavreel. Have you met him before?"

"No, I'd only heard about him. He's a good friend of Ruwach's."

Levi had a million more questions, but he suddenly didn't want to talk anymore. He didn't even care if they ever got off the mountain. He had his father with him, and that was all that mattered. Thayne was gone. The fortress was destroyed. They'd done what they came to do. He put his arm around his dad's broad chest and lay still, letting all the pain and fear he had experienced wash away.

Then he thought he heard someone calling his name.

"Levi! Brianna!"

"Did you hear that?" he said, sitting up. Brianna looked at him, confused.

"What was it?"

Levi fished out the Glimmer Glass and peered through the smoke.

"It's Xavier!" Brianna cried. "Over here!" She waved one arm wildly. "We're here!"

Through the Glass, Levi saw Tannyn turn and head their way. Maybe they would be rescued, after all. "He's coming!" he said, turning to his father. "Come on, Dad! Let's go!"

Mr. J. Ar had risen to his feet.

"No," said Mr. J. Ar. "You go on, son. Both of you."

"What do you mean?" Brianna asked.

Levi glanced up to the top of the mountain. The fortress was gone. But Ruwach was there, the little figure in the purple hood, beside the tall, majestic Gavreel. And the blind king in the tattered robe was there too—Nameless.

Levi felt his chest cave in, his throat close. He threw his arms around his father, clinging so tightly he could hear the thud of his father's heart.

"I'm not going without you!"

"Yes, you are," said Mr. J. Ar as he wrapped his son in his arms and held him close. Then he gently disengaged and took Levi's chin in his hand, smiling into his eyes. "It's okay, son. Everything is going to be okay. I promise."

"But . . . why?" Levi could barely speak through his tears.

"You will understand one day," Mr. J. Ar said. "All you need to remember is this. I love you, son. I'm proud of you. You are a Prince Warrior. You will carry on my legacy. And it won't be long before we are together again."

"How long?" Levi cried, sobbing now.

"Take this." Mr. J. Ar lifted his sword to Levi. "I pass this to you, father to son. It will serve you as faithfully as it did me. And one day, I hope you will pass it to a son of your own."

Levi took the sword in both hands. It was far bigger than his own, but it did not feel too heavy for him. He held the blade aloft, as if in salute. Mr. J. Ar put a hand on his shoulder.

Mr. J. Ar turned and began to climb up the rampart. He joined Ruwach, Gavreel, and the blind king at the top and gave his son and Brianna one last wave. Then he turned to follow the king over the top of the mountain, disappearing in the mist.

In the ICU of the Cedar Creek Hospital, Dr. Arthur grabbed hold of her husband's hand. His eyes had started to flutter, and his hand flinched a tiny bit. She bent over him, peering into his face.

"James . . . I love you."

Mr. J. Ar's body went still. The beeping on the monitor over his head became erratic, the little red dot jumping up and down. Dr. Arthur held her breath, clutching her husband's hand as the little red dot fell one last time, the rapid beeps slowing to a single, soft, unchanging tone.

Tannyn crashed down on the ramparts. Levi heard Xavier's voice calling out to them.

"Guys! Hurry! Let's go!"

Levi's eyes were blinded with tears. He dropped to his knees, thrusting the sword into the ground and rested his head against the hilt.

"Levi!"

Brianna tugged on his arm. She was crying too. Levi wouldn't move.

"We have to go," she said urgently.

Levi didn't answer. He lifted his head to look at his father's sword. There was something inscribed in the blade, a jumble of letters in a strange language.

עֲמוֹד

Surprisingly, he could decipher exactly what those letters meant.

Stand firm.

Something flashed through his mind. A memory. But it wasn't his own memory. He recognized his father as a young boy, standing before a tall Warrior in fine armor who was handing him the sword. Mr. J. Ar had grown up without a father. So who was this Warrior who had given him the sword?

The memory flashed again. This time the tall Warrior turned his head, and Levi could see his face. It was not a face he knew. It was a kind face, and yet it was strong and fearless too. Just like his dad's.

Carry on my legacy.

Brianna knelt down beside him and put her hand on his shoulder.

"Come with me, Levi. One step at a time. It's going to be okay."

She got up slowly, her hand still on his shoulder, and Levi got up with her. *One step at a time.* He walked with her to where Tannyn and Xavier waited. The ground shook, and he almost fell, but Brianna held on to him, and he stayed on his feet. When he got to Tannyn, Xavier pulled him up onto the dragon's back. He noticed the new sword but didn't say anything. Brianna climbed up behind him. She took out her root and put one end in his hand. His fingers closed over it.

"Let's go, Tannyn," Xavier said.

Tannyn leapt into the air, breaking through the smoke that ringed the summit. Levi was surprised to see that away from the mountaintop the air was clear and the sun was shining. The battle below seemed to be almost over. The sky was filled with gentle snowflakes . . . at least they looked like snowflakes. Levi pulled out his Glimmer Glass and looked through it. The sky and the land were filled with tall, majestic, shimmery Warriors. The Sparks in their true form. They were there, just as they had been at Cedar Hill. Levi smiled through the tears still streaming down his face.

And then a bone-chilling roar filled his ears, and an enormous red dragon suddenly dropped out of the sky.

CHAPTER 50

The Dragon Returns

Its wings were wider than an ocean liner. Each of its many spikes was actually a tongue of flame. The dragon was on them before Xavier could react, clamping down on Tannyn's tail and flinging him away. Tannyn wailed as he was thrown head over tail, Xavier, Brianna, and Levi barely clinging to his spikes.

Tannyn struggled to right himself, flailing his wings as the red dragon dove toward the Prince Warriors on the battlefield.

"Get him, Tannyn!" Xavier cried, urging the dragon to follow.

"No, wait! It's Ponéros!" Levi shouted.

The fiery red dragon sped toward the unsuspecting Warriors on the ground. Xavier directed Tannyn to land, thinking they could better help their friends on foot. As Tannyn headed for the ground, the Warriors saw the Sparks—the army of the Unseen—rise up from the ground. They surrounded Ponéros, slashing him with their gleaming swords and deflecting his fire breath with their golden shields.

All the Warriors stood silent and in awe as the fight went on. The red dragon looked like a streak of fire in the sky. The Sparks' swords were like long sleek icicles; with every pierce, one of the dragon's flaming spikes went out, leaving a blackened scar. Ponéros was covered in many scars, and yet he kept fighting, yellow flames erupting from his great jaws. He refused to give up.

Then the sky lit up with a brilliant flash, like a nuclear blast. And from the light came another dragon, this one pure white, with fiery white spikes. A small purple figure was perched just behind its magnificent head.

"Ruwach!" Brianna cried. Everyone shouted his name.

Ruwach rode the white dragon directly into the midst of the fight. He raised one of his long, shining arms. A glittering spear appeared in his hand. Ruwach threw the spear, which streaked through the air like a lightning bolt. Ponéros screamed in pain and rage as the spear pierced his heart. A blackness spread from the wound, consuming his flaming scales, his enormous wings. He fell from the sky, spinning helplessly, and disappeared.

None of the Warriors saw where he landed. But they heard a sound like thunder inside the earth, and saw a plume of dark smoke rising into the distant sky. And then it was quiet.

CHAPTER 51

Victory

There was nothing left of the Lava Forgers except piles of ash.

The Askalons lay in heaps of twisted, smoldering metal.

The fortress was gone. And a thin wisp of smoke rose up from the flattened top of the Mount of Rhema, peaceful and serene.

The Breath had returned.

The Prince Warriors were at first too stunned to understand what had happened—that the battle was suddenly over. They stood still with blank stares on their faces, the only sound their panting breath.

And then, gradually, they began to cheer. First one voice, then two, then a whole chorus of praise rose up, swords piercing the air in victory.

Ivy, Finn, and Evan ran to Levi and Brianna as they slid from Tannyn's back, shouting with happiness. Ivy threw her arms around Brianna's neck.

"I'm so glad you're okay," she said.

"Me too," said Brianna.

"How was it up there?"

Brianna smiled weakly. "Stellar."

Evan gave Levi a high five. "Wow. You did it, man. Awesome!"

"Thanks," said Levi. "So did you."

"Where'd you get that sword?" Evan pointed to the sword that Levi still held in both hands. "It looks like Mr. J. Ar's."

Levi's head dropped.

Brianna spoke for him. "It is."

"Mr. J. Ar was there? On the mountain?" said Xavier, astonished.

"Yes. He came to rescue us. He fought Thayne."

"Well, where is he?"

Brianna glanced at Levi. Her eyes filled with tears. "He's . . . not coming down."

The friends were quiet, looking from one to the other. No one wanted to believe it.

The moment was interrupted by Mary Stanton, who came bounding toward the group, waving excitedly.

"Guys!" she said, nearly colliding with Finn. "We made it! I'm actually getting to like Ahoratos, although it could really use a Starbucks."

"Where's Manuel?" Evan asked, looking around.

"Here I am." A bedraggled Manuel limped up to them. "I ended up next to a big Russian dude who stepped on my toes numerous times. I think several of them might be broken."

"Kalle! Kristian!" Ivy said as the twins came over, looking tired but triumphant. They all high-fived each other. Bupe and Ravi and their friends came to join in with high fives and fist bumps and Bupe's secret handshake, which all the Prince Warriors soon adopted as their own. They talked excitedly about the events of the battle and the fall of the great red dragon from the sky.

It was Evan who first noticed it.

"A leaf!" he cried. He pointed to a tree branch over-head, where a single green leaf was gently unfolding before their eyes. Everyone stopped what they were doing to stare at the miracle taking place before their eyes. Suddenly there was hope again, and life, and peace.

Evan grinned. "I think the Winter is over."

Back to the Beginning

The rec center was full of people. Levi couldn't even find any place to sit. So many people had come out for the memorial service; most of them Levi had never seen before. Levi's mom had decided to have the reception for Mr. J. Ar at the rec center since it had been such a big part of his life. People brought a ton of food. They cried as they told their stories of how Mr. J. Ar had affected their lives. Everyone was eating and talking and crying, but there was laughter sprinkled in with all the tears. Happy memories. A sweetness they wanted to savor a little longer.

After a while, Levi went outside to the playground. There had been a thaw, and the snow had melted. It wasn't as cold as before, and tender green patches of grass were starting to break through the dead ground. He wandered over to the swings and sat on one. It was still wet from the melting snow, but he didn't care. He could see the skateboard park and thought about going to get his board. Maybe he could do a little skating. He needed to do something.

Then he looked over at the basketball court, where his father had spent so much time. He smiled at the memory of his big, burly dad charging up and down the court with his famous whistle, encouraging and correcting the players in his booming voice. Levi had never really liked playing basketball. Now he wished he had so he could have spent even more time with his dad.

Levi reached into his pocket and took out the Glimmer Glass. He held it to his eye. He didn't know if it worked on earth the same as in Ahoratos, if he could see what others couldn't see. He aimed it at the basketball court. But it was still empty.

"Looking for someone?"

He flinched, startled. He looked up to see a beautiful white bird sitting on a branch in a nearby tree. The bird appeared to be looking right at him.

"Did you just . . . talk?" he asked, staring at the bird.

"You've never heard a bird talk before?"

"Okay, I'm imagining things now." Levi stood up to leave.

"Levi."

Levi turned slowly around and looked at the bird. "Are you . . . who I think you are?" he asked. But he didn't have to ask. He knew already. This wasn't Ru, or his father. This was the Source.

"Look for me, and you will find me," said the bird. "Look not with your eyes, but with your heart."

Levi felt dizzy, his vision blurring with tears.

"Levi!" a voice called from the rec center. Brianna. The bird suddenly flew up into the sky and disappeared. Levi got to his feet, though his legs were shaking.

Brianna came running up to him. "We were wondering where you went." The others came also, his friends. Levi turned around and smiled at them. Their faces were kind, sympathetic, a little anxious.

"Oh, hey," Levi said.

"What are you doing out here?" Ivy asked. "It's kind of cold."

"Oh, I was thinking it might be fun to . . . play a little basketball."

The others were silent a moment, looking at each other.

Then Evan spoke up. "Good idea! I'm in. I'll go get the ball." He raced back to the rec center.

"I'll play," said Finn.

"Me too," said Ivy.

"I'm not very good, but I'll give it a try," said Manuel.

"I can't play," said Xavier, indicating his crutch. "But I'll ref, if you want."

Evan returned with a ball and Mr. J. Ar's whistle. He handed them to Xavier, who lifted the whistle carefully and put it over his head. They all went out onto the basketball court, which was filled with puddles from the melting snow. They picked teams—Evan, Ivy, and Finn against Levi, Manuel, and Brianna. They gathered around Xavier, waiting for the whistle. Xavier put the whistle in his mouth and held the ball out for the toss.

"Ready?" Xavier asked.

"I'm ready," said Levi.

Xavier blew the whistle, and Levi jumped higher than he'd ever jumped before.

To discover the
hidden secrets of The Prince Warriors, go to

www.theprincewarriors.com

Acknowledgments

B&H Publishing, Michelle, Rachel, and Gina. This project has made a family out of us—a tribe of mothers committed to mentoring the next generation. I'm so honored to be a partner with you.

Joshua Thomas Farris II. Welcome to the world, Prince Warrior. An army of godly men and women in this family are cheering for you. I'm so honored to have a great-nephew like you.

To my sons, Jackson, Jerry Jr., and Jude. When we first started dreaming up this series together, you were elementary-age children. Jude, you were still in diapers. Now, nearly a decade and four books later, you are all young men—teenagers forging your way through the tender transition of adolescence. Your father and I are watching each of you journey toward your God-given destiny in awe of how your character is building, your strengths are being magnified, and your weaknesses are becoming mighty platforms on which God's power will be displayed. You are mighty Prince Warriors, and we are full of expectation and enthusiasm about the impact you will make for the kingdom of God. You are our life's greatest joy and privilege.

Never forget that this series was always meant—first and foremost—to be a gift to you, to equip you for victory and give you a written account of the spiritual inheritance we desperately want you to have from us as your parents. So let Mr. J. Ar's final words be a constant reminder of our hopes for you. . . .

> *"All you need to remember is this. I love you, son. I'm proud of you. You are a Prince Warrior. You will carry on my legacy."*

> *Mr. J. Ar lifted his sword to Levi. "I pass this to you, father to son. It will serve you as faithfully as it did me. And one day, I hope you will pass it to a son of your own."*

About the Authors

Priscilla Shirer is a homemade cinnamon-roll baker, Bible teacher, and best-selling author who didn't know her books (*The Resolution for Women* and *Fervent*) were on the *New York Times* Best Seller list until somebody else told her. Because who has time to check such things while raising three rapidly growing sons? When she and Jerry, her husband of nineteen years, are not busy leading Going Beyond Ministries, they spend most of their time cleaning up after and trying to satisfy the appetites of these guys. And that is what first drove Priscilla to dream up this fictional story about the very un-fictional topic of spiritual warfare—to help raise up a new generation of Prince Warriors under her roof. And under yours.

Gina Detwiler was planning to be a teacher but switched to writing so she wouldn't have to get up so early in the morning. She's written several novels, including the YA fantasy *Forlorn* and its upcoming sequel, *Forsaken*. She is honored and grateful to have the opportunity to work on The Prince Warriors series with Priscilla and the wonderful B&H Kids team at LifeWay (and hopes there will be a #5!). She lives in Buffalo, New York, with her husband, Steve, and three beautiful daughters.

THE PRINCE WARRIORS

Don't miss the other great adventures in this series!